SEVENTH DIMENSION
BOOK 6

THE HOWLING

LORILYN ROBERTS

A YOUNG ADULT FANTASY

SEVENTH DIMENSION
BOOK 6

THE HOWLING

LORILYN ROBERTS

To My Sister Alison Paige

What a blessing

"Time is an illusion until God's appointed time."—Lorilyn Roberts

INTRODUCTION

"A spiritual kingdom lies all about us, enclosing us, embracing us, altogether within reach of our inner selves, waiting for us to recognize it. God Himself is here waiting our response to His Presence. This eternal world will come alive to us the moment we begin to reckon upon its reality."-- A. W. Tozer, *The Pursuit of God*

The Howling is the sixth and final book in the *Seventh Dimension Series*. If you have not read the previous books, I would encourage you to read those first. Profound truths build, like reading the Bible from cover to cover. While you will understand the gist of the story in *The Howling*, the backstory will be like a hidden gem that I don't want you to miss. I've kept the price low on ebooks, and the first book in the *Seventh Dimension Series, The Door*, is free on all ebook platforms.

Thank you for trusting me with your time. May my words uphold the truth of God's Word, and may my Lord and Savior, Jesus Christ, receive all the glory.

Daniel Sperling enters the Seventh Dimension shortly before the return of the Messiah. As one of the 144,000 Jewish evangelists called by Yeshua, the horrors of the Day of the Lord take center stage. Discernment in the seen—and faith in the unseen—can mean the difference between life and death as God teaches perseverance. Daniel's love for Shale and Shira grows amid revelations concerning the future and the fate of his father. As the Kingdom of God draws near, a new world order, built on a matrix of deception, makes Daniel's calling more perilous and deadly. His race to the finish, where time is an illusion until God's appointed times, is heroism at its finest—and demonstrates God's profound love in the heart of all of those who seek Him.

PREFACE

From *Seventh Dimension – The Prescience, Book 5, A Young Adult Fantasy*

THE ROARING CROWD and horses' hooves pounding the dirt track shook the stadium. Tariq viscously whipped his horses. It didn't take long for disgust to settle in my stomach.

The overwhelming truth consumed me that the guy was a cheater—a Nephilim from the future. He came here and made a mockery of the races.

What had he done to Daniel's father? He was a hybrid without a conscience, without a soul. I felt stomach contents threatening to disgorge. I slumped over pressing my arms into my midriff.

The two chariots sped down the track neck and neck into the first turn. Daniel lost ground on the outside, and Tariq took the lead. Daniel thrust his reins.

Tariq glanced behind him. Seeing Daniel gaining, the Nephilim whipped his horses, and I heard their cries. The animals were at the mercy of a demonic tyrant.

Daniel caught Tariq at the turn, but Tariq wouldn't let him pass on the inside. Daniel tried to go around him on the outside, and he lost ground.

Tariq cut the turn sharper. Daniel dropped back. He'd have to find a way to get around Tariq on the inside.

The first metal cut-out dolphin fell.

Shira grabbed my arm. "Auntie, look."

"Yes, I see." My voice shook.

She noticed. "Are you all right?"

I nodded. I couldn't speak. Three-year-olds could be so perceptive.

Daniel charged ahead. The chariots zoomed around the turn at the far end. Daniel trailed. Could he sneak up on the next straightaway?

One of Tariq's horses took a misstep. Daniel seized the moment. He plunged ahead of Tariq on the inside.

When Tariq caught up, he hurled his whip at Daniel. The unexpected attack left Daniel wobbling. He struggled to regain control. The chariot lurched sideways.

I held my breath. When my betrothed recovered, he whipped the reins once more. His horses swooped forward, but Tariq passed him. Daniel maneuvered around the turn tighter this time. Could he catch Tariq? I couldn't watch.

The spectators chanted, "Daniel!"

Daniel exited the turn behind Tariq but inched closer. Perspiration beaded on my forehead, and I felt faint, leaned over, and vomited on the stone pavement. Shira looked away, disgusted. No one else noticed —they were too busy watching the race.

Tariq pulled ahead going into the next turn.

A second dolphin fell. Five more laps.

Daniel crept up on the outside. Again, the hybrid creature slashed his whip on Daniel's back. How was Daniel going to get around him without being attacked? That couldn't be legal. I covered my eyes. Five more laps to go.

"Is Daniel going to lose?" Shira asked.

"Pray," I urged.

The gladiators hurtled down the track, but Daniel still trailed. I shook my head. The Nephilim was demonic. Making the turns so fast, one would think the centrifugal force would sling him through the air.

Daniel kept losing ground on the turns. Then he would have to make up the distance on the straightaway. If Daniel could pass Tariq on the inside, he could win. Daniel's horses were faster.

The excitement reached a fever pitch. Most of the fans stood at their seats and waved banners and hankies. Fortunately we were in the front, or unfortunately. If something happened, I'd see it.

Daniel and Tariq rounded the turn and entered the straightaway. Daniel once again came within a horse's head, but couldn't pass. They galloped into the next corner.

A third dolphin fell. Four more laps to go.

The thunderous roar shook the stadium. The two chariots passed us. I shouted, "Go, Daniel."

Daniel was pushing the limits of the horses. Unexpectedly, he slipped past Tariq. Could he maintain it through the next turn? Daniel went low so Tariq couldn't overtake him on the inside. Tariq almost careened into Daniel. I held my breath. Both chariots wobbled, but Daniel charged ahead.

The crowd roared, "Daniel, Daniel!"

Tariq lashed the whip on the horses. Again I heard their cries. They ran harder. Tariq shot even with Daniel.

"No," I cried. "Don't pass him."

The Nephilim stuck Daniel with the whip. He jerked, swaying back and forth.

"No," I shouted. I raised my fists in the air. "No, you"—I stopped when Shira looked up at me. "God, please help Daniel," I prayed.

The hybrid creature whacked the whip again at Daniel, and the belt wrapped around Daniel's neck. Gasps came from the spectators.

The trumpet sounded. Was it over? Daniel struggled to extricate himself. He managed to get the whip off before entering the next turn.

Tariq, enraged, pursued him.

"God," I cried.

The fourth dolphin fell. Three more laps to go.

Daniel regained control pivoting into the turn. Tariq smacked the whip hard. Instead of hitting Daniel, the cord got stuck between the spokes. Tariq jerked forward, almost falling. Daniel surged ahead.

I waved my hands. "Go!"

Then I noticed Tariq's whip was on the ground. "Thank you, Jesus."

The fifth dolphin fell. Two more laps to go. If only this were the last lap. If only.

Daniel plunged forward, flashing the reins. Tariq thrust ahead nipping at Daniel's back wheels. They sped into the next turn, and Daniel cut sharply. Any sharper, he would have overturned.

Daniel's opponent again tried to plow into Daniel's biga. They came out of the corner and hit the straightaway. Daniel's chariot seesawed before leveling out. They entered the final turn with Daniel in front. Tariq was a hands-breadth behind.

The sixth dolphin fell. One more lap to go.

Tariq snuck up from behind. His front chariot wheel was even with the back of Daniel's. Then I saw what Tariq was doing. There was a sharp spike on his wheel. Could he saw off the spoke of Daniel's biga?

They entered the corner with Daniel leading. Tariq bore down. A horse's head separated them. Daniel pulled out in front. The distance widened, but as my beloved neared the next turn, Tariq gained ground.

"Please, God," I cried, "protect Daniel's wheel."

They passed in front. Too much dust hampered my view as the horses went into the far turn. Daniel stayed tight. Tariq was desperate. Thankfully he didn't have the whip.

They came out onto the straightaway. Tariq pressed even harder, but his horses were tiring. He couldn't torture them anymore. Daniel blazed forward into the final corner, and I held my breath. The spectators stood waving their hands and shouting, "Daniel!"

The racers pounded the track, and the horses stormed toward the finish line. Tariq made one last attempt to catch Daniel, but his efforts were futile.

The last dolphin fell, and I joined in the cheers. My hero won.

Then, momentarily, I didn't see either chariot. Seconds later, they were back. I saw the chariots and the horses, but where was Daniel? I glanced at Tariq's chariot. Where was the wicked one?

The riotous crowd seemed to notice something was amiss. A hush fell over the Hippodrome. I peered through the settling dirt on the turn and straightaway. Where were they? Had they gone into the center island? My heart pounded.

"Where is Daniel?" Shira asked.

I stared at the unmanned chariots. "I don't know."

Shira pointed. "Look, Auntie."

Distracted and upset, I didn't want Shira bothering me. I ignored her, straining to see down the far side of the track. I glanced at the Roman socialites—some stood, gazing at the chariots.

Shira shook my arm. "Auntie, look. There's a white dog."

I peeled my eyes away from the track to see what Shira was pointing at. "My God," I cried. I touched my hand to my heart. "Much-Afraid, is that you?"

She ran toward me, wagging her tail, avoiding where I threw up. "Shale, you've left such a mess."

"It is you!"

CHAPTER 1

My horses, Mosi and Oni, took the lead. I could taste victory—sweet victory. They could run like gazelles when I let them. Just one more lap. I heard the roaring crowd chanting my name.

"Run!" I shouted. We passed Tariq, and a scowl covered his brow. He slapped the reins at me in a last-ditch attempt to yank me off the chariot, but I was a seasoned racer now. No chance of that happening.

We rounded the first turn, and I kept my distance. I didn't want any more trickery or sleight of hand—like Tariq sawing off my wheel. The other racers had been knocked out or given up. Only Tariq was left, but dropping farther behind. The finish line called my name.

Less than a minute later, I threw up my hands triumphantly. I flicked the reins to slow the horses, and the people drummed their feet in the stands. Celebratory flowers littered the Hippodrome as the fickleness of the spectators never ceased to amaze me. The Romans believed I was a criminal and a Jewish one at that. Now that I was the winner—making risky gamblers wealthy— the crowd was on my side. Besides, everybody loved an underdog.

I relaxed for a moment in all the accolades. The Roman authorities wouldn't dare arrest me. The last thing Pontius Pilate wanted was a riot on his hands and be called back to Rome.

Now was my turn for sweet revenge. What had Tariq done to my father? And that time traveler who terrified Shale at the inn, Tariq must know who sent him.

I searched for my betrothed and Shira behind Pontius Pilate and his entourage, but I couldn't find them. Out of nowhere, I saw Much-Afraid scurrying across the racetrack. What was Shale's dog doing here? Horses and chariots were everywhere. Fear that she might get trampled made me panic.

As I was scheming how to help her, a mysterious cloud settled over the racetrack. Amid the fanfare, I heard someone whisper, "Daniel, the race isn't over."

Of course, the race was over. I looked around. Who said that, but I couldn't see anyone in the fog.

The noise of squeaking wheels and cheering fans began to fade into the distance. When the haze lifted, I saw an open scroll, and Tariq and I were racing again—this time among the stars.

I head a familiar, angry voice. "Michael, he's finished the race."

"Not so fast," the authoritarian voice replied.

The forgotten event happened on my way from Hurva Square to the first century—the argument between these two invisible creatures. I arrived at the inn with an injury to my forehead and couldn't remember how it happened. Dr. Luke bandaged it—the first time I met the impressive doctor.

"Time is an illusion until God's appointed times," Michael replied.

The angry voice retorted, "I'm outnumbered two to one. Isn't that like God, to stack the odds in his favor?"

"The Lord rebuke you. No one is taken until God's appointed time." Michael's answer seemed to settle the matter, and an uneasy silence followed.

Suddenly, my biga became unstable as Tariq appeared beside me in his chariot. He smiled, flipped his reins, and took off ahead of me.

"The race is over," I shouted to Tariq. The race had to be over. I won, despite what Michael said. The powerful angel must be referring to something else. I tried to catch Tariq, but everything was a blur until the earth came into view. A man appeared galloping on a white horse across the planet. While he was far away, he was also near. As the horse cantered, the rider's hair rippled around his smooth face. His narrow brown eyes matched his skin tone. Handsome, charismatic, and mysterious, he held a bow with no arrow. He was poised and self-assured. I continued to watch as reptilian-like hands placed a crown on his head. The rider turned his eyes toward me. He mouthed, "Mine," and galloped across the Middle East.

A second man riding a red horse appeared. I recognized him when I saw his face. He had become more powerful, more famous, and more profane. He held a sword in his hand and seized control of the kingdoms of the world. He took great delight waving the weapon as he galloped across Europe.

A third horse followed. The black stallion's rider held a pair of balances, and cries of mourning reached into the heavens. Burning grasslands crisscrossed the former breadbaskets of the world as the black horse turned into death. The rider had grown into a monster—deceptive, cunning, and evil.

Soon a green horse appeared. Whoever rode him was longer human. He was possessed, and wretched creatures followed him. The earth, wounded, hung limply in space. Death lingered over the planet and clung to me like poison.

I saw killers roaming the earth in the guise of beasts, plagues, wars, and famine. After much sadness from seeing so much suffering, I looked toward the heavens and saw an open door among the stars.

Through the door I could see under the altar the souls of them who were slain for the word of God. They were dressed in white shining robes. A heavenly counter was counting upwards with a number so significant I didn't know how to read it.

I heard one of the souls ask, "How much longer?"

"Rest a little longer," an angel said.

A holy quietness followed until a tsunami-like wave exploded. Shockwaves battered the solar system, and a blood-stained moon cast shadows over the earth's surface. The sun became blackened, and a cold wave of icicles clung to my bare skin.

Balls of fire fell upon the earth. The mountains shook, the islands split, and the seas roared. The earth reeled like a drunkard. Terrified earth-dwellers cried out to the rocks and mountains, "Fall on us. Hide us from the face of him who sits on the throne and from his wrath."

As quickly as it all began, the open door closed and a seal was stamped on the closed scroll so it couldn't be opened again except by the King.

A scarred hand touched my forehead. "Remember."

CHAPTER 2

I remembered what Yeshua said to me during my first appearance on the Mount of Olives. "It's not your appointed time now, but I'll bring you back when it is."

The trumpet blew from the Third Temple. Across the Kidron Valley, the Kohen were performing animal sacrifices. To perform such rituals in remembrance of Yeshua Hamashiach's death and resurrection would have been inspiring if the Jews hadn't missed the King's first coming.

As I stood dressed in white with the one hundred forty-four thousand Jewish evangelists, he quoted Scripture. "Many of you will be thrown into the flames, flogged, ripped in two, beheaded, and tortured. However, those of you who endure will be saved."

As I watched the Temple sacrifices, I was sad. Judaism promised so much more. Even two thousand years of wanderings did not soften the hearts of most Jews to consider Yeshua was the Son of David, the promised one. Despite that, God kept his unconditional covenant to Abraham, giving him land and millions of descendants so that through him the world would be blessed.

"You'll rule with me when I establish my kingdom," Yeshua

proclaimed. "However, my return won't happen until my people mourn for me."

The building of the Third Temple was the most significant sign of the King's return. Most missed its magnitude. The impressive structure rose prominently against the backdrop of modern society—big cars, hurried people, and a mishmash of iconic ruins from empires that rose and fell. Vainglory snuffed them out, but time etched its passage. Walls had been built and rebuilt. Trees had been chopped down and replanted. Through thousands of years, Israel had been conquered, freed, and reconquered.

Unexpected tears welled up. An imposter now ruled Jerusalem. Soon two witnesses would appear on the streets of Sodom. Their appearance would be another sign.

Yeshua finished with this admonition, "It will be more tolerable in that day for Sodom than for that city that receives you not." Following our commissioning, we sang a song. "Salvation and glory and honor and power are given unto our Lord and Savior. True and righteous are his judgments."

Millions of voices responded from the heavens. "Praise our God, all his servants, and fear him, both small and great."

A heavenly trumpet sounded, and an angel flew overhead. He'd soon share the everlasting Gospel with the earth-dwellers. "Fear God and give glory to him, for the hour of his judgment has come. Worship him who made heaven and earth, and the sea, and the fountains of waters."

As I gazed into the throne room, the door closed.

Yeshua's voice brought me back. "Why are you staring into the heavens?"

I lowered my gaze and met his eyes. He pointed to a wooden door that stood upright on the Mount of Olives. Through the opening, I could see a different place, but it wasn't well defined, more like shadows.

As I contemplated my future, I noticed thousands of doors were visible. Two by two, Yeshua was sending evangelists through them. He placed his hand on my shoulder. Another man whom I did not know stepped forward, and Yeshua put his other hand on his shoulder.

"Daniel and Jonathan, I've chosen you to be my faithful servants in the last days. Over one million nomads have never heard of the Kingdom of God. Demons and unclean spirits burden these wanderers. Fear not the signs in the heavens or the strange wonders on the earth. I send you out in power and strength. You will cast out devils and heal the sick. Receive visions and dreams. Remember, I have overcome the world."

With my eyes closed, I claimed Yeshua's power, and my new brother, Jonathan, and I stepped through the door.

CHAPTER 3

Sand—as far as I could see. The skull of an animal with antlers still attached rested on a shifting dune. Dozens of rock formations jutted into the sky creating a ghost kingdom of sand. Against the horizon, sand-dragons, dark faces, and steep pillars reminded me of images from the moon.

A strong gust of wind blew. I dug my head into my shoulder, but the dust was so fine my eyes burned before tears flushed it out. The sheets of wind eventually subsided, and I rested on a rock studying the endless, faceless terrain—bizarre but breathtaking.

Jonathan stood nearby brushing the sand out of his hair.

"We should look for a water source," I suggested. "Nomads can't live without water."

Jonathan crossed his arms leaning against a rock. "We can't either."

I tapped the water canteen Yeshua gave us. It wouldn't last more than a day.

"Which continent do you think this is?"

"The Sahara," Jonathan replied. "I often watched YouTube videos posted by hikers to unusual places. Desert videos fascinated me the most."

A sharp plateau rose in the distance. The only purpose I could see the sand spires served was shade for desert creatures before they died. "Why would anyone want to live in such a hostile place?"

"This is nothing like Florida, that's for sure."

I studied the young man. Jonathan was bulkier and more muscular than me. I could imagine him playing American football. "You're from the United States?"

He nodded. "Orlando. I was a freshman at the University of Florida. I wanted to study anthropology."

"Yeshua must have put that desire in your heart. This would be an anthropologist's paradise."

Jonathan looked away. "Life can change quickly, can't it?"

That was an understatement as I thought about the illusion of time in the seventh dimension. Earlier today I was in the first century. Now I was in the future on another continent.

Unusual structures jutted up at the oddest places. I flipped the sand with my sandal. "I've seen something similar in the Arava Valley, but the sand here is almost like dust. This looks like Mars."

"Disneyworld could make a fortune here," Jonathan quipped, "without spending millions."

I half-smiled. Disney is child's play—or is it? "Disney is a temple of the imagination," I heard a voice say. I looked around but saw no one. My imagination must be playing tricks on me. "I'm from Jerusalem, never been to Disneyworld."

"You're Israeli?"

I nodded. We stopped talking to conserve energy. The air was hot but not oppressive—just enough to make me sweat and wish I were somewhere else. It didn't take long to come upon leg bones of more dead animals. Sand bugs scurried among the wind-blown drifts.

After a while, my thoughts darkened. Why did Yeshua choose this door for us? Where did those other doors go—Brazil, a delightful Pacific Island? My disgruntled spirit fed itself until I recognized the source. I glanced at Jonathan. The upside was, we were in excellent physical shape.

The sun rose high in the sky. Heat exhaustion was a real possibility.

I drank most of the water, more than Jonathan. We would die out here if we didn't find potable water. At least it wasn't tortuously hot.

Sometimes hopeless prayers in hell-holes work. I saw something moving against the horizon. I broke the silence. "Jonathan, I see a car. Over there, isn't that a car?"

"Or a mirage." `

A mirage—I hadn't thought of that. It was hard to tell if it was coming toward us or away from us.

Jonathan threw up his hands and waved. "We should try to get his attention."

Less than a minute later, the driver pulled up and stuck his head out the window. "An intelligence officer said a drone picked you up. We received an alert—two sightseers missing. How'd you end up here?"

"We're looking for nomads," I began.

He interrupted. "Never mind. Get in."

The vehicle was old and junky-looking, but at this moment worth more than gold. The driver turned his head. "You're insane adventurers. I take you to town."

Jonathan and I immediately jumped in. Our driver put his foot on the gas pedal, and we took off bobbing on the road-less sand.

Low-lying scrubs and scraggly trees clung to life. Strange-looking spires sprouted from the sands. "What are those rock formations?" I asked the driver.

"They're the Towers of Ennedi. Some have never been touched. Did you come here to rock climb?"

"No. We're here to visit nomads."

The driver snorted. "I'm not getting close to those savages. They're untamed. You must want a real adventure. Some trekkers never return. That's why those tours stopped. No customers."

"Tribes are nearby?" I asked.

The man laughed. "Cow herders."

Jonathan and I exchanged glances.

"Can you take us to their encampment?" You would have thought I wanted an ocean in the desert.

He nodded. "But I'm not getting near them."

Soon we came to a roadblock, and three teenage soldiers approached us. They were dressed in full uniform, and one sported an M16 over his shoulder. Another held a copy of the Quran.

After a brief conversation in an Arabic dialect, the soldier shone a flashlight in the back seat. "Any Bibles or weapons?"

I shook my head. "No, nothing."

He stepped back and waved us on.

I noticed a map tucked inside the back pocket of the front seat. I pulled it out. "We're in Chad, Africa."

"Are you speaking English?" Jonathan whispered.

I nodded.

"Our driver is speaking English?"

"I guess so," I replied. I glanced down at the map. "At least we know what country we're in."

"And that soldier spoke English?"

I got Jonathan's point. "That seems odd, doesn't it?"

Jonathan leaned over the front seat. "How long before we get to the nomad encampment?"

The driver glanced in his rearview mirror. "Not long."

I stared at the map. All roads lead to heaven or hell.

CHAPTER 4

I leaned over and whispered, "Tell me about America. After the EMP attack, we didn't hear much."

"You mean after the electromagnetic pulse or after the rapture?"

"Tell me about the rapture first."

Jonathan's lips quivered. "Many professors and students at the University of Florida disappeared. They closed the doors thinking it was a terrorist attack. My mother teaches at a middle school, and all the kids twelve and under disappeared. Most students older than that remained, which was hard to explain unless you were a Christian.

"Suicide rates soared when parents couldn't find their children. Nursery and elementary schools went into lockdown. Most churches were empty. At least in Gainesville, only a handful remained open."

Jonathan bowed his head, shuffling his feet under the front seat. "The stock market crashed. Many companies closed. Unemployment shot up into double digits. You'd be surprised at how many people are employed in service industries related to children. Washington shut down. Riots broke out on the streets, and Martial law was declared. Karma eventually pays wages."

Even though Jonathan had lowered his voice, I was worried the driver could overhear us. I leaned forward. "Can you put on some music?"

He flipped through several stations and landed on one playing African rap.

"That sounds good. Thanks."

Clasping my hands behind my neck, I sat back. Jonathan was articulate and intelligent. He lived in America, and because American laws protected religious freedom, he should have heard about Yeshua. "Why are you still here?"

Jonathan kept his voice low. "Even though I'm Jewish, we were non-practicing. My family wasn't—still isn't—interested in Judaism."

He waved his hand dismissively. "We have a copy of the Ten Commandments on our dining room wall and a menorah in the foyer. Besides that, there is nothing to identify our heritage."

"Was that intentional?" I asked, thinking they had experienced anti-semitism.

Jonathan thought for a moment. "No, I think we were just comfortable. My dad works for the State. As I said, my mom is a teacher.

"I had a friend who was a Buddhist that I hung out with in high school. I thought it was brilliant that only five rules governed Buddhism.

"I liked Buddhist philosophy because it was based on reason—cause and effect. I thought I was a righteous person, and I believed if I lived an honest life, good karma would follow. I was convinced I could live by the Five Rules of Buddhism."

"What are they?" I asked.

"No killing, no stealing, no slanderous talk, no greed, and another one I've forgotten. I thought I could keep the Buddhist Golden Rules and find Nirvana. I realized later the rules were almost identical to the Ten Commandments."

"What did your parents think about you becoming a Buddhist?"

"That's hard to answer," Jonathan said. "We never talked about it. I don't think they cared that much."

I could relate.

"Anyway, I discovered I couldn't keep the Five Rules of

Buddhism. I never did anything terrible, but I wasn't righteous at all. I mean, I could hardly look at a beautiful woman without having lust in my heart. Actually, that's the fifth Golden Rule that I forgot—sexual purity. I eventually realized my lousy karma would cause me to suffer forever."

"Sort of like trying to earn your way to heaven?"

"Exactly. My high school friend told me I couldn't pay for my bad karma in this life. I would have to come back and pay for it in my next life."

"Like reincarnation?"

"Yes, reincarnation. I had so much bad karma I'd have to keep coming back. I needed to work my way out of suffering, so I was more enslaved than ever."

"So how did you learn about Yeshua?"

Jonathan tilted his head against the backseat. "I knew you would ask. That's the big question for Christians now, isn't it, why did you get left behind? Well, things only got worse when I went to the University of Florida. I had a dream one night that I died and turned into a black snake. When I tried to enter the gates of heaven, a light-covered man who identified himself as Peter wouldn't let me in. When I asked him why, he told me it was because I was a snake. I said I used to be human and tried to be good. I pleaded with him. 'That must be worth something.'

"Peter shook his head. He told me no matter how much good I did on earth, if I did one bad thing, one wrong thing, even if it was just telling a small lie, that it was enough to keep me out of heaven.

"Of course, I was devastated. I argued with him. 'No one can be that good.'

"As I was speaking to Peter, I heard the delightful sounds of heaven that were so near and yet so far away. I looked through the gates and saw other beautiful light-covered people. Then the most beautiful of the heavenly beings started walking toward me, but when he saw me, he turned away.

"I was devastated. 'Why did he turn away?' I asked Peter.

"Peter looked straight into my eyes and said, 'Yeshua, who took away the sins of the world, never knew you.'

Jonathan pinched the bridge of his nose. "Panic welled up inside of me. I asked, 'Is there anything I can do? If Yeshua will give me another chance, I'll return to earth and tell everyone I meet how to get to heaven.'

"Peter's shoulders sagged and he looked very sad. He had a book in front of him and he read through the page several times, making sure he didn't miss my name. Finally, he said, 'At the bottom of the hill is a fork in the road.' Peter pointed. 'Read the sign at the fork. You missed the sign when you were on earth, but perhaps God will give you another chance.'

"So I slithered down the hill as fast as I could. When I arrived at the fork, the sign had two arrows. One arrow pointed toward a wide road labeled destruction. The other arrow pointed toward a narrow road. That road didn't have a name. It only said, 'Enter here to take the narrow road that leads to life. Very few will find it.'

"I was so sad I coiled up as a rope beneath the sign and wished for snow to freeze me to death. There were no second chances. I couldn't go back. I didn't want to go forward.

"I remembered my days on earth, the choices I had made, and how I never gave Jesus a second thought. My longing sent me searching for another way to heaven. I thought Buddhism was the answer, but even good karma wasn't good enough.

"When I woke up, I was covered in perspiration. I needed to find someone who could tell me about Jesus. I didn't own a Bible. I needed to find one. I asked around campus if anybody knew any Christians. Someone suggested I go to the Christian Study Center.

"I started attending classes there. They had many philosophical discussions and apologetic lectures.

"When the purge happened, all those students and faculty disappeared. They were the only Christians I knew. I listened to the news to find out what happened, but I didn't believe what the media said."

"What did they say?"

"They said those who disappeared were taken by aliens. They called them Enki."

"Enki?" I repeated.

"Yes. They said the aliens left the good people here to save the planet." Jonathan shook his head. "That was an inadequate explanation for the disappearance of the kids."

"What happened at that?"

"Well, for one thing," Jonathan said, "I was more depressed than ever. The following weekend, I sat in the empty building at the Christian Study Center, took one of the Bibles off a bookshelf, and read the Gospel of Matthew. I got down on my knees and told God I was sorry. I asked him to forgive me for all the wrongs I'd done. I knew at that moment Jesus, who I prefer to call by his Jewish name, Yeshua, was the Messiah."

I took in a deep breath as I thought about his story. "It's so much harder for Jews to see the truth than anyone else, isn't it?"

Jonathan sighed. "I don't know why, but it's true. I read the New Testament that weekend. When I got to the book of Revelation, I knew we were in the last days. God spoke to me and said I was one of the one hundred forty-four thousand Jewish evangelists, and I needed to make Aliyah to Israel.

"A few days later, I called my parents. I told them everything. They were skeptical, but they let me come. I took the first flight I could catch and found some Jewish believers in Tel-Aviv. By then, thousands were arriving in Israel from all over the world."

Jonathan fell silent. "What about you?"

I drew in another long breath and exhaled slowly. My story was so strange, I wasn't sure Jonathan would believe me. I began by telling him how I had gone back in time in an alternate universe, a place that I called the seventh dimension. I told him how, in this other domain, we lived in a spiritual reality, and the choices we made in that dimension determined our eternal destiny. I finished with sharing how I left Shale in the first century. "That was the hardest part, is leaving my fiancée behind with a little girl we were taking care of because her parents had died."

"So you time traveled?" Jonathan asked, as if it was a common occurrence.

I chuckled, "Yeah, it was definitely interdimensional time travel. Like you, I did not believe Jesus could be the Messiah, until I met him at the cross and witnessed his resurrection."

Jonathan nodded. "I believe you, Daniel. I do. When I read the book of Matthew, it was as vivid and real to me as if I were there. It must be hard to be here and those you love not to be."

I swallowed hard. "It hasn't truly sunk in. Everything happened so fast…but I knew God would call me back. He told me he would bring me back when the time was right." I lamented, "I wish I had prepared Shale, but I had no way of knowing God would return me to this time and not Shale and Shira."

Jonathan comforted me. "I understand. But, you know, things are only going to get worse. If there is anything good in all of it, be thankful they aren't here."

"I'm definitely thankful they aren't here. I'd be so worried about their safety…"

Jonathan's spirits lifted. "The one good thing God provided for me was that international flights had finally been restored after the EMP attack. Otherwise, I don't know how I could have made it to Israel."

I nodded. "That's true."

"You know, Daniel, you would think that the electromagnetic pulse would have woken me up, but it didn't." Jonathan puckered his lips. "I guess you know about the Ezekiel War, how God intervened, and the rise of the new leader who took credit for Israel's victory."

"That was happening when Shale and I went back to the first century, with Shira."

Jonathan rolled his shoulders. "Most countries are under his control now, except for a few in the West."

"I suppose Europe is at the forefront of his empire?"

Jonathan nodded. "Turkey and Iran suffered severe losses when they invaded Israel." He pointed out the window. "Look."

CHAPTER 5

Straight ahead, brown women wearing brightly-patterned dresses and scarves stood with their hands planted on their waists. Their bodies were covered, unlike some African tribes, but what caught my attention were the animals. Several dozen cows, goats, and sheep were circumnavigating a couple of camels hunched in the middle of the circle. I couldn't tear my eyes away.

"Have you seen anything like that?" I asked.

Jonathan shook his head. "Looks like the animals are doing the Hajj in the Sahara."

A

long rectangular water trough came into view. A few cows left the main group and were walking toward it. The women were placing bowls on the ground.

"We stop here," the driver said.

A little farther, a community of tents appeared anchored to the desert like appendages. Waves of uncertainty flooded me. We didn't know the people, the culture, or the language.

The driver pointed. "These are the Shuwa nomads, a subgroup of a larger tribe, the Baggara. They're cattle herders.

"The women are doing the evening watering. I don't want to get any closer. They're known for their brutal raids. They plunder nearby villages so they can steal the cows."

"How much do we owe you?" Jonathan asked.

He rattled off a figure which I didn't understand. Jonathan and I looked at each other. Where were we going to get the money?

At that moment, several men became visible running toward us. The driver yelled, "Get out—they got guns!"

As soon as we jumped out, the driver took off, leaving behind a parachute of dust. Suppose he came back and accused us of not paying? Too many men were descending upon us to worry about that now.

I shouted to Jonathan, "Hold up your hands. Make it clear we don't have any weapons."

The nomads closed in on us. We kept our empty hands visible. White thobes with Arabic head coverings meant they'd had contact with Islam in the past. They also wore brown, leather amulets around their necks associated with animism. I suspected their worship was a blend of both. The men slowed down as they neared. I didn't see any guns or knives as the driver said. They abruptly stopped at a distance.

An awkward silence separated us. Then one of the Shuwa nomads stepped forward. "How are you?"

I was surprised he spoke English. "We're well. Thank you."

Satisfied with my answer, the man turned to Jonathan. "How is your mother?"

Jonathan's eyes widened. "My mother is fine. Thank you."

The Bedouin spoke to his compatriots, and they whispered among themselves.

The man who greeted us spoke again. "We would like for you to come to our tent and drink tea."

Jonathan and I exchanged glances. Were we walking into a trap? None of this fit with the horrid description the driver gave us.

"Would you like to have tea with our new friends?" I asked Jonathan.

He nodded. "Yes."

The leader motioned with his hand to follow. "Come."

The women stopped what they were doing and watched with curious eyes as we walked by. They were coaxing the rest of the animals to the water and feeding troughs, but their strange behavior stayed with me.

As we neared the village of tents, coldness crept up my arms, and I inhaled a whiff of foul air. I glanced at Jonathan, but he remained quiet.

A fence of native thorn bushes surrounded the encampment. Two women sat on the ground stirring food in large pots with long, curved bamboo sticks. The men stared at us, but I saw no signs of aggression.

The leader of the group who brought us spoke to one of the women. Then he pulled some reed mats off the top of his tent and placed them inside. The woman followed him in and brushed them off. After she finished, the leader signaled for us to join him and another man.

"The women will bring us tea," he said.

Jonathan and I removed our shoes before entering the tent and sat cross-legged on the mats. I didn't feel threatened by them, but I couldn't imagine why they brought us here. And how could we speak with them in English? Speaking in tongues was not unknown in the Bible. It was even a common practice by some in the twenty-first century, but I'd never experienced it.

After a while, a young woman brought us drink and extremely thin flatbread, also known as Bedouin bread. She offered it to each of us. Once we all shared, the woman left the tray if we needed more.

I took a sip. "This is very good."

The men smiled, happy that we appreciated their hospitality.

The leader held up his tea. "God is good. God is great, yes?"

I nodded. "Indeed. God is good. Very good."

The other man in the tent nodded.

They repeated this ritual a second time. Then the leader asked again if our mothers were well and if we were well. Finally, the leader appeared to relax and offered his hand. "I'm Amare."

Telling one's name must be a sign of friendship. I reached over and shook it. "I'm Daniel."

Jonathan said his name, and then the other Bedouin man stated his name as Cesar. After a couple of minutes of name sharing and drinking tea, another awkward silence followed. I wasn't sure what would happen next, so I took another sip of my drink and finished the bread.

When I began to think this was all there was to the visit, Amare held up his mug. "Let me share why we have been waiting for you to come."

CHAPTER 6

Jonathan raised his eyebrow. We both reacted the same way. The Shuwa nomads were waiting for us?

I edged closer. "Why have you been waiting for us to come?"

Amare set down his tea, stood, and strolled over to the doorway. He thrust his hand out the entrance. "What do you see?"

I ran my fingers through my hair. I wasn't sure what Amare meant.

Shifting from one foot to the other, he pulled the tarp away from the opening.

I peered outside. "I see men, women, animals—sheep, goats, cows, a donkey, two camels."

Jonathan interrupted. "There're no children. They were taken in the rapture."

Despair crossed Amare's face. He held up his palms and drew in a long breath. "We weren't fighting anyone that day. No sickness. The sun was high in the sky. My daughter was getting water. My son was with me."

His breathing quickened. "Rafa disappeared in front of my eyes," pointing to his own. He wiped his face.

"It happened everywhere," Jonathan said. "Not just here, all over the world."

Amare wept. "We miss our children." He returned to his mat. "Our old men have no young wives. The old women have no one to bring them water. Our little ones aren't here to tend to the goats and sheep."

He pointed to the watering area. "Now the women have to do the children's jobs. I prayed to Allah to send our children back and to bring the rains for our cows and animals. The desert rains have been few. Allah didn't answer.

"It's been months, years." He slapped at an insect on the mat. "I still have my children's clothes they were wearing the day they left us."

My mind wandered. Without the truth, how could anyone make sense of what happened?

"There is more," Amare said. He clutched his chest. "One day insects swarmed in on the hot desert winds. They consumed our crops. They hid inside our tents. They ate our clothes. We were afraid to destroy them. Suppose they were our children?

"Birds dropped out of the sky, and our land became contaminated. The air smelled foul. Everyone believed it was the desert demons. They're angry, and the clouds have withheld their rains," Amare said.

"After that, Ennedi fell from the sky. The earth broke apart. Chasms appeared in the rocks and cut open our sacred places. Kadir, our leader, went into the city to talk to the Imam."

Amare dropped his shoulders and hung his head. "Nothing helped. The days became nights, and the nights became days. Hot became cold, and cold became hot. The sun rose when it should have set and set when it should have risen. No one knows the times or seasons anymore. Our animals act strangely now, walking in circles from sunrise to sunset."

Amare threw up his hands. "We prayed for God's mercy. The Imam told Kadir a neighboring tribe cursed our animals. So we raided the tribe that put a spell on us. We killed many and stole their cows, but their cows did the same thing. Our leaders met. We couldn't agree. Some thought the unclean spirits in the desert were getting too powerful.

"Three nights ago, I had a dream. A man was coming toward me from the desert dressed in a white robe wearing brown sandals. I went out to meet him.

"He said, 'I am Isa.'

"Terrified, I dropped to my knees. Isa lifted my face with his hand and said, 'I have heard your prayers. Two men will come from the desert in three days. They will tell you about your children. Listen to them and do what they say.'

"Then he turned and left. A strong wind arose, and he disappeared in the swirling dust. I remembered everything when I woke up.

"Today is the third day. We've been watching and waiting all day. I began to doubt. Perhaps the dream didn't mean anything. Then I saw the van, but there were three men and not two. How could I know if these were the men Isa told me would come?

"As we neared, I saw two men get out of the van. Then the vehicle fled. My dream must be true. Still, I needed to be sure. Now I'm sure. Please tell us about our children as Isa promised and what we're to do."

Anxious eyes waited. I glanced at Jonathan. He wanted me to answer.

"Do you know who Isa is?" I asked.

Amare nodded. "Yes. He's a prophet and messenger of God. Peace, be upon him."

The other Bedouin, Cesar, added, "The Imam said he performed miracles and healed the sick."

Jonathan squared his shoulders. "Isa, also known as Jesus, is more than a prophet. When you say, 'peace be upon him,' Jesus will give you his peace."

As Jonathan spoke, we heard faint voices and footsteps outside. A man stuck his head inside the tent. Two others were behind him.

"The elephant has fallen," the messenger shouted. Amare's face froze. "Kadir." His eyes fell on Jonathan and me. "I must go see our leader."

"Can we come?" I asked.

He nodded, gesturing with his hands. "Come."

CHAPTER 7

I didn't know what Amare meant by "the elephant had fallen." The late afternoon rays cast long shadows through the thick, muggy air as we followed the messengers to the other side of the encampment. Nomads were gathered outside Kadir's tent when we arrived.

Inside the tent, two women sat on a mat with tears streaming down their faces. A sheet covered a body. A masked man wearing a beaded headband with bird feathers was uttering incantations. Beside him were potions. We appeared to have been too late.

Amare pulled the sheet away from Kadir's face, leaned over, and listened. "I hear no breath sounds."

"How long was he sick?" I asked.

The witch doctor replied, "Several days."

Amare replaced the sheet. The room was quiet except for the women sobbing.

I whispered Amare's thoughts to Jonathan. "He had a toothache. Amare feels overwhelmed as the new leader."

Jonathan looked strangely at me. I should have told him I could read human thoughts, my special gift.

Amare shook his head in disbelief. "The witch doctor failed, the incantations failed, and the sacrifices failed."

I heard a voice speaking. "Listen to the men."

Amare looked around the tent. "Isa, is that you?" He turned his eyes toward me.

I prompted Amare. "Kadir had a toothache?"

"Yes," Amare said.

A tooth abscess was deadly in the desert because the infection could spread to the brain. I whispered to Jonathan. "We should pray."

"Amare, if we pray in the name of Jesus ..." Jonathan's voice trailed.

"Can we pray for Kadir?" I asked.

"Kadir"—he shrugged—"is dead now. No breath is in him."

"Can I still pray?"

Amare nodded and pulled the cover back from Kadir's face.

Jonathan and I laid hands on the dead man. I prayed, "Dear Father, we come to you in the name of Jesus. We ask you to show the nomads the Kingdom of God and raise Kadir from the dead. In Jesus' name we pray."

Jonathan prayed after me. After a few minutes, we finished and waited. I hoped to see a miracle that would reveal God's superiority over the demons. Disappointment set in when nothing happened. An awkward silence spoke to the lack of a healing miracle.

Amare's face remained expressionless. After a respectful amount of time, he got up and left. Jonathan and I followed him. Moved with compassion when I saw tears in Amare's eyes outside the tent, I told myself not to be angry with God.

"Thank you," Amare said. "I'd hoped Isa would be more powerful than our witch doctors. He told me to listen to you. I did what he asked."

Before I could answer, Amare's face became white.

I turned and saw Kadir standing in the doorway of the tent.

"I feel better now," he said. "The witch doctor healed my tooth."

❋

A strong gust of wind steepled up around the encampment. A couple of goats began fighting. We could not allow the powers of darkness to snake into his healing. Vultures circled overhead. I squinted. No, those weren't vultures. They were drones. The spy planes the driver spoke of? I didn't know.

Before I could think, Amare ran to Kadir. He held his hand in front of his nose. "The breath of life is in you."

"I'm alive," Kadir said. "You speak as if I was dead." Kadir's eyes looked past Amare and studied us. "Who are these men?"

"You died," Amare said. "These men, through Isa, brought you back to life."

Murmurings filled the crowd.

Kadir stared at us. "My tooth no longer hurts. The incantations worked."

Amare walked back to me and stood within inches of my face. "Daniel, tell me about Isa."

After Amare asked the women to provide food and drink to Kadir, we went back to Amare's tent. It didn't take long for word to spread. Dozens of nomads showed up. What seemed like a small tribe in the Sahara turned into a large gathering of cow herders.

After an evening meal, we sat around a fire drinking tea. Amare had picked out a few men he wanted us to share about Isa. "Tell us about our children. Isa said for me to listen to you."

Kadir insisted on coming, to everyone's surprise. Several men had confided to me they had a hard time believing Isa was more powerful than the demons. They wanted to learn more.

The crackling of the fire and whispers of night creatures filled the air. A full moon cast shadows of light and darkness. It was one of those moments when everything seemed perfect.

"As you know," Amare said, "many unusual things have happened in recent months. Our children are missing. The Imams haven't been able to answer our questions.

"Three nights ago, I had a dream. I saw a man walking above the drifting sands. A white light surrounded him. He came toward me and said, 'I am Isa.'

"I noticed he had scars on his hand. He said 'I've heard your prayers. In three days, two men will come out of the desert sands. They will answer your questions.'

"When I woke up, I remembered my dream. Today is the third day. When I saw the van, I thought this must be the men Isa said would come." Amare pointed to Jonathan and me. "I invited them to have tea with us.

"As they began to tell me about Isa, messengers came. 'The elephant has fallen,' they said.

"We ran to Kadir's tent. Daniel asked if they could pray. Kadir, can you come up here?"

He stood beside Amare.

"Isa used Jonathan and Daniel to raise this man from the dead, the men Isa promised to send. We've seen that Isa is more powerful than the demons. Can we listen to Daniel speak?"

Nods spread through the listeners.

I whispered to Jonathan, "Pray for me."

I stood. "A great prophet lived long ago. You know him as Isa. He's also known by Christians as Jesus. Jews call him Yeshua.

"The Quran is correct. He was a great prophet, but he was more than a prophet. He was the Son of God. Your leader has shared with me there is a great fear among you. Curses from your enemies bring diseases and hardship. Demons come from the desert and torment you. Kadir died from a tooth infection. Your doctors couldn't heal him. The Kingdom of God is here. Through Jesus' power, we raised Kadir from the dead."

Kadir stood. "Amare, did you pay money to these men?"

"No," Amare said. "They've not asked for money from us."

I continued. "At thirty-three years old, God's only Son, Jesus, was killed by evil men. He was a perfect man. He died for the sins of the Baggara. To receive God's forgiveness, you must become a follower of Jesus."

"He died for our sins?" a man asked.

I nodded. "You must, in a sense, be born again, and repent of all the wrong things you've said and done."

A stunned silence followed. After I returned to the mat, I remembered I forgot to say why their children were missing.

Discussion ensued as the men broke into groups. I answered a few questions as several asked me to explain more. Amare came up to me. "The men want to discuss what you've shared. They're asking about their children. Can you tell them where they are?"

When everyone was quiet, I explained, "The power of Jesus raised Kadir from the dead. But Jesus' judgment is upon the world now. Jesus took all the children away to save them from the wrath to come.

"Soon the Kingdom of God will come to earth and Jesus will reign from Jerusalem. Even now his kingdom is spreading.

"Think how hard it would have been if your children were here. Isa will keep them safe until he returns. Take comfort that your children are in heaven."

I glanced at Amare. He nodded.

I looked up. "Thank you, Father." I knew the powers of darkness among the Baggara would not surrender without a fight.

CHAPTER 8

As the men were leaving, Amare took me aside. "Sleep here."

Later that night, as I lay on the mat inside his tent, I flashed back to the race. My joy lasted only seconds. At least Dominus could pay off the financial mess I created by breaking my horseracing contract, and Shale could live off the winnings and take care of Shira, the three-year-old orphan God wanted us to adopt. I'd taken a huge risk racing, but I beat Tariq, something that seemed impossible. I wished I'd asked him about my father when I had the chance. The worst part was my guilt over Shale. Her face flooded my thoughts as I left Theophilus' house. I recalled her last words, "Goodbye."

Why didn't I listen to her and get married? All she wanted was to be my wife. I hated to think she might become a betrothed widow in the first century. As one of the one hundred forty-four thousand, death would hunt me down every single hour of each day from now on.

I knew Theophilus would protect Shale as long as she stayed with my sister and extended family, but what if she didn't? I could see my betrothed going to the inn and asking Jacob to send her back. My brother would do whatever she wanted—Shale could be quite convincing and quite persistent.

And, of course, what about Shira? Maybe that's why God wanted us to adopt her—to prevent Shale from searching for me. She would protect Shira at all costs, even staying in the first century.

And Much-Afraid? What was she doing on the racetrack? Had God sent Shale's favorite dog back in time because I might never return?

As my eyes became heavy, the strange conversation in the chariot haunted me. Those voices—I'd heard them another time also, arguing over my future. God had kept the vision from me until now—but why? When I closed my eyes, I remembered it, but this time, I knew the dream was slightly altered.

Someone called my name. "Daniel G. Sperling." I looked and saw a very tall creature wearing a black robe. He held a large book in his hand.

Another well-built supernatural creature dressed in a shimmering white robe appeared, blocking the other's path so he couldn't reach me. "You can't have him. His name is in the book now."

The supernatural being gritted his teeth. "He's mine."

The authoritative voice raised his voice. "Your power is diminishing, Lucifer."

"I'm still the prince of the air, Michael."

"His soul has been purchased, and you can't have him."

"Michael, his death is imminent."

"His time has not yet come, you fallen one, and you are not all-knowing."

The two argued back and forth.

The man in the white robe held up his hands. "The race is not over, Lucifer." Michael turned his eyes to me. "Finish your journey, Daniel. Know you are highly esteemed, and keep seeking the truth."

Distressed voices awakened me. I felt something cold and slimy on my legs, and I jumped up slapping my thighs. Jonathan and Amare were shouting.

I searched in the darkness. "What is it?"

Jonathan answered. "Snakes!"

Amare scrambled out of the tent and shouted, "Wake up, horned vipers have invaded." He ran to the tent next to ours. "Vipers are in our tents."

Jonathan and I followed him. I could see horror-stricken faces from the light of the moon and the stars. One of the men stirred up the fire embers. "We need torches."

Amare was running from tent to tent. I rushed to another one in the opposite direction, "Snakes!"

By the time we counted them, six tents were infested.

Exhausted, I asked Amare, "Has this ever happened?"

"No," Kadir interrupted. "Isa put a curse on us."

"Isa would not do that," Amare fired back.

"Isa's cursed us," he said. "These men brought a curse on us."

Amare shook his head. "These are good men. Isa is good. He saved your life."

While they quarreled, I pulled Jonathan off to the side. "What are the chances that six tents would have snakes unless it was demonic?"

He reached over and grabbed my tunic. "Zero. The demons must obey the voice of Yeshua. We should tell the demons to go back into the desert."

Jonathan let go of me, and I straightened my cloak. We returned to the encampment where two men were lighting torches. The displaced women took refuge in safe tents with friends. A couple dozen men guarded the others.

I found Amare. "We can make the snakes go away. The demons must obey Jesus."

Amare took one of the torches. "Let's go," he said. "I believe you."

We opened up his tent, and he waved the torch in the air. At least a dozen shapeshifters were crawling on the mats. Two were shimmying up the poles. With the light, I could see the horns over each eye. The snakes flicked their tongues and coiled backward as if they wanted to strike.

"You do it," I told Jonathan.

He stepped in front of me. "In the name and power of Yeshua, I command you to leave and return to the desert."

At once, the snakes came toward us. Those slithering on the pole fell to the ground.

Jonathan backed into me. "Let's get out of here."

It didn't take long. We waited as others gathered. Within an hour, every snake in Amare's tent was gone.

Murmurings filled the air. We went to the other five cursed tents and commanded the vipers to leave. When we arrived at the last one, I suggested to Jonathan, "Amare should cast out these. He can exercise the same power we have, in the name of Jesus."

Jonathan wasn't sure. "Suppose it doesn't work? They aren't believers. Don't you have to believe in Jesus to exercise his power?"

"The demons don't know what we know, but they must obey what they're told to do in the name of Jesus."

Jonathan nodded. "That makes sense."

I tapped Amare on the shoulder. "We want you to cast the snakes from the last tent. The demons must obey Isa."

Doubt filled Amare's eyes.

Kadir pointed his finger. "Amare, you brought these men here. Isa supposedly spoke to you in a dream. Do you not trust them?"

Amare stood up straighter. "What do I need to do?"

I told him what to say, emphasizing again the demons must obey.

He entered the tent with Jonathan. This time Jonathan held up the torch. Amare's voice was clear. "In the name of Isa, I command you to leave and return to the desert."

Within seconds, the snakes left and joined the others departing. The first rays of light revealed the mass exodus. I wanted to crush their heads. Every time I walked on a dune, now, I'd be thinking about stepping on a desert horned viper.

The event took a few hours, long enough to ponder Yeshua's power over the forces of nature. When the last of the snakes were gone, the men dispersed, and the women returned to their tents. The world of the Baggara wouldn't be the same.

A couple of men came up to Jonathan and me. "What must we do to have that kind of power?"

"Become a follower of Jesus and repent of your sins."

Amare pleaded, "Stay with us for a few days and teach us every-thing about Isa."

The Baggara began to call Isa by his Christian name Jesus—abandoning the common Arabic translation. Many repented. Jonathan and I took turns preaching the Gospel of the Kingdom, emphasizing his soon return. We told the nomads about the seven years of suffering. We stressed that impostors would come, claiming to be Jesus; that preachers would preach there were many ways to heaven and that we were already in the tribulation. We told them since the Kingdom of God was near, Jesus commissioned one hundred forty-four thousand Jewish evangelists, and he sent Jonathan and me to the Baggara people. We shared with the nomads that many would die, but those who endured until the end would be saved.

One day as I was venturing out to the sand dunes alone to be with God, I overheard some men talking. They were discussing raiding a nearby village to get camels. I knew man's heart was wicked, but how could they go on this killing spree, continuing in their old ways, and believe in Yeshua?

I returned to the village and found Jonathan, explaining to him what I heard.

He answered, "The Baggara need to go and witness to those they want to kill. Otherwise, they've no testimony."

I crossed my arms and gazed off into the desert. "What do you think the chances of that are?"

Jonathan rolled his shoulders. "Remember how surprised I was when you told me you could read minds?"

That was a change of topics. I nodded.

"After I became a believer, I started seeing things in the future before they happened."

"Like a prophet?"

Jonathan laughed. "I'm no prophet and wouldn't want to be one because they often die early deaths. No, it's more like God gives me a word of knowledge."

I waited for him to continue.

"Many things have happened since Yeshua sent us here, and some of those things I knew before they happened. That's how I knew snakes were attacking us in the tent before anyone else."

"Why didn't you tell me?"

"Because I knew you would ask me what other word of knowledge God might have given me, and I didn't want to tell you."

My heart pounded. "Like what?"

"Like right now, some of the men are going to attack a nearby village. That's why I'm here praying. A few will blame Yeshua for their heavy losses. Some will grow weary, seeing Yeshua as a heavy-handed taskmaster. Even so, many will recognize their sin and repent, even after we're gone."

I studied Jonathan. "I can read your mind if you don't tell me everything."

Startled by my response, he glanced away. "I could always be wrong."

I shook my head. "I'm sorry, I shouldn't have said that." Frustrated, I planted my hands on my waist. "It doesn't change anything, does it, what we say here?"

Jonathan shook his head. "But prayer will strengthen us, and why should we put limits on what God can do because of our lack of trust? We already know most of the one hundred forty-four thousand evange-lists will be martyred."

I glanced at Jonathan's hands as he wiped the blade of a knife. I plopped down, and we bowed our heads in prayer. When we finished, I returned to the common area.

CHAPTER 10

Amare rushed up to me. "Where have you been? Kadir and a group of men confiscated all the weapons from the shed and went to the Teda tribe. I tried to stop him, but he wouldn't listen. What should we do?"

I clasped his shoulders. "Pray for God's mercy, and pray God will give you an opportunity to share Jesus with the Teda nomads."

His eyes bulged. "You think our enemies will listen to us after we attack them?" He flung my hands away and stepped back. "I fear God now. This is all wrong. And Kadir, he knows the truth. Jesus raised him from the dead. I am sick at heart."

I grabbed Amare by the shoulders again. "Gather all your men, those who will come, and let's meet in front of your tent."

"Yes, we can pray," Amare said.

I watched as he approached some men. The conversation seemed to go well, so I raced back to Jonathan. Together we went to Amare's tent. While we waited, three women approached. "We are followers of Jesus. Can we come and pray also?"

It was customary for the men and women to pray apart, but I agreed. More women joined us, and soon we had a large gathering.

Amare, Jonathan, and I assembled the prayer warriors into small groups of four or five. I told them to join hands and pray. Those too afraid watched from a distance. Fear covered their faces—a familiar fear that I hoped Yeshua would take away.

Suddenly, we heard voices. It happened quickly—loud shouts and movement of people.

"The Teda are coming to kill us," Amare said.

"Keep praying, don't move."

I heard weeping from the women, but their prayers intensified. I prayed for God's mercy, deliverance, and a chance to share Yeshua.

Minutes later, the place was swarming with bodies. The Teda warriors wore different colors, and when they saw the onlookers fleeing, they took off after them with their knives and spears.

"Keep praying," I shouted.

The warring factions disappeared behind a wall of shifting dunes. Shouts echoed across the desert sands followed by silence.

Then something unexpected happened. Emerging from the dunes were two men and a woman. One of the men was from the Baggara tribe, and the other man was a Teda nomad. As they approached, I noticed the woman was carrying a child. The remaining members of the warring factions stayed back—those who survived the ambush.

Jonathan and I exchanged glances.

Amare whispered what no one could believe. "The Baggara woman is carrying a baby." Surprise spread through the prayer warriors. One of the women cried out, "My daughter is alive." Some of the men started to get up, but I told them to wait. "Let them come to us."

Amare acknowledged the Baggara peacemaker, and he greeted the Teda leader by exchanging hand gestures. It never occurred to me there would be a language barrier. "Yeshua," I prayed, "please give them the gift of speaking in tongues."

The woman stepped forward. "I will speak."

What she said was understandable to me and appeared to be so with the others. She seemed capable of speaking both languages at the same time.

The woman explained. "I was with child when our children were taken. I didn't tell anyone I had life within me, so no one knew, except one man. Like Hagar, one of Abraham's wives, I packed up food and water and went into the desert. After two days, I had nothing. What was I going to do?

"A Teda man found me and offered me food and water. He took me to his tent, and I stayed with him and his wife. They lost their son when the children disappeared. After the birth of my son, they loved my child as if he were their own.

"The Teda treated me well. I learned their language. I learned the Teda nomads are like the Baggara. They've camels, goats, and eat the same food. They sing, recite poetry, and dream.

"Today, Baggara thieves wanted to plunder. I took my baby and hid. I feared for my life and my baby's life. Would the Teda retaliate by killing us?

"After the Teda slaughtered some of the Baggara, the Teda took off in revenge to kill more of my people. I cried. When will the killing end? I speak both languages. What can I do?

"I knew a shortcut through the dunes and chased the Teda. The fighting stopped when they saw me. No woman would ever come between warring parties. One of the Baggara men knew me. I felt shame, but I wanted to speak. I spoke in the language of both.

"This is what I said. 'I offer my baby and myself as a blood sacrifice if you will stop fighting and killing each other. I want peace between us.'

"The Teda shook their heads. They dropped their weapons. Then the men from my tribe, the Baggara, did the same.

"The leader of the Teda walked over to me. He said, 'This is the only baby in the world. He's God's gift to the Teda. He shouldn't have to die to bring peace. And you, his mother, are blessed.'

"A man from the Baggara came forward. He said something I didn't understand, but I translated what he said to the Teda. He said, 'God has already sent a baby to bring peace—a long time ago. Only now do I understand we must change our ways. In my village are two men. We will take you to them. They will share about another baby greater than this one. We don't want this baby to die. We have no babies in our village. Perhaps we can learn how to live together.'

"Now, I want to meet these two men who can tell us about a baby who came long ago to bring peace. Please share—so my baby and I can live, so we can all live, and suffer no more bloodshed."

A pregnant silence followed. All eyes turned toward Jonathan and me as we joined the leaders and stood beside the woman.

"She is right," I said. As fear lessened, the listeners moved closer. The woman's story was similar to Hagar's and was a good segue to explain the Kingdom of God. Sadly, however, despite God's supernatural grace poured out on one brave woman, Kadir and many others were dead. If Kadir had believed, he would have lived, but he did not endure because of his unbelief.

CHAPTER 11

Many earth-dwellers became believers in the weeks following that day. Word spread among neighboring tribes there was peace between the Baggara and the Teda. How could two mortal enemies become friends? Visitors came to see for themselves.

I knew that not all the seeds would fall on fertile soil. I feared the coming persecution—perhaps mostly because we didn't know what form it would take, but Jonathan and I knew the Day of the Lord was here, and billions would die. What we didn't expect was how soon the authorities would detect our proselytizing.

The day was overcast and gloomy when the familiar vehicle pulled up to the encampment. I recognized the driver. Perhaps he'd returned to be paid. A second man got out of the back seat. I knew him also. He was the man holding the AK-47 at the checkpoint who asked if we had a Bible.

The curious walked over to see why they were here. Visits of this kind were rare because no one trusted the Baggara.

"They've come for us," I heard Jonathan say.

I turned and saw him approaching. "The driver just wants his money, right?"

Jonathan didn't answer. His eyes confirmed my fears. We could run away, but what kind of example would that set for the new believers? Besides, did God call us to flee from persecution?

Instead, we walked over to greet the two visitors. Amare was gesturing with his hands, but he didn't give any indication that something was wrong. I was still hopeful, but when the driver saw us, his friendliness turned to angst.

The soldier stepped toward us. "Proselytizing isn't permitted under the New World Order. You have disobeyed the High Command. You are under arrest."

"We have no Bibles," I said.

"You are telling nomadic tribes Jesus is the Messiah. You are spreading falsehoods and undermining the authority of the New World Order. Disobedience isn't allowed. We must take you to the nearest headquarters for treason."

"Treason?" I repeated.

The driver added, "You also never paid me. I told the authorities I didn't know your purpose. They almost arrested me. I thought you were tourists, not Christians."

Amare interrupted, waving his hand in front of the men. He turned to me and said in a depressed voice, "Tell them in the last month, peace has come to the Sahara. When has there ever been peace between the Teda and Baggara? Tell them you're peacemakers, nothing more."

It was apparent the soldier and driver didn't understand the tribal language, but they understood Jonathan and me. I repeated what Amare told me to say, albeit reluctantly.

The soldier replied, "Anything done in the name of Jesus is evil. He's the great deceiver. Just wait until the rains stop and the plagues come, like in the rest of the world. You'll be fighting again. The only peace that can come is through Prince Adonikam."

A crowd gathered a safe distance away. I didn't want to put Amare at risk. He was the new leader since Kadir's death. The Baggara needed him, and we were expendable.

I spoke to Amare, hoping to strengthen his faith, believing the soldier and the driver would not understand my words. "Amare, trust in the one who died for you. Your freedom is bound up in him. Don't be deceived, and endure."

Jonathan added, "We'll see you again. Whatever you do, don't accept the mark."

I was glad we told them about that. I didn't see the need, but Jonathan insisted.

I looked up at the overcast sky. Several drones were flying above us. Had they been watching us for the last month, monitoring our activities?

The soldier put us in handcuffs and nudged us with the rifle tip to his van. The cows, goats, and sheep were circumnavigating the camels —just as when we arrived. It was a ritual that defied explanation. In one sense, nothing changed; in another, everything changed.

As we climbed into the van, the Sahara seemed surreal. We had arrived a month earlier with no idea what we were doing. Many nomads would make it to heaven because of our witness—their names now etched in the Book of Life.

I whispered to Jonathan, "If we pray, maybe God will save us."

Jonathan nodded, and for the next two hours, we prayed.

CHAPTER 12

I clenched my eyes as I sat in the back seat and recited all the Bible verses I knew. Voices from the front drifted to the back, and despite my desire to pay no attention to our captors, I would succumb to the temptation of listening. My eavesdropping filled me with paranoia, so then I would pray. I was caught up in an endless cycle of trying to trust God and failing. I exhaled and inhaled purposefully, remembering all the martyrs. How did they have such faith?

I glanced at Jonathan, and his peaceful countenance strengthened me. To allow my mind to drift would take me to divers' places—where monsters hung out and wreaked havoc with men's souls. It wasn't the thought of dying that made me afraid. It was the process—would it be quick and painless or slow and painful?

Thank goodness God appointed man to die once. For that reason alone, why would anyone want to worship another god or believe in another faith? The thought of dying over and over to achieve Nirvana was not appealing.

I cast aside my broodings. "Yeshua, help me." I prayed for the nomads and everyone I could think of—my beloved Shale, Shira, my family, and those whose lives we might touch if God allowed us to live. I prayed that God would increase our reach into the remotest regions of the Sahara.

The sand drifts had no beginning and no end. They all looked the same—rivulets disappearing into nothingness. As we navigated in and out of dunes, the wind began to howl. Long breaths emanated from the trackless sand beneath the vehicle, followed by a thump-thump-thump that reminded me of a beating heart. Dust clouds accumulated from the loose sand, and the floating islands slammed into the vehicle. A protracted trumpet blast sounded, but the swirling islands blocked my view. I couldn't see anything.

"The sand is roaring," Jonathan whispered.

"What?" I asked.

"When the sand is ripped by external forces, it roars," Jonathan explained.

I didn't know what he was talking about, but before I could say anything, shouts from the front erupted. The engine hissed and sputtered, and I could feel the tires sinking into the dune. The wheels spun, pushing the limits of the vehicle, and then the unthinkable happened. The engine stalled, and the vehicle died. A long blast echoed through the desert that reminded me of a trumpet. Where was the sound coming from?

I heard the driver moaning. I looked toward the front seat and saw the soldier waving a blood-covered knife. The driver was squirming to get away from the blade. With great difficulty, he pushed the door open and fell out. Within seconds, the supernatural storm blasted him, covering him in sand. Blood oozed from his shoulder as he stood. Confused and disoriented, he lumbered away directionless in the howling wind.

The soldier, waving the bloodied knife, spoke roughly. I recognized in his Chadian Arabic the word Allah. I prayed he wouldn't reach for his gun. At that moment, a wicked gust entered the driver's open door. Shouts of anger left the soldier's lips as sand lodged in his eyes. He dropped the knife.

Jonathan and I exchanged glances. "Cover your eyes," I said.

We flung open the back doors. I fell out, unable to brace my fall because of my bound hands. The sand was scaling up the sides of the vehicle, and I pulled myself up with great difficulty. I dug my face into my robe and leaned into the van for balance. Then Jonathan bumped into me, and we almost knocked each other over.

"Should we stay here?" I shouted over the roar. That AK-47 haunted me, and the soldier who wouldn't think twice about using it. I also felt a twinge of guilt for leaving him in the makeshift coffin, but I didn't care. We needed to focus on saving ourselves.

The blast funneled through the sand as the waves rippled like a burrowing worm. We might be dead by the time the storm ended. The van would soon be submerged. We couldn't do anything but pray.

Jonathan saw him first. He pointed as best he could with his shackled hands. A dark figure was approaching. At first, I thought it must be the driver. Who else would be out here? But as he neared, the roaring ceased. A sudden calmness filled the area, like the eye of a hurricane. I couldn't imagine anyone being able to walk through this maelstrom except a supernatural being. I pulled my hands apart, and the bindings fell off.

At the same time, Jonathan shouted, "Look."

When the figure reached us, I knew who it was.

The man reached over and covered my face with his hand. "You are my messenger."

CHAPTER 13

I heard voices singing, "How beautiful on the mountains are the feet of those who bring good news."

My Lord uncovered my eyes, and I was standing in a chariot of fire. I clenched the reins and swallowed hard, thankful to be alive. I hoped my path crossed Jonathan's in the future.

Over the whisperings of space, I heard discordant, tinny noises. They reminded me of the sound of water dripping into an empty cup or well lined with tin. The sounds were from earth.

"We did it," a voice said.

Applause erupted.

"Where are they going?"

Silence.

"There is a disturbance in Eilat."

"I think we opened a Pandora's Box."

"Close it."

"What is that writing?"

"It's Hebrew."

"What does it mean?"

The Israeli voice spelled the letters. "T-e-k-e-l."

An anxious female in a French accent asked, "What does Tekel mean?"

"You have been weighed in the balance and found wanting."

Emerging from the black stardust, Tariq shot past me. I'd forgotten we were still racing. I glanced down at my gladiator clothing as my heart pounded in my chest. Ice pellets and fiery meteors swooped past.

The horses descended toward earth as we passed through ash-like feathers. Soon we dipped through layers of clouds, and when we broke through, I was delighted we were almost to the ground.

The blinding, unnatural light burned my eyes. Squinting, I could see bits and pieces of a mountainous desert that extended way out in the distance. A large body of red water bordered the barren terrain.

Tariq interrupted my musings as he came alongside me. His lips were turned up in an annoying smile. He wiped his mouth with his shoulder, reminding me of a savage. "I knew the money would lure you back," he quipped.

Was it appropriate for a Jewish evangelist to call someone a jerk? I bit my tongue. I wanted to ask him about my father. Some sense of civility could make that happen.

Wherever we were, our gladiator apparel would not endear us to the natives. I checked the sheath on my belt. I still had the knife.

I wanted to curse the blinding light. Fortunately, the horses didn't seem bothered, and the animals brought us to an oasis. I stepped off the chariot, edged over, and cupped my hands. The horses had already dipped in their nostrils.

After having my fill, I stood, studying the surroundings. Tariq was a short distance away. He seemed disinterested in hydrating himself. How could he not be thirsty?

Suddenly, I heard a swishing noise. Our horses and chariots were gone. Had God returned them to the first century? More edgy about their disappearance than I cared to admit, I looked straight ahead. A stone walkway led through palm trees and disappeared. I couldn't distinguish much because of the sunlight, but I could see a wall.

I started along the pathway, and Tariq trailed behind me. Impressive columns accentuated the trail with palm trees providing some relief from the overbearing sunlight. The trees also offered a place to hang cameras. I first noticed them when I heard a clicking sound. When I examined the columns, I saw more cameras, and then I realized the columns were really 5-G towers. Someone was watching us.

I put my hand over my knife—just in case.

CHAPTER 14

The walkway led to a stone wall that was about three meters high. An old wooden door was built into the wall so I couldn't see through to the other side. A voice spoke in English with a thick Middle Eastern accent. "Step forward, please."

I juggled the door open, and Tariq slipped in behind me. Why was he following me? On this side, the path continued, fortified by succulent desert plants and trees that seemed more appropriate for a temperate rain forest. The vegetation was so thick I couldn't see more than a few meters in any direction.

Soon a white cubicle came into view. While quaint looking, it wasn't what I expected—perhaps something more secure and less flimsy. The door was white with peeling paint around the edges of a small window. A suave-looking man was gazing at us through the hole.

"Please approach," he said.

I walked up to the cubicle.

He smiled. "Welcome."

I expected Tariq to join me at the window, but he didn't.

The man handed me some dark glasses and pointed. "Go that way, and I'll open the gate."

I appreciated the sunglasses. "Thank you."

"Also," he added, "once you put them on, don't take them off. You don't want to be blinded, do you?" He smiled again.

"Where am I?"

He looked puzzled. "You don't know where you are?"

I shook my head.

The man shrugged. "No worries. You'll find out soon enough."

I left the window, thinking Tariq would need to "check in" and get some sunglasses also, but the man in the cubicle didn't seem to notice him.

I approached the open gate with Tariq following me. Upon entering, I stepped onto a large stone slab that abutted the wall. Three dark-complexioned men dressed in throbes were seated in wooden chairs by the gate. Perhaps they were the gatekeepers. They gave me a dismissive gaze.

Straight ahead, pyramidal skyscrapers sprouted out of the desert sands. The only pyramids I knew of were the ancient ones in Egypt. The city of spires, filled with black obelisks stretching into the stratosphere and five-sided buildings, would have been a mathematicians' dream destination. Gold, sapphire, ebony, white, and blue skyscrapers glistened. Red-laced water lapped the shoreline, and pink mountains spread across the horizon.

Suddenly I felt a severe blow to my head, and searing pain shot across my forehead. I started to take off the dark glasses, but the sunlight was too unbearable. I wiped my brow, and when I looked down at my fingers, they were covered in blood.

Who struck me? Out of the corner of my eye, I caught Tariq lunging at me again. I pivoted and was able to avoid him the second time.

I remembered Shale's strange comment about Tariq when we returned from the stables in Caesarea. "The horse told me he didn't smell like a human or an animal."

After the unprovoked attack, the gatekeepers took an interest in our sparring, but only for entertainment. No one came to my aid. I had a sudden impulse to leave, but without the horses, where would I go?

I pulled out the knife and held it up, never imagining I would use it to defend myself. Tariq circled me, but the element of surprise no longer gave him an advantage.

"I'm ten times stronger than you," he mocked.

"What about my father?"

He smacked his smiley lips.

I braced for another assault. As he came at me, I ducked, ramming my knife into his torso. I'd never stabbed anyone and didn't know what to expect, but the horror of what I'd just done soaked me with guilt. Did I kill him? Something seemed wrong, but in my confusion, I didn't know what. I pulled the knife out and fell backward, landing on the pavilion.

A gasp escaped from his lips. He bent over, turning away. Then I scrambled to my feet. Crouched in a defensive position, I waited for him to come at me again. I glanced down at the knife. There was no blood on the tip, and it was bent.

The men at the gate were boisterous. Cheers, boos, and applause showed their pleasure and displeasure. My anger burned.

Tariq turned toward me.

I blinked. Broken circuitry filled his abdomen.

"You're a robot!"

"No," he quipped. "I'm a hybrid."

"What's that?" I scarcely realized I'd spoken.

"I have the body of a robot but the mind of a human."

He couldn't have the mind of a human. I couldn't read it. Why was he racing horses in the first century?

A voice spoke through a hidden speaker. "Why did you attack Tariq?"

I recognized the voice as the man in the cubicle. How did he know Tariq's name?

I pointed at the three men sitting by the wooden gate. "Tariq attacked me. Ask them."

Tariq positioned himself.

I brandished my knife. "Don't come any closer."

He bared his teeth. "You're a dead man."

The final word "man" was long and drawn out as if a plug was pulled. Tariq's eyes became stuck in a blank, fixated stare.

I looked at the gatekeepers for answers, but they no longer showed any interest.

I heard a different voice. "Follow me."

I turned and saw two men approaching from the city of pyramids. They were dressed in white throbes and wore blue and white Keffiyeh scarves. The men looked identical to each other with protruding sideburns, mustaches, and thick eyebrows.

One of them held out his hand. "Knife, please."

I handed it to him.

"So much for the welcome," I muttered under my breath.

"Come with us," the other one said.

I followed them reluctantly. "Where are we going?"

"No questions." I couldn't tell which one spoke. Their voices sounded the same.

A stone walkway took us near the water as loud seagulls squawked and darted through the waves. In the distance, the tall obelisks drew nearer.

We came to a city block where stores were interspersed with restaurants and waited at a street corner. A black cube shot up from underneath the ground. The door slid open, and the men pushed me inside. The door closed, but the black cubical didn't move.

One them said, "We must blindfold you first."

My uneasiness increased. "Why?"

"We need to take you to the numberless floor. Remove your sunglasses."

Once the blindfold was on, the cubicle moved, but I couldn't tell if we were going up or down.

The black box hummed, and a female computer voice spoke. "Welcome to Bavil, Gateway of the Gods. Today's quota met. Population in habitable territories – three point five billion. Good work by the New

World Order. Don't miss happy hour tonight. Enjoy plenty of food, wine, and perpetual delights."

The cube stopped, and I heard the door open. One of the men shoved me forward. Our sandals clicked on the numberless floor as unsettling noises filled the hallway. We made a few turns, and then I heard another door open.

"You can remove the blindfold," one of them said as the door closed behind us.

My blood covered the white cloth, and I threw it in the garbage. My forehead bled more than I realized.

Plain chairs lined the bare walls, and unfamiliar magazines written in Arabic were displayed on a table. A TV played in the background.

A woman receptionist sat at a desk. She spoke in Arabic to the men, and then she turned to me and motioned for me to step forward. "I have some papers for you to fill out."

I hesitated. "I don't have any money to be seen by the doctor. I don't think I need to be here. I'm not even sure where I am."

"I see," she said. "Just fill out this paperwork. We'll take care of billing later."

Along with the clipboard and a paper attached, she handed me a towel. "Your forehead is bleeding."

I took the hand towel as I scanned though the sheet that asked the standard medical questions. I sat in a chair and checked off the boxes. The two men kept one eye on me and another eye on the TV.

I returned the clipboard as another woman appeared in the doorway. "Daniel Sperling?"

I followed her down the hallway, and she escorted me into a private room. Before she said anything, a man walked in behind us. "Thank you. I can take over now," he said.

"I haven't taken any vitals."

"I can do that," he assured her.

Puzzled by the doctor's hurriedness, she left, closing the door behind her.

The doctor washed his hands. "I'm Dr. Ahmad Arntz. I hear someone attacked you."

"I nodded."

"Do you mind if I take a look?"

He examined my forehead. "You'll need stitches."

After cleaning the wound, I noticed he put some blood in a tube and labeled it with my name. Someone came and took it. Another man with a camera took pictures of my forehead.

After the doctor finished stitching me up, he held up a mirror for me. Tariq slashed me where God had placed the seal. Disturbing as it was, there was nothing I could do. The numbing cream was wearing off, and the injury burned.

The doctor removed his gloves and handed me a bag. "We have some appropriate clothes for you." He pointed to an adjoining room. "There is a shower where you can wash up, but keep the wound dry. When you're finished, someone will be waiting to take you back."

"Take me back where?"

He smiled without responding to my question. "Hope you're feeling better."

"What are you going to do with my blood?"

"Blood?" the doctor repeated.

"You put some of my blood in a vial."

His smiled evaporated. "Oh, we just need to make sure you don't have an infection."

After he left, I disrobed and stepped into the shower. For a few minutes, I was able to forget everything as the hot water poured down my back. Until I looked up and saw a camera with a blinking light. Why were they videotaping me?

CHAPTER 15

The camera clicked. Horrified, I turned off the shower and grabbed the towel. With the towel wrapped around me, I opened up the bag and found a white thobe and black sandals.

I quickly dressed. Taking video or photographs of someone in the nude without their permission was wrong, whether it was in a medical facility or not. I opened the door and stepped out were two men were waiting. They were tall and lanky, younger than the two who brought me. Again, they looked identical with a mustache, a short triangular straight beard, and dark sideburns. How many twins could work in one place?

One of them handed me dark glasses. "Put these on, and we'll blindfold you over your glasses until we leave the numberless floor."

I did as instructed, and they escorted me down the hallway, I presumed, to the black cube. The same female voice spoke in the same monotone, "Welcome to Bavil, Gateway of the Gods."

Once we exited the cube, I took off the blindfold. The sun seemed hotter in long sleeves, so I was thankful for the dark glasses.

"Are you hungry?" one of the men asked.

I handed him the blindfold. "Yes."

As they talked in Arabic, I noticed how crowded the city was. Bodies in various shapes and sizes and ethnicities pressed up against one another on the streets and in the stores. They all wore dark glasses, and they all appeared rich and happy, in contrast to me. However, I saw no children and no one with gray hair. I might have risked trying to escape, but guards stood on street corners holding semiautomatics. Since I had no idea where I was, where would I go?

Drones circled overhead, similar to the ones in the Sahara. The idea of being watched made me uncomfortable, especially after being spied on in the shower.

One of the men interrupted my thoughts. "What do you want to eat?"

Many restaurants were within walking distance, but some of the names were very unappetizing, like the Snail's Shell and Eel's Crevasse and Hell's Angels. I pointed to the Falafel House.

As we approached, I smelled sandalwood incense, a scent I recognized from Nepal. Star and crescent moon lampposts lit the walkway. Golden bulls guarded the door. Despite the line, the hostess quickly seated us.

I started to take off the glasses, but one of the men cautioned me. "There is still too much light. You risk blindness."

Whatever country this was, people were drawn to it. The lavishness of decadent decor—extravagant excesses, from majestic water fountains to sparkling gondolas to driverless cars—spoke of desire. Could there be too much prosperity? I saw large diamonds on women's hands and gaudy gold watches on men's wrists. Everywhere I looked were paradoxical contradictions—like too much sunlight and too many twins, and so much wealth it was trivialized. Where was I?

One of my handlers dumped some painted, half-moon shaped pieces of wood on the table as we waited. Each piece was round on one side and flat on the other. The twins spent the next few minutes laughing and throwing the blocks. I caught the words yin and yang.

"What are you playing?" I asked.

"These are Jiaobei blocks," one of them replied. "We're divining your future. Is our newest patient going to live or die?" He slammed the ill-shaped blocks on the table. When they stopped moving, the men exchanged glances but did not tell me what the pieces portended. I didn't care. I knew divination was of the devil.

The restaurant was packed with too many bodies, and to figure out my location based on clothing was futile. A few women wore the hijab, but they were in the minority.

I ordered some tabbouleh and swallowed the whole glass of water in one gulp.

In the distance on the Red Sea—I called it that because it was red —ships were coming and going. Seaports dotted the coastline between luxurious beaches. Cargo ships were delivering loads in truck-size containers; others looked like cruise ships. That would account for the hordes of people.

Four cellists entertained restaurant patrons with soft music. I made a half-hearted attempt to read the minds of the men who brought me here but couldn't.

After we finished, they paid the bill, and I followed them outside. We walked along a sidewalk that sprouted into several smaller ones. At times, the walkway took us close to the beach where sunbathers worshipped the sun. Massive umbrellas and white tents provided shade for those who didn't. Many women were dressed in bikinis. Until now I thought I was in a Muslim country, but that couldn't be the case.

We passed covered walkways where servers were delivering food and drinks along the beachfront and in heavily trafficked areas. We must have walked four kilometers when we arrived at a two-story establishment. A flashing sign read "Europa Theater and Casino." A movie theater was on one side, and a casino was on the other. We walked toward the theater that displayed alluring advertisements of movies I didn't recognize. Upon entering, one of the men spoke in Arabic to the man selling tickets, and the attendant waved us through.

Once we were away from the sunlight, we removed the dark glasses. We passed a turnstile and walked along a red-carpeted, dimly-lit hallway. The men opened the door and directed me to enter.

The multiplex screen covered the front of the small auditorium that might have seated fifty patrons, but the three of us were the only ones in the room. Getting out of this place was impossible, but I liked the idea of being close to the door, so I sat on the back row.

One of the men leaned over and whispered to me, "Don't leave once the movie starts. We're watching you."

I nodded. The curtains opened, and the words flashed across the screen, "Welcome to Bavil, Gateway of the Gods."

CHAPTER 16

Soft music filled the theater as memorable scenes appeared on the screen. I was in a boat on the Red Sea. The breeze buffeted my back, the sunlight warmed my face, and the familiar saltiness of the ocean transported me back in time. More photos shimmied up through the waters and gave way to forgotten memories of family and friends—planting, watering, tilling, reaping, cooking, eating, and celebrating. These heart-warming scenes brought me comfort.

It was as if my thoughts were being tapped into with cinematic clarity. Then uncomfortable truths were dramatized. I was forced to think about things against my will—of war, famine, sickness, and death. The horrors lingered, and the familiar feeling of oppression returned followed by the putrid smell of death. I resisted, and grace remained.

I prayed, and my depression left—almost as if my resistance caused the presentation to shift. I saw myself as a young boy with my father. He was reading the Haggadah to me. Longing filled my heart to be reunited with him. More video from Israel awakened my past. I could taste the freshwater from the Sea of Galilee as I dove in and out of the gentle waves. Mount Arbel beckoned me. I remembered the times I climbed the ridges, chased butterflies among the flowers, and teased hapless toads on moonlit nights. I remembered fishing for legendary sea monsters and exploring rainbows through prisms.

Now I was a man. I could rappel off those same cliffs, but my desires were magnified when I discovered I could fly. I wanted to go to Jerusalem, but instead, I found myself in Bavil. I saw a woman sitting on an unusual animal. She offered me a glass of wine—that's what I presumed it was—and called to me in a sweet-sounding voice, "Daniel."

A quartet of cellists played soft music in the background. I wanted to linger, mesmerized by the sounds of the strings. The glass of wine was tempting, but there was more to see. Curiosity pulled me away.

I headed to the Red Sea. Dozens of ships were hauling in delicacies from around the world. My eyesight was as sharp as an eagle's, and I could see inside the shipping containers. The boats contained objects of worship—idols of various kinds. I saw carved images from the cedars of Lebanon, fine linens from Nepal, and exotic tea from India. I was captivated by the high-tech secrets in sealed containers that represented inventions from the future.

Hundreds of mega-barges arrived filled with gold, precious stones, pearls, ivory, wood, brass, iron, and marble. The flotilla of cargo boats was too many to count. I swooped down low to inhale the finest in perfumes and essential oils. I was rewarded with whiffs of champaca, cannabis, and frankincense.

My amazing eyesight empowered me, and I was obsessed with knowing what was in every container, from crude oil shipped from wells in the desert and stacks in the oceans to items of vanity.

I soon discovered Bavil had an insatiable appetite. Greed fed it. The kings of the earth lived well. The merchants waxed rich in abundance, and I had no trouble imagining what I could do with all that wealth.

After a while, however, I grew bored looking at jewels belonging to others. While I could have stolen anything I wanted, I knew that was wrong. Wanting those things, however, filled me with envy.

I left the waters of the Red Sea and flew into town where I found craftsmen, musicians, and artists of exceptional talent. My longing to be like them tugged at my heart.

I came to a wedding. Laughter filled the halls as the wine flowed. Some guests were full of themselves, and others were drunk. Shale flooded my thoughts—I wished we were married, and then reality returned.

"Daniel," I heard a voice whisper, "evil is tempting you."

My quickened spirit urged me to pray. "Dear God, please break the spell cast on me." I was hoodwinked by my desires, unaware of the depth of my sin. The devil's deception blinded me, luring me into a mindset of involuntary slavery.

Perfect love always revealed the right choices—if I listened. While God was eternal, the World of Bavil was a Gateway to the fallen world of useless depravities, temporary pleasures, trivial pursuits, and a chasing after the wind. All was vanity.

CHAPTER 17

The spell was broken. No longer was I soaring among the clouds. I was sitting in the movie theater. More disturbing pictures filled the screen, but the evil one didn't know God had intervened.

I saw statues oozing blood—the occult using deception to gain power over the masses. I saw dimly-lit candles carried by people wearing strange clothing. Why would anyone among the living want to contact the dead? Yeshua communes with the living.

I saw a woman sitting in heaven—the queen of heaven, she called herself, gloating over her stolen position. How many acolytes did the harlot deceive? The true Mary would never allow herself to be worshipped.

I saw babies murdered in the womb—bodies dismembered and parts sold off to the highest bidder. Mind-altering substances filled the coffins of the young and the innocent, precious lives destroyed by poor choices. I saw billion-dollar companies that sold themselves to the devil, taking huge profits and hiding the truth—some of their products caused cancer.

I saw the Hollywood temple of creativity, where actors and actresses created fake worlds beholden to unclean spirits. Millions wanted to be like them and worshipped them at altars of soon-forgotten legacies. What a waste.

I saw the media running around with mics seeking stories to tickle the ears of gullible listeners. They were the voice of the enemy—his mouthpiece, his platform, his agenda, his New World Order. The sensationalistic, questionable news stories were tweeted and Facebooked across the internet and broadcast into homes to poison listeners—the uninformed who submitted to blind, corrupt, misguided leaders. Where were the Christians when it began, when the lies and deception went viral?

When I thought I would be sick to my stomach, God revealed that the ability to taste evil is limited by the purity of one's heart. Another scene appeared, and this one was more personal.

The Sea of Galilee returned to the screen. Seagulls flapped overhead, and several boats were off in the distance. The camera moved to the shoreline, and I could see myself picking up a pebble and throwing it into the water. Nathan, Shale's half-brother, was with me. He was running back and forth into the water.

I remembered that day. I took him there when I was depressed. I'd lost my ability to talk to him when he was mute. Brutus, Shale's father, hired me to tutor him. At first, God gave me the ability to read minds, but I turned from God and lost the talent. I was sad that I could no longer help Nathan.

I was also depressed because Shale and I had parted ways. I didn't know what to do. I heard myself tell Nathan, "I'm going to walk up to that embankment, and then I'll come back."

Nathan nodded.

"Don't go anywhere," I said. "I'll be watching you."

As I walked along the shore, a black shadow appeared alongside mine.

"Can you see me?" the voice asked.

An old bag woman came into view. She wore a green dress, had a balding head, hollow eyes, and sunken cheekbones, just like I remembered from our first meeting in the seventh dimension.

"Where are you going?" the bag woman asked, who I later knew as the ventriloquist.

I walked over to the stone embankment that butted into the water. I climbed up the ledge to get a better view. I remembered I had been concerned for Nathan, and I saw myself searching for him along the shoreline.

The old woman stayed below. I called out to her, "Who are you?"

"I'm your benefactor," she replied.

"Come on," I objected. "You aren't my benefactor."

I could see myself rubbing my nose. I remembered, despite the freshness of the water, I could smell rotten eggs.

The old woman laughed. "What do you want?"

I knew what happened, and it made me sick. I heard my voice. "I want my gift back."

She answered, "To read minds?"

I remembered wondering how she knew without me telling her.

She continued. "I can give you that ability." She told me why I was depressed. "You are upset with Shale. She's met a man she calls the king, the one Christians call Jesus. You're troubled, disturbed about events surrounding Yeshua. You want to convince Shale he's a charlatan."

I felt myself becoming nauseated. Everything the bag woman said was true, and I knew now, as a follower of Yeshua, how much I had broken his heart in that moment. I heard myself asking, "How do you know these things?"

"Does it matter?" she replied.

I watched as I continued to talk to the old woman, my biggest mistake. I knew she was evil even back then, but I had wanted my gift back more than anything.

"You can give me back the ability to read Nathan's mind?"

"Anyone's mind," she replied.

I remembered being disturbed. A voice had spoken to my heart. "The woman is wicked."

But another voice spoke to me back then, too. Nathan's life would be more fulfilling, and I would know things that Scylla, Shale's step-mother, and Judd, the farmhand, had kept from me. I could be a better friend to Shale. Even if the ventriloquist was wicked, I would use it for good. I would be my old self again, having restored to me that which was taken.

I shut my eyes, unable to block out the lies of the old woman.

"Daniel, you are trying to be a better friend. Let me help you. I told you I was your benefactor."

"What's the cost?"

She laughed as if it was a stupid question.

I brushed her off at this point, irritated that she laughed. "I need to head back."

I watched myself on the screen as I climbed down the rock wall with her trailing me. I almost escaped her seduction, but before I reached Nathan, she spoke to me once more. "Nathan is hungry, but you wouldn't know that without being able to read his mind, would you?"

I sobbed. I wanted to be Nathan's mentor, and without being able to communicate with him, how could I do that? He couldn't understand what happened between us. Was it wrong to want back a gift I used for only good?

I heard myself ask, "What do I need to do to get the gift back?"

The old woman smiled. "It's done."

Then she disappeared as if she had never been with me. One shadow remained—mine.

The scene continued to play out to its bitter end.

I continued to watch myself on the screen. I approached Nathan. "Hey, are you hungry?"

He nodded, and a smile crossed his face. I reached over and squeezed his shoulder. "Come on, let's head back."

The movie stopped.

The room was dark, darker than I remembered when I entered. I was grieved in my spirit. "God, help me to understand. I'm just a stupid man." Tears filled my eyes.

I heard a voice inside my head. "Daniel, what is truth?"

I tried to grasp what God was saying. "Discernment." That was it.

Discernment. God wanted me to look for truth. Deception was the god of the last days.

The lights came on, and when I looked up, I saw the ventriloquist sitting across the aisle on the front row. I wanted to jump up and run out of the theater. She was eating popcorn, and I flashed back to seeing her at the Hippodrome in Caesarea. Still balding, with a few whiffs of hair, holes between her gaping teeth, and wearing the same green dress, God showed me something I'd fail to notice before—wickedness never changes.

She smiled at me. I sat frozen, stunned into silence. I imagined the woman finding lurid pleasure in tormenting me. Then she shapeshifted into Shale Snyder.

<h1 style="text-align:center">CHAPTER 18</h1>

Nothing was as it appeared. I'd not sold my soul to the devil, and Shale wasn't sitting across from me eating popcorn.

The devil knew me too well. He wanted me to think I was lost or insane. After all, I had spent time in a mental institution. It was my choice to allow him that much control over my thoughts. Psychological warfare was a formidable weapon—otherwise, he wouldn't use it.

The twins stood in front of me. "We need to leave now."

I looked across the aisle. The ventriloquist was gone.

"Where are you taking me?"

"Prince Adonikam."

"Who is he?"

"You know who he is," one of them said. "Put on your glasses."

Why did they wear dark glasses? I couldn't read their minds. I was perplexed by this seeming contradiction. Maybe it was psychological warfare, to make me doubt what I knew to be true.

We entered the lobby, and moviegoers waited in a long line for tickets. The smell of piping, hot-buttered popcorn was bittersweet. I wasn't sure I could ever eat popcorn again.

As we left, one of the men said, "A car will be here to pick us up in a few minutes."

People started pointing at the sky. A fiery, spherical object skimmed across the heavens. It burned without being consumed, disappearing below the horizon. Then smaller balls of fire fell in an umbrella-like canopy over the sea waters.

Panicked voices filled the evening air. "Suppose some of the ash comes inland?"

His words spread fear among the onlookers.

"Nothing can touch us in Bavil," someone else said.

Nevertheless, the fires falling over the ocean gripped onlookers.

"Meteor," I mumbled to myself. But I didn't know what it was. The large object had deep crevasses and holes through which long streams of molten fire glided across its surface. It moved too slowly for a meteor, and it didn't disintegrate in the atmosphere.

The gondolas stopped, leaving people trapped inside. The festive lights strung through the trees burned out. The overhead fans cooling those waiting for movie tickets stopped. The music streaming in from the casino froze, and the cars on the streets stalled.

An uncomfortable silence followed, and then everything returned to normal. Contagious sighs of relief filtered through the crowd as murmurings began. "What was that ball of fire? Why did the electricity go out? Did the meteor hit the earth?"

Even as people questioned, a hot wind tore through the streets, and lose items flipped across the ground. The trees swayed. Seconds later, a loud blast filled the air.

A woman screamed, "I'm tired of all this death. When is it going to stop?"

"Shut up," a man shouted, standing next to her.

Another woman spoke. "She's right. How can we pretend everything is fine when half the people are dead? That's insanity."

A police officer came over and grabbed the first woman by the arm. "You need more happy medicine. When is the last time you took yours?"

She hesitated.

"Come with me," the officer said, "so I can take you to the number-less floor."

Gasps filled the crowd.

She tried to resist but a second guard came over and helped the first one. Her husband dutifully followed behind them.

Another policeman hauled off the second woman and spoke to the rubberneckers. "If you're out of your happy medicine, come see me. You don't want to become like these derelict women or be taken to the numberless floor, not here, where life is perfect and everyone is happy."

A woman held up a bottle. "I've never been happier."

The crowd nodded their approval.

Soon the people dispersed, and a car with no driver pulled up to the curb.

Wishing I could escape, I climbed into the back, and one of the men sat beside. The other man sat up front. Before we took off, I felt the ground moving. Aftershocks. I hated being in a car with no driver and the earth trembling.

We left, and no one said a word. I couldn't get the woman's terrified face out of my mind. So they drugged people to make them happy.

The car followed the coastline, and we traveled in and out of mountains as the sun touched the horizon. Hazy dust settled on the windshield, and the wipers came on. I could smell smoke even inside the car. Wherever the fiery ball landed, it was close.

We turned onto a road that came to a guard station. The man in the front seat showed an I.D., and the guard waved us through. The gate lifted, and a spectacular pyramidal glass structure rose in front of us. Light from the setting sun hit the sides of the building that reflected into the heavens. I imagined the building could be seen for miles.

The car parked itself along the front curb, and two soldiers with semiautomatic weapons approached. I opened my door and stepped out.

After a quick conversation, one of the soldiers latched onto me. I was surprised the twins were not coming with us.

The door to the guarded building opened upon command. As I

entered, the décor and majesty of a futuristic castle entered my thoughts. What would it look like? Glass walls, high ceilings, marble floors, and soft lighting from gold chandeliers spoke of unmatched elegance. Musicians played in the background.

We came to a moving spiral stairway that wound upward like a DNA strand. Beneath the spiral was an enchanting pond. Strange creatures appeared and disappeared in a game of hide-and-seek. Fountains of water sprayed from the woman's midriff as she sat on a scarlet beast. Seven heads and ten horns protruded from the strange creature's body.

I recognized the woman. She was draped in purple pearls and held a golden cup filled with something that smelled vile. The smoke from the cup bubbled up the staircase. A red substance oozed out of her mouth as she smiled like a sloppy drunkard.

One of the men pushed me forward when we reached the top. "Let's go. We don't want to keep the prince waiting."

CHAPTER 19

Our footsteps tapped on the tan marble floor as we passed several checkpoints, and we arrived at a room decorated in earth tones with hanging Oriental lights. One of the guards spoke in Arabic to an official behind a desk. He turned to me and translated. "We wait here until he's ready to see you."

A few minutes later, the double wooden doors opened, and we entered into a room befitting a king. A young man, seated on an ornate, golden-red throne, rose to greet us. He was Hollywood handsome with deep-set brown eyes and thick, jet black wavy hair that was partially covered by a gold keffiyeh. He spoke in Arabic to the two guards. They saluted and left, and the doors closed.

I recognized the prince as the one sitting on the horses traipsing across the planet on my way to this strange country. He gestured toward a plain chair next to his pontifical throne.

"Have a seat."

His English was so perfect I couldn't tell his ethnicity.

As I edged over, I could see through the tinted windows the red waters that must be the Red Sea. Not because they were red, but because of the desert-like mountainous terrain. Even the sand had a reddish hue.

I noticed a yellow crescent moon and the Star of David stitched into the red velvet on the back of his throne. Did that mean he was Jewish, Muslim, or both?

The man studied me before extending his hand. "I'm Prince Adonikam."

I shook his hand with reservations.

"Do you know who that makes me?"

I was surprised I could read his mind. Perhaps I was wrong, and he wasn't the Antichrist, but the resemblance to the man I saw riding the four horses was compelling.

He arose and edged over to a tall, portable cart and poured himself a drink. With his back turned, I looked around. Photographs of UFOs covered the walls. Some of the pictures looked like clips from Hollywood movies. Several photos of animalistic hybrids made me shudder.

On the wall behind his throne were photos of the supposed leader in various official capacities—meeting heads of state, posing at a military installation, and riding on a white horse leading a parade. One photo showed him standing with Adolph Hitler at Pergamon's Altar of Zeus—the altar of holocaust. My stomach churned. Someone must have photo-shopped that one—unless he was a time traveler.

Other photographs of him with world leaders included Emmanuel Macron with the caption, "United Nations Opens New World Headquarters in Babylon." There were photos of him with celebs in Berlin, London, and Astana. The most distinguished photograph showed him at a special event with many heads of states, including Saudi Arabia, Jordan, UAE, Kuwait, Bahrain, Oman, Egypt, Israel, United States, England, and U.N. representatives. Signatures were shown beneath the photograph confirming a seven-year covenant. That was the most indicting evidence I'd seen that Prince Adonikam was the Antichrist.

Data appeared on a computer screen written in a language I couldn't read. A black snake-like plant had wrapped itself around a table, and the room smelled like cigarettes from ash-scented candles. That dark crystal orb—what was it? It occupied a very conspicuous location.

When Prince Adonikam faced me, he held up a crystal glass containing a red liquid. "It's time to celebrate."

I didn't say anything, but glanced at the ceiling that bore a likeness to the Sistine Chapel. Colorful, hand-painted scenes from the creation story rivaled it in intensity except this display was disturbing. The garden scene showed Adan reaching out to touch the hand of the serpent—if you could call it a hand.

The prince's voice was smooth like silk. "It's a spectacular painting, isn't it? I brought in the finest artists from Italy. I think scenes from history when correctly interpreted add a lot, don't you?"

I remained equivocal. Who was Prince Adonikam? I wished I could be sure, but as he stood in front of me, I could read his mind. If he were supernatural, I wouldn't be able to. I always thought the Antichrist would not be human—perhaps a Nephilim, perhaps Satan himself, but it was hard to comprehend the Antichrist would be fully human.

A golden tree covered the front of his white thobe, matching the gold in his outer robe, and a wide red-belted sash accented his waistline. I also noticed the gold bracelet on his right wrist. His hair was rather long underneath the keffiyeh. He was clean-shaven with olive tone skin. His most disturbing feature was his eyes—deep, penetrating, and reptilian. Everything about him seemed…perfect, a specimen of enviable looks, intelligence, and persona.

He moved sleekly across the floor to his throne, made himself comfortable, and took a sip from his glass. After setting down his drink, his eyes drifted. A beautiful sunset hypnotized him. His words broke the silence. "I didn't have to accept this position, but the enlightened one asked me to be the leader of the New World Order."

He lifted his drink and gulped the rest of it down. Crossing his legs, he asked me again, "Do you know who I am?"

Was he testing me? I shook my head. "No."

His eyes focused on the red waters. "I have brought peace to most of the world—Europe, the Middle East, Asia, and many smaller countries. A few have sunk into chaos. They aren't worth remembering. However, we're on the precipice of our biggest accomplishment. The time has come to invade Israel." His eyes bore into mine. "As a Jew, what do you have to say about that?"

"God will prevail."

His eyes narrowed. "The ships of Chittim won't succeed this time. The United States and its allies are weaker, and my strength is growing."

"What about the United States?"

"Since the purge, their place on the world stage has—how should I say it—diminished. After Hillary Clinton won the election..." he shrugged. "The U.S. still hasn't recovered from the EMP attack."

My ears perked up. "Trump won the election, not Hillary."

He replied flippantly. "I changed history. Do your research. Everyone knows Hillary Clinton won, not Trump, just like the United States lost the War of Independence from England."

"You can't rewrite history."

The lines of his mouth twisted unnaturally. "He who controls the past determines the future. We must control all truth, and then rewrite history to where the earth-dwellers believe my version of what happened."

I sat numb, not sure how to respond. Then I replied, "So the United States was never a free country?"

Prince Adonikam laughed. "England gave the United States their freedom. They didn't win it. That was simple. No big deal, the Mandela effect on steroids. I control the truth, the World-Wide Web, and update it to where people believe what they're told."

"Why are you telling me this?"

His reptilian eyes narrowed even more. "Because you have something I want."

CHAPTER 20

He pointed to the computer. "Rewriting history is nothing. Time travel allows altered history. But scrolls and antiquities—including books—must be destroyed. They're a waste of resources."

"Because what's written can't be altered," I mused.

"You see," Prince Adonikam said, "time is nothing more than an illusion. If we keep starting time over, the usurper's plans remain unfulfilled. Time measures change."

He leaned into me. "That's what I need to talk to you about. Your time travels."

I shifted uneasily in my chair.

He made a steeple with his hands. "I was chosen. I didn't ask to be the world leader."

"I don't understand."

His eyes froze in an unnatural stare. "I want to talk to you about the scroll."

"What?" I pretended I didn't know what he was talking about.

"Your fiancée wrote it."

My heart pounded.

He walked over and swiped the crystal ball, gazing at the dark, blurry images inside it. "Bibles have been destroyed. Historical documents and archeological discoveries with any connection to the Bible have been burned, even the writings of your beloved Josephus."

His eyes bore into mine. "History is different from what you remember."

I stared at him.

He waved his hand in the air. "I must control all truth, all knowledge, and all history. I want the scroll."

How could Shale's diary garner that much interest? "God has hidden some things for a time, but before Yeshua returns, the Mystery of God will be finished." I shrugged. "I'm not sure where it is right now, but it is insignificant, I assure you."

His eyes narrowed. "If I were to guess, I'd say Shale has it. We have our ways of getting what we want." His voice trailed off.

"I could get it for you, but it would take some time."

He smiled. "If you want to see Shale again…Christians have perpetuated a lie. Jesus is not the Son of God. He never was."

"The Lord rebuke you," I said in my heart. I wasn't going to argue with him.

He walked over and peered out the window. "You've been gone many years. More than you know. You will soon discover things have changed. You should consider yourself honored to have this private meeting with me."

I folded my arms. "It makes me sad what you will do."

His interest was piqued. "And what will I do?"

"Many will die because of the wars you start, and those who refuse to worship you will die."

He whirled toward me. "You are blind, my friend, and stupid. Why do you think Tariq slashed your forehead?

His sudden outburst took me by surprise. I remained quiet.

"You're no longer one of the one hundred forty-four thousand."

"The Lord knows."

He smiled coyly. "Perhaps you've forgotten. You sold your soul on the shores of the Sea of Galilee. You belong to my father, Lucifer."

Regret pierced my soul. "The blood of Jesus is my salvation. Nothing Lucifer, the devil, does can change that."

Prince Adonikam's words were like quicksilver. "Even Jesus can't violate your will." He jerked his thumb toward his chest. "I will soon possess all the kingdoms of the world. It is my destiny. What I want, I take."

I shook my head. "Everything you have has been given to you. That does not include me. I've been sealed by the blood of Yeshua Hamashiach."

Adonikam hissed. "How stupid you are. You sold yourself to my esteemed father."

"I was tricked by the ventriloquist."

"Do you want to see Shale again?"

"I'm still one of the one hundred forty-four thousand whether I have the seal or not."

"The one hundred forty-four thousand Jewish babblers are too late. The Enki took the Jesus freaks years ago."

"No, they didn't. Those believing in Yeshua were raptured."

Prince Adonikam strutted up to the wall across the room and pointed. "These photographs are a reminder of the dangers we face today. The Enki want to take over the earth. In this case, those green men did us a favor. We've been much better off without those misguided religious fanatics. We've achieved peace, thanks to me."

So that was the strategy of the political leaders. The Enki were good aliens who helped to rid the earth of troublemakers, but how did that explain the disappearance of the children? Of course, if those in power could pass laws legalizing infanticide, was alien abduction that far-fetched?

He returned to his throne, leaned back, and puffed out this chest. "We have some business matters to tend to."

"Like what?"

"The chip."

Again, I pretended I didn't know what he meant.

"We have perfected it. Your friend, Nidal, wore a prototype for testing purposes, so you can't pretend ignorance. Scientists have refined it, and when I assume absolute power, I will force everyone to receive the mark to buy and sell. My power increases with each passing day. Once I control all the money, if people want to eat, they will need to be chipped. That way, the dwindling food supply can be allocated fairly to everyone."

"What does that have to do with me?"

Prince Adonikam studied me. "I like you, Daniel. You are a great specimen—young, smart, articulate, handsome—when people see you've been chipped, they will follow you. I'll give you a few days to mull it over. You'll find this a spectacular place. I promise you, you won't be disappointed. Once you are chipped, I'll appoint you as leader over many."

"No, thank you."

He laughed. "You're deceived. Let me tell you more."

I bit my lip.

Adonikam went off on a tirade pontificating his powers and hopeful future exploits. "Look at this," Prince Adonikam said, pointing to the symbol on his throbe. "The tree of life heals every disease. Think about it."

I shook my head.

"It's just a chip," the prince said, "the size of a grain of rice."

I knew what the significance of the chip was. "I don't want it."

"Are you a fool?"

His mockery made me more determined.

"What would you take in exchange for my offer? Make me a counteroffer."

"I don't have a counteroffer."

His eyes grew cold.

Had Prince Adonikam already become the serpent? Perhaps that was still future. I wanted to fit the pieces together. Anyone who received the mark could not be saved. I suspected the chip altered human DNA. Whether it did or not, I knew worship of the prince preceded the chip, or the mark of the beast, and I could never worship Prince Adonikam.

The Prince interrupted my thoughts. "I brought peace to Israel, uniting forces that had never known peace."

He paused as if waiting for me to respond.

"So you confirmed the peace treaty?" I asked. I already knew the answer.

He smiled. "The Jews credit their God, but it was me. Now they're more prosperous than they've ever been. Jerusalem is the focal point of the world."

I loathed his gloating.

He spoke into an unseen listening device. "Guards, please."

The men who brought me returned.

"Take him to his accommodations." Adonikam's eyes turned cold like a snake's. "My time has come. I shall increase. You and your ilk shall decrease."

He returned to his throne and grabbed the sides in a fit of lustful revelry. "I shall take my seat in the temple of Jerusalem, the greatest city in the world, once I've finished my conquests."

The guards escorted me out as he ranted on in blissful self-absorption. Before the door closed behind us, I heard his parting words. "I want that scroll."

The twins were standing by the driverless car in the parking lot when we returned. The trip back to the city was a blur. The sun set, and the waters were dark along the road. Few cars passed us from the opposite direction.

My worry for Shale and Shira increased. I thought they were safe, but now I was concerned. Prince Adonikam would think nothing of killing Shale to get it, and with the New World Order at his command, nothing was impossible for him—except God's restraining hand. I couldn't accept the mark as a ransom to protect Shale, but if I let Prince Adonikam believe I was willing, that might give me a chance to come up with an escape plan.

The car pulled up to the curb where we had left. The streets were packed with moviegoers, casino patrons, and loiterers. Some of the women were dressed scantily, and the open solicitation of drugs turned my stomach.

Dozens of lanterns flickered against the rising moon. Smoke-filled salons of ill-repute drew many, and barrooms entombed with rowdy drinkers lined the streets. As we neared the beach, foul language polluted the night air.

We walked along the stone walkway, and dozens of eyes followed me from the darkness. Did they belong to demons or animals? I didn't know.

CHAPTER 21

We left the stone walkway and went inside the Old Palace. The check-in area was a cross between a museum and a hotel. Raised platforms along the perimeter of the lobby displayed statues of horses standing guard over guests. The outer walls were inlaid with hand carvings. An ornate chandelier hung from the beveled ceiling.

It was late, beyond check-in time, so the lobby was quiet. A woman smiled, indicating she could check us in. One of the twins stayed with me while the other one handled the details. When the paperwork was completed, the receptionist handed over two keys.

I was too far away to eavesdrop, but I wondered why two keys were given. We left the check-in area and proceeded to a circular stairway that went up one floor.

When we entered our room, a bright light from the living room revealed roomy accommodations. A sofa and two chairs faced a large glass window that I imagined overlooked the Red Sea. The curtains were pulled to either side, and I could see a few lights, perhaps from ships, in the distance. On the left was the bedroom and on the right side was a small kitchenette.

However, it wasn't the opulence of the accommodations that

caught my attention. It was the man sitting in the living room that shocked me—Tariq.

He stood as the three of us entered. After the perfunctory greeting, his eyes turned to me. He was wearing the traditional Arab garb and head covering. A fake smile crossed his lips. "So we meet again."

I stared at him, so caught off-guard I couldn't think of anything to say. Was he going to stay in the room with me?

The twins spoke to him in Arabic. I was not conversant in Arabic, although if I listened, I could often decipher a few words here and there. After a short exchange, they handed Tariq the keys, glanced at me as they walked by, and left. Tariq edged over and locked the door behind them

I stood in the foyer of the suite. I was going to be locked up with someone who tried to kill me? No, it was worse than that. I was going to be locked up with a hybrid who tried to kill me.

"You recovered quickly," I quipped.

"Yes, we're superior to humans."

I glanced at my bed and then back at Tariq. "Are you going to murder me while I sleep?"

Tariq smirked. "Not unless I'm told."

I stared at him. "Have you been told?"

He laughed again. "I wouldn't tell you anyway."

Of course, the men took my knife when I arrived. As I scanned the suite room, I saw cameras. I felt hopeless. I was in a godless kingdom with hybrid creatures and cameras that spied on me in showers. Was I going to allow this monster to control me? Tariq might kill me while I slept, but he couldn't destroy my soul.

I walked over and sat on the bed, took off my shoes, and lay down. As soon as I closed my eyes, I fell asleep.

CHAPTER 22

I knew the world was different when I flushed the toilet and the water swirled counterclockwise. The clocks always stopped at 6:16 p.m. for six minutes, and the sun moved west to east instead of east to west.

I slept almost two full days although I wasn't sure if a day was twenty-four hours anymore. I walked into the kitchen and saw Tariq gazing out the tinted window overlooking the Red Sea. The hybrid never slept. In some ways I envied him. How much more I could accomplish if I didn't have to sleep. However, Yeshua slept—and it was good.

I was watched by cameras twenty-four hours a day. I couldn't shower or relieve myself without being observed. I had access to nothing—no computer, no television, no phone, no humans, not even snail mail, if that even existed anymore. Because Tariq wasn't human, I couldn't read his mind. Escaping wasn't within the realm of possibility.

I made myself some coffee and sat on the sofa. At least with the tinted windows, I didn't have to wear sunglasses. I felt rested enough to ask Tariq about my father—knowing the answers might be disturbing. I'd start with something open-ended and non-threatening. "Tell me how you got involved with my father."

Tariq turned from the window and walked over to sit in the chair. He stretched out and propped his feet on the table. "I work for the New World Order. The scientists created me. I was engineered for the specific task of finding the scrolls given to your father by the antiquities dealer."

I didn't know science and technology had advanced that far, but it still was not sophisticated enough to predict human behavior. I simply hid Shale's diary among the Dead Sea Scrolls because Shale forgot them when she returned home to Atlanta. My father snail-mailed them to Jerusalem after an antiquities dealer bought them—who just happened to be my father's friend. I shook my head. God chooses the simpleton to confound those who think they are wise.

Tariq continued. "I met Nidal in Syria. Remember, we were racing partners."

"I know who Nidal is."

He scratched the back of his neck as he talked, even yawning. His mannerisms were so human I found it hard to believe he wasn't.

"I was sent to find the scrolls. The antiquities dealer told us he gave them to your father. We found your father, but he didn't have them. He never told us where they were.

"When you and Shale gave the scroll to Scylla in Jerusalem, that's when we learned he mailed them. None of the scientists could believe he shipped them in an unmarked box. We assumed he hid them."

"Is my father still alive?"

Tariq threw up his hands. "Your guess is as good as mine. The last time I saw him, he was in Perlsea Castle."

"Where did you go after you left him there?"

"The New World Order decided we needed to go back in time and retrieve them from Qumran or get them from you before you hid them. Access to you was easier than Shale. Days seemed to go by when she never came out of the house."

That was because Scylla kept Shale locked up for days at a time. It never occurred to me that God might be protecting her from being kidnapped. "If you were after the scrolls, why were you racing chariots in Caesarea?"

Tariq laughed. "Once the bankers realized they could get rich by having us compete in the chariot races, they became as interested in making money as in finding the scrolls. Gold became quite an enticement. Of course, the New World Order wanted the scrolls, but they needed the bankers to finance their time travels, and they needed the scientists to actually do it. That's as much as I can say about that. Not everyone had the same priorities."

I leaned forward. "So you left my father in the Perlsea Castle. Could he escape?"

Tariq half-shrugged. "Nidal was the last one to see him. I don't know of any reason why your father wouldn't have been able to escape. The scientists didn't want him killed, and they controlled the time portals that the New World Order needed."

"Tell me about my father. Did he have food?"

Tariq nodded. "We tied him up for a time, but it didn't matter. Your father wasn't going to tell us anything. We provided him food. There was no point in starving him to death."

"How long did you keep him in the castle?"

"A few months. Not that long."

"But a couple of years went by. What happened during that time?"

"Our interaction with him wasn't that long." Tariq stopped to think. "We detained him in Syria for several months, and then the war got too bad to stay. We went to Nepal and solicited the help of the Shaman."

"So you decided to stay in the first century and keep racing to fill up the coffers of the New World Order?"

"As long as you and Shale were there, we knew there was a good chance we could get the third scroll in the first century. It was just a matter of when. Certain things needed to happen that the New World Order couldn't control."

"What do you mean?"

"The elitists needed to wait for the right opportunity. I was making them rich. They didn't mind the delay."

"Why are we here, then?"

Tariq raised his eyebrow. "Something intervened. This was never meant to happen, to bring you here."

My curiosity was piqued. "What is this place? And why did you try to kill me."

"First, I didn't try to kill you. I was instructed to remove the seal on your forehead."

"Instructed?" I repeated.

"They tell me what to do. Someone's brain has been imprinted into me. That makes me part human."

"Who?"

"You wouldn't know him. He's a higher up."

How could I find out more? If I had a computer…I'd seen the 5-G towers. There had to be internet access. Of course, Prince Adonikam controlled the information highway, so what help would a computer be anyway?

Tariq expounded. "I'm part human and part robot. We're smarter than you, have heightened senses, are stronger, and immortal. No matter how much we're damaged, we can be restored. Humans can't. Even our brains are backed up in case of a fatal flaw. They can be restored, just like a hard drive on a computer."

I stared at Tariq. "So you think that makes you superior to humans?"

"Do you think you could be restored in a few hours? Your forehead hasn't healed yet, and it's been three days."

"Why did you strike me?"

"I was told to strike you on the forehead."

"You knew I had the seal?"

"I was told it was the wrong seal and it needed to be removed so the proper seal could be applied. Since you came to Bavil, the opportunity presented itself."

"What is the proper seal?"

"It's a chip that goes either on the right hand or on the forehead."

"You mean the mark?"

Tariq shrugged. "Call it what you want."

"And what is this place?"

"Bavil, Gateway of the Gods."

"What country?"

Tariq puckered his lips. "It's not a country. It's a location identified by 666, and it's also a system."

"Identified how?"

"W-W-W stands for 6-6-6. It's the World Wide Web. We have augmented reality at this location. We exist in a matrix, but we live everywhere across the network and across the world."

"I wasn't supposed to come here?"

Tariq shook his head. "Unexpected."

So God must have brought me here, I mused, remembering the conversation I overhead in the biga.

"What year is it?"

Tariq put his hands behind his head. "The times have been changed because of past events, so a new calendar exists. The clocks seem unable to adjust. That's why they keep getting stuck on 6:16."

"What's going to happen to me?"

He shook his head. "I don't have that information."

I stood and looked out the window. "Why is the water red?"

"The seasons have changed. That's the new norm."

"Can you bring me a Bible?"

Tariq laughed. "Those no longer exist."

I closed my eyes in silent prayer. I never imagined I would want to be a prophet, but to have that gift now would have been helpful. I knew God would win, but it was all the stuff before Yeshua's return that made me anxious. I could see it all unraveling right before my eyes, and I couldn't even express what little faith I had in Bavil.

I went back into the kitchen to refill my coffee when someone knocked on the door. Tariq shuffled over just like a human to open it. I edged closer to listen. I couldn't hear what was being said, but I recognized the other voice. I shook my head. It couldn't be Shale's father.

Tariq invited the guest in, and as he walked into the living room, my eyes met his. He looked the same, but he was also different. A little heavier than in the first century, but it was his eyes. People's eyes don't change.

How could Shale's father be here? I knew this wasn't Brutus from the first century, but his nemesis in the twenty-first century. Or, in reality, this was Shale's real father, and I met his nemesis in the first century. How did he know I was here?

Brutus reached out his hand to shake mine. "Daniel, it's good to see you."

I returned the handshake. I read his mind to make sure he was human.

"Very nice view," he remarked.

At least a dozen ships were coming into port or leaving.

He was definitely Shale's father. "Yes, it is."

Brutus's eyes lingered on me for a moment—as if he needed to make sure it was really me, and then he spoke to Tariq. "You're doing an excellent job. I hear the Illuminati are pleased with the unexpected turn of events. No doubt your keen intelligence and quick thinking played an integral role in Daniel's arrival. You are to be commended for bringing him here."

Tariq nodded. "Thank you. However, the third scroll is still missing."

Brutus reassured him. "All in good time. No worries. We'll get it." He turned to me. "What happened to your forehead?"

"Tariq attacked me."

Brutus glanced at Tariq.

"I was instructed to remove the seal."

"I see," Brutus replied, showing little emotion.

An awkward moment followed. Brutus broke the silence. "Tariq, would you like some fresh air? You're probably due for a recharge. After all, we must remember you aren't a machine, but a hybrid, and we should treat you well."

Tariq smiled. "Indeed."

Brutus gestured with his hand. "Take as much time as you need. Enjoy yourself for a few hours."

Tariq required no coaxing, and he was soon out the door.

Questions filled my mind, like what was Brutus's position? While I could read his mind, unless he was thinking about what I wanted to know, I couldn't always get the specific answers I sought. I knew he held a prominent position in the Roman government in the first century, but what about in the twenty-first century?

I remembered his fondness for ancient scrolls, his extensive collection, and the manuscripts he let me keep, including the book of Joel. It never occurred to me that he might hold a similar position in America. I couldn't remember what Shale told me about him. Because of their poor relationship, it didn't seem important that I ask her those questions.

All my emotional energy right now was focused on Shale. I ran my fingers through my hair. "Have you seen Shale?"

He shook his head. "Not recently."

I couldn't imagine what brought him to Bavil, but at least no news was good news.

CHAPTER 23

"Do you have sunglasses?" Brutus asked as he put on his.

I grabbed them off the table and followed him down the hallway. At the double arching stairway, he held up his iPhone. A handwritten note covered the screen. "Don't talk—too much surveillance."

As we passed through the lobby, I put on the sunglasses before reaching the entrance as blinding light poured through the doors. Scorching heat blasted us as soon as we stepped outside. Within seconds, I was soaking in perspiration and thinking how cool the pool or sea would be.

We took a pathway that led toward town. Palm trees provided scant relief from the heat but did provide shade from the sunlight. Brutus pointed to clusters of cactus, bristle brush, and soaptree yucca. "Even though weapons were confiscated from people years ago, cameras and 5G towers still keep a watchful eye…for aliens."

Aliens? I wanted to ask what he meant, but he told me not to talk. He pointed to other random places, even hanging baskets in front of stores and on posts at street corners. Once I knew where to look, it seemed as if every cluster of green plants or palms contained hidden cameras or 5G antennas.

We walked along the winding trail. Songbirds chirped from the canopy and flittered from tree to tree. Not being an avid birdwatcher, I was surprised I recognized a few—a falcon, a flycatcher, and a bunting. If Shale, with her unique gift of talking to animals, were here, she could ask the birds to tell us about Bavil.

Brutus waved his hand. "The dream of dreamers, the vision of visionaries, the playground of artists—this place is a utopia. The New World Order wants to make it a reality all over the world. 666 is making that possible. More highways and connectors are being built."

We went toward the shoreline as a gentle breeze blew in from the Red Sea. Brutus leaned against a palm tree to scratch his back. "Bavil covers over ten thousand square miles. Everything is powered by wind and solar. Most of the work is done by hybrids, like Tariq, allowing humans free time. Why should humans be burdened by mundane things that can be done by robots?"

We walked along the shoreline, but it was too hot to stay out in the sun, so we returned to the hub of restaurants and stores. I saw drones circling overhead.

"Constant surveillance," Brutus reminded me.

He tapped me on the shoulder. "Let's go to the forest."

We took another trail that led away from town. I hadn't seen this area before. A pleasing scent reminded me of a different time when I was young. Splotches of filtered sunshine reached the green carpet under our feet, breaking through here and there. The temperature was pleasant and the air was misty. Conifers and evergreens grew well here.

I saw more cameras. Had I missed them before, or did they become visible when I started to think about them?

I heard the sound of horses' hooves and saw the graceful movement of several in the distance. I started to go to them, as I loved horses, but Brutus stopped me. It was then I noticed other creatures in the forest. Some looked like two-headed dragons. Others walked like humans with hooved feet and wimpy tails. A winged lion was stalking us. As my perception increased, my awareness of the unseen stirred up concern that all was not as it appeared.

Brutus whispered, "Don't look into the eyes of the chimera."

Chimera? My heart pounded, and I willed my legs to walk. Sleep called my name, and my mind was consumed with taking a nap.

Perceiving my sluggishness, Brutus urged me to keep moving. "Don't let the enchanted forest seduce you."

Enchanted? Fear entered my thoughts as creepy sounds filled my ears. The trees appeared to have been awakened by our appearance. They groaned if a tree could do such a thing, and piercing, unsettling screeches whizzed through the air. Yellow eyes popped out from behind green needles and tree stumps.

When I couldn't go any farther, the forest ended. I was surprised at how quickly my strength returned. I shook my head to clear my mind.

We left the forest and came to a large inlet of water surrounded by mountains. Snow covered the mountaintops, and wispy clouds floated around the highest peak, enclosing it in a white ring. The cold air made me shiver. The band of white horses I saw in the forest feasted on the grass in front of the blue waters. One lifted its head, and catching our scent, alerted the others. They took off cantering to a safer area.

After watching until they were gone, snow began to fall. The blue sky turned gray as snowflakes covered the grass. How could it be summer and winter at the same time?

I'd had enough of being silent. "I'm freezing. Let's go back."

We reversed directions, but where the forest had been a massive stadium replaced it. The peaceful silence was broken by cheering fans. As we approached, two teams were ice skating chasing a black object with long sticks. Goalposts stood on each end. They looked like hockey players with thick pads covering their shoulders, elbows, shins, and knees.

I'd never seen ice hockey in person. I followed Brutus into the stands, and we found a seat. The stands were full and the faces were human, not weird creatures—at least they appeared to be human. They even wore sweaters and hoodies, unlike us wearing light robes.

I wasn't familiar with the rules of ice hockey except how to score. As I watched, however, some things seemed strange. All the players wore the same team outfit—black socks, shorts, leggings, gloves, and helmets. How could they tell which team was which?

I noticed crows sitting on the shoulders of some of the players. They were pecking at their faces and heads. Some were cackling in their ears. One net was being used. The goalpost on the other end was empty. How could two teams play hockey using just one net?

The crowd was loud, throwing coins on the ice. Wasn't that dangerous to the skaters? One of the players scored, and cheers shot up. As the player held up his hockey stick, he grew taller.

Play resumed on one side of the rink. Players struck each other with their sticks, tried to trip each other, and body slammed whoever got into their lane. There were no referees calling penalties. Getting the puck into the net was all that mattered.

A player attacked the player who grew taller. Teammates knocked the goal scorer to the ice and beat his head against the floor. Two men ran onto the rink with a gurney and carted him off. Another player came in to replace him. Play resumed.

It didn't take long for another player to score. He scored twice more, and now he was the tallest player. Suddenly, hockey sticks covered the ice and gloves flew through the air. The giant fell, and the other players piled on top of him. Crows swarmed above the players dispensing a litany of grating caws. The annoying birds turned the whole affair into a full-blown riot as they sky-bombed anyone they could victimize.

The crowd watched in rapt attention. After several minutes, when things calmed down, the giant lay still on the ice. He was carted off and replaced with another player. Two players were dead, and the game resumed.

I heard doves cooing, and I looked up and saw them circling. Some attempted to shoo away the crows that crouched on the shoulders of some players, but the crows fought back. A battle ensued, and I became as interested in their mischief as in the game

My focus returned to hockey, and now the players were making little effort to score. Some just skated in circles. After a few minutes of boring play, the crowd grew restless.

Then a skater raced over and chased down the puck. When he captured it with his stick, he surprised everyone by skating to the empty goal at the other end and slapping the puck into the net. A bird was on his shoulder—a dove this time.

Shock covered the players' faces. Did they not know there were two nets on the court? The player that scored grew taller. With the dove still on his shoulder, he crouched in front of the empty net.

Play resumed, but the players struggled to figure out which team they were on. Another goal was scored, and then another and then another. Now several very tall players were skating. A fight erupted. When things settled down, more players were carted off. Other players were brought in to replace the fallen ones.

Play continued until another fight erupted. The crow team attacked the dove team, and blood covered the ice. When the fighting ended, no one offered to retrieve the bodies on the dove team. The crowd became quiet.

Someone announced, "It's not right to leave those players on the ice. They need to be taken away."

The grumbling grew as no one could agree on what to do.

"There is too much at stake to stop the game now," someone said.

Many in the stands were unhappy. Several stood to voice their displeasure and fans stepped on the ice. Soon so many people were on the ice play stopped. Sympathetic souls removed the lifeless bodies, but some of the players didn't like it. They attacked the fans.

I stared. "Lord, what happened? I don't understand."

"Apart from God, what is the goal?" a voice asked.

"Isn't there always redemption?"

"Not here," the voice said. "Not now. Sometimes the score isn't settled until the game of life is over."

I felt Brutus slip a rolled parchment into my hand. He held up his iPhone, and I read the message. "I've handed you Shale's scroll. Hide it and give it to the medic when he sends for you. Don't tell anyone you have it or speak about it."

I hid the scroll inside my pocket, and we arrived at the hotel room without a word being said between us. Tariq was waiting for us.

I asked Brutus before he left, "Can you bring me a TV or a computer?"

He hesitated. "Perhaps a television would be permitted."

There were no cameras inside the bedsheets and that's where I hid the scroll.

CHAPTER 24

The next morning, a television woke me up. I poured myself some coffee and went into the living room. Bloomberg World News was airing, and across the screen flashed the headline, "Israel's Market Economy Thrives."

The anchor reported, "Israel's gross domestic product is outpacing the rest of the world, far surpassing the United States, China, and England when adjusted for population. Prince Adonikam's staunch support of Israel through the New World Order Treaty has made the country the envy of the world.

"Despite the ten-nation confederacy's economic incentives, most of the world languishes following one economic crisis after another, fueled by rising oil costs, crop failure, climate change, and uncertainty in global markets. Here's more from our correspondent in London, Aaron Walstrum."

"Good afternoon, Emily. With only 6.5 million people in Israel, it's remarkable that their GDP has risen to almost $500 billion. By comparison, in the last three years, the U.S.'s GDP has dropped by two-thirds, to $6 trillion. With the dramatic decrease in population due to the purge, the Middle East War, and a litany of natural disasters, the numbers reflect a shift in wealth and productivity.

"How long this will continue, however, is uncertain. Pressure is being exerted by the New World Order to 'spread the wealth,' should I say, to areas of the world that have been hit by earthquakes, famine, and pestilence.

Earlier today I spoke to Professor Rohrich, a professor of economics at the University of Cambridge. I asked her what she thought about the inequality and what can be done."

The camera switched to a middle-age woman wearing glasses and heavy costume earrings that pulled on her ears.

"Thank you, Aaron, for inviting me to speak on this important topic. Inequality is ravaging the economy of this great planet. Take Israel. They've so much oil they could never use it all. The Jews could help the countries that are on the brink of economic collapse. Minister of Truth Father Haman Urhammu says the chip will spread equality across the world because it regulates the buying and selling of food. Even as we speak millions have already received it, and countries are reaping the benefit. It's allowing those in less fortunate countries to have access to at least one meal a day. Who knows if the Enki might strike again if we aren't gracious with one another?"

"Is socialism better for the world in these trying times than capitalism?" Walstrum asked.

"Socialism will save our world," Professor Rohrich said. "Capitalism has failed. Look at the crop failures, stock market collapse, trade wars, and tariffs. Look at the increase in pestilences because of pharmaceutical companies overcharging for medicines people need and can't afford.

"The New World Order wants to ensure equality for everyone. Globalization will make that happen. With all the inequity in the world, what better way to show how much you care than by being generous and sharing with those less fortunate? Prophet Urhammu wants to ensure that happens. The NWO is in the best position to enforce graciousness. We belong to each other, right? And money should unite, not a divide."

The reporter interrupted. "What about a person's individual rights and freedom? Should the NWO be given authority to take from those who have to give to those who are impoverished?"

The professor appeared taken aback. "The New World Order knows what's best for everyone."

"In every instance?" the reporter asked

Professor Rohrich replied, "In today's world, we need stability and security. Prophet Urhammu and Prince Adonikam are providing the leadership we need. And let me add, I don't understand how those two so-called holy men who appeared in Jerusalem out of nowhere can threaten to withhold rains from desperate countries. Calling down fire on countries without cause should be a crime. What kind of holy men are they? I hope Prince Adonikam will address it at the next NOW meeting in Paris. Perhaps those prophets are in cahoots with the Enki —to give them an excuse to return. Haman Urhammu has set up a commission to investigate their possible ties. I hope their report will be released to the public soon."

The Bloomberg reporter glanced down at his notes. "I'm sure it will. Switching topics, what do you think about making the chip mandatory?"

"It's already mandatory in the areas that Prince Adonikam controls."

"What about the resistance from those who call themselves Christians? Some of them say they will never take it."

Professor Rohrich rolled her eyes. "When they've no food to eat, they'll take it. And that's what's coming. We need the fair allotment of food because it's growing scarcer by the day. Plus, all the gold is in the hands of the World Bank. You know as I do it's illegal for people to own gold, so their meal ticket is the mark. If people want to eat, they will need to take the mark."

"What about the United States? They seem to be the lone holdout among the countries not directly under Prince Adonikam's control."

The professor was nonplussed. "The dollar is worth nothing. The chip is now the world's default currency. I'm surprised the U.S. hasn't implemented it yet, but they will. Even now, they're experiencing food shortages that will get worse."

"What do you think is going to happen with global markets in the next six months?"

Professor Rohrich drummed her fingers. "That's a good question. Some countries in the Middle East have been at war for the last several years. The hope is that Prince Adonikam can bring those warring nations under his jurisdiction. The latest nuclear attack sent shockwaves across the Middle East. The ramifications are being felt in the market sector and in natural resources. I hear some of the water supplies in the region have been contaminated by nuclear fallout.

"I would say if the chip is implemented across all borders, even beyond Prince Adonikam's territory, it would be another critical step toward peace and a one-world government. You have to remember, it's the inequality that sparks wars and violence, especially when food is short. I'm sure we'll see him do something as a result of the latest nuclear attack by Iran on Saudi Arabia.

"Regardless, something has to be done about Israel. The treaty Adonikam confirmed with them I'm sure he now regrets."

"Thank you, Professor Rohrich, for your insights. That's it from here, Emily. Aaron Walstrum, Bloomberg Global News, London."

Reporter Emily looked into the camera. "We'll be back right after this short break."

I was about to ask Tariq what other channels we could receive when the commercial caught my eye. On the screen was an overhead shot of Bavil. I recognized it from the shimmering pink mountains and towering iconic structures rising from the sands. Streaming across the screen was the advertisement, "Gateway of the Gods." I recognized Prince Adonikam as the narrator.

"There is no other place on earth like Bavil—where you can enjoy spectacular scenery, romantic walks, relaxing meals, and exciting tours. Indeed, Bavil is the Gateway of the Gods.

"And now, thanks to the work of our top scientists, the chip has become the gateway of the mind, soul, and spirit. The number of the chip is 6-6-6. Win a trip to Bavil, the eighth wonder of the world.

"In this fast-paced world that's changing by the hour, the chip is more than money. It's a necessity." Adonikam's voice was as smooth as well-told lies. He chuckled. "It will allow easier access to personal data, job information, and social networking. Everything you need like medical records, passwords, financial information, and credit reports will be at your fingertips. It's like wearable money. You won't have to worry about going to the bank ever again.

"How many times have you lost your credit card or overdrawn your bank account? Remember when you had to recall dozens of pass-words? Remember when the store shelves were empty at the grocery stores? Using 666 will ensure everyone has access to food. Remember when your I.D. was stolen? Now you wear it on your right hand or forehead. This is the most amazing A.I. technology ever developed.

"For a limited time, everyone who receives the chip will be entered into the Bavil Sweepstakes. Plan your getaway today." The scene panned out with excited people waiting in line to be chipped. A number to call flashed across the screen as the programming went into the next commercial.

I glanced up at Tariq. "What other stations are there?"

He clicked his iPhone until he came to CNN.

"You can leave it there," I said.

The screen showed a church service. A young African-American woman was singing to a crowd of mourners. As the camera panned around the room, I could see people dressed in western clothing and some women wearing the hijab. At the front of the church on a green emblem outlined in black appeared the word "Chrislam." Beneath it were the words "One Lord, Three Faiths." A cross cut through the crescent moon.

The scene returned to the CNN Atlanta studios. "Breaking News" flashed. The anchor looked up from his cheat sheet and peered into the camera. "We have a news alert. More trumpet sounds have been heard across America, Europe, and Asia. People are reporting a significant reduction in sunlight when it's day and a similar decrease in light at night. In the U.S., one-third of the sky is starless. The moon has shrunk by one-third. In Europe, sunlight is also reduced." A video appeared on the screen showing people staring into the sky.

"If you're experiencing any reduction in light where you live, please let us know on Twitter with #darkened. We would love to hear from you."

A bold knock at the door startled me.

CHAPTER 25

T ariq went to the door, and I rose from the chair to see who it was. When he opened it, a man in scrubs and two guards holding AK-103s filled the doorway. Alarmed, I edged closer to listen, but I didn't know Arabic well enough to understand what he said.

"What is it?" I asked.

"We need to take you to the clinic," the medic said in thick English.

"Why?"

His face twitched. "The doctor wants to check your stitches."

I attempted to read his mind—and I was surprised I could. He was human—and lying. I glanced down the hallway.

"I see. I need to use the facility."

One of the guards gestured with his hand. "Go ahead."

I closed the bedroom door and retrieved Shale's scroll from the bedsheets. I'd hoped for more time to plan an escape. Discouraged, I threw up a half-hearted prayer.

Not only were they going to chip me to cover up God's seal, but they were going to feature me on the news—a propaganda ploy to encourage others to take the mark. That's what was in the medic's mind.

According to the book of Revelation, anyone who took the mark could not receive salvation through Jesus. Of course, worshipping the beast was required, and I hadn't done that. Did that mean God would protect me? I couldn't think of a single instance in the Bible where anyone received the mark that didn't worship the beast first.

To stall for time, I used the facility.

I recited out loud John 3:16: "For God so loved the world that he gave his only begotten Son so that whosoever believeth in him should not perish but have eternal life."

Every move I made was calculated, slow, and deliberate. I didn't want to go. I didn't want to think about what would happen.

Shale's beautiful face filled my thoughts. I wished we were married. I grabbed the sink, leaned forward, and clenched my eyes. "Father, I need not worry about the future because you are already there." I stared defiantly into the camera and opened the door.

CHAPTER 26

Tariq handed me my dark glasses, and I left with them. In the foyer, a quartet was playing Baroque music. A flower shop must have delivered fresh roses as the scent of rose petals filled the lobby. I remembered how much Shale loved flowers, and I noticed one lying on the floor. I stopped and picked it up, stuffing it inside my hidden pocket.

The hotel lobby was crowded. We approached the entrance, and when the double doors opened, once again, the outdoor heat punched me like a boxer. What if I ran? Without a second thought, I took off, losing my sandals. The hot, stone pavement seared the soles of my feet. I didn't hear any footsteps, and no bullets whizzed by. Seconds later, however, drones circled, and guards approached from all directions. I'd forgotten about the cameras. It was pointless to try to escape as I stared into the muzzles of a dozen guns.

"Mr. Sperling, put up your hands," an unidentified voice ordered. A growing group of oglers enjoyed the unexpected excitement.

One of the guards tied my hands and shoved me forward. The other one squeezed my shoulder. They escorted me to the black box waiting at the street corner. Once inside the cube, the guards blindfolded me and stuffed earplugs in my ears. This time I could tell we were descending. The female computer voice gave the same greeting as before, though muffled with the ear plugs. "Welcome to Bavil, Gateway of the Gods. Today's quota met. Population in habitable territories—three point zero billion. Good work by the New World Order. Don't miss happy hour tonight. Enjoy plenty of food, wine, and perpetual delights."

After a few seconds, the door swished open, and the guards pushed me out of the box into what I presumed was, again, the numberless hallway. After walking a fair distance, even with my ears plugged, I heard a door open. Once I was in the room, they yanked off the blindfold.

Scientific equipment filled the laboratory—tables, scales, charts, apparatuses, chairs that moved in odd directions, contraptions that must have dated back to the dark ages, and machines I'm sure someone rediscovered to torture their victims all over again.

A fancy display monitor showed a computer-generated image of a human body with floating heads above it. To my horror, one of the heads was mine.

The medic pointed at a dentist-like chair and said something I couldn't hear.

"What?" I asked.

One of the guards untied my hands, and I removed the earplugs.

"Why did you do that?" the other guard asked.

"Do what?"

"Untie his hands."

"The doctor may want to put the chip on his hand instead of his forehead." The guard motioned to me. "Sit."

I sat in the chair and waited, I presumed, for the doctor as the technician filled out paperwork.

Next to my room was an adjoining room separated by a glass partition. It looked identical to the one I was in.

After a brief wait, the doctor arrived. He was not the same doctor as before. He introduced himself while he washed his hands. "I'm Doctor Aiken. I understand you injured your forehead."

I nodded.

He dried his hands, put on some gloves, and pulled up his chair. Then he removed the bandage and inspected the wound. "It's healed nicely. The chip will cover the scar. You'll never see it."

I wanted to tell him it was the seal of God, but instead, I grabbed his arm. Dr. Aiken flinched with surprise.

"I have something Prince Adonikam wants. I want to offer it in exchange for my freedom. I do not want to receive the chip. I mean, I refuse to accept the chip."

The doctor leaned back in his chair. "What do you want to give me?"

I pulled the scroll out of the inside pocket and handed it to him. The parchment was in poor shape and not well preserved, but perhaps its poor quality would intrigue the doctor enough to investigate it.

The guards edged over to see for themselves. The doctor examined the outside of the scroll but was reluctant to open it. "Just a minute."

He went to a table, picked up a magnifying glass, and returned to his chair. He turned it over several times to look at it in closer detail. "I'm afraid if I open it, it might fall apart."

At last, he removed his glasses and slumped back. "I need to call someone."

He pulled out his cellphone and wandered out of earshot. His back was turned as he was absorbed in the conversation. Too bad the guards were still here. Perhaps I'd blown my only chance to escape by trying too soon.

I grew impatient. This was taking too long. I peered again through the glass partition, and my heart stopped. Staring back at me was a body double. The room became quiet. I could have heard a feather drop.

I rubbed my hands and touched my face. Now I knew why they had videotaped me. They were making a humanoid, or a half human, or a chimera, or who knew what—of me!

I wanted to run into the other room and smash him, pull the plug on the computer, dump it on the floor, and pulverize it. On second thought, I felt revolted at shattering an image of myself. What kind of A.I. was it? Did it feel pain?

I knew it didn't have a soul, but what did it have? Was it a hybrid or a transhuman? What was the difference? Did it have snippets of my brain in its head? DNA from my blood? I couldn't think.

My eyes flittered about the room. It was then I noticed the guards, medic, and doctor were frozen, or I was moving a thousand times faster than they were. I was beginning to think I was insane when two dazzling white beings appeared next to me. I shielded my eyes, wondering what happened to the sunglasses.

"Come with us," one of them said. "God can't do anything until we rescue you. Put on these sandals. Don't waste a second."

I did as instructed, casting one last glance into the other room. Transfixed, the double stared at me. I wanted to ask God's messengers about the mannequin, but they were in too big of a hurry.

I thought about wiping the computer clean. What else would someone do with my medical information? They had my DNA, photos, and videos. They created a twin of me—without my consent. Since arriving, they had documented my life in the minutest detail. How could I leave the information behind, but the two angels' priorities were so urgent, there wasn't time.

"We must take the stairs and not the cube," one of them said.

They hurried me down the hallway of the numberless floor as we passed glass rooms full of strange-looking creatures—half-formed beasts, hybrids, and gargoyles. Oversized test tubes lined walls. Filled with cloudy concoctions, I suspected they were growing things— creatures from hell. I remembered the two hundred million-man army mentioned in the book of Revelation.

Disturbing animal sounds filled the hallway as a rotten smell poured through the air-conditioning vents. I averted my eyes. The numberless floor was the abode of monsters that carried out secret experiments.

The messengers of God broke a lock on a door and whisked me inside the stairwell. I grabbed one of them by the arm. "I don't have my dark glasses."

"You don't need them," the angel assured me. I lost count of how many floors we climbed.

We reached ground level, and the door opened. Fearful of the sunlight, I hesitated. The angels pulled me through the door, but something unexpected happened. Everything I saw in Bavil—the people, the buildings, the restaurants, the driverless cars, the shops, the cameras—everything faded away. As when one wakes up from a dream, the world that was so real and familiar evaporated. The matrix of Bavil was gone.

"Please don't take away the memories, Lord," I prayed. "What if I need them in the future? What if I come back here?"

All I saw was a barren landscape. The Red Sea was off in the distance, but there were no structures. No drones flew overhead, or hidden cameras tracked me with an all-seeing eye.

I stared at the angels. "I don't understand."

"The things of this world are temporary," one of them said. "God's light blinds evil and delivers the righteous. We're taking you out of the City of Sin before its destruction."

I followed them down to the shoreline, and we ran along the beach for several minutes. The waves, the wind, and the birds—everything was frozen.

One of the angels spoke urgently, "You see that red boat?"

I nodded.

"There is someone on the boat you know."

"Okay," I said, breathlessly.

The other angel handed me what I thought was a flashlight. Why would I need that?

"Don't give this to anyone," he said, "and it must not be used on a human."

"What is it?"

"A weapon not of this world. We must go. The days are shorter today than they were yesterday. At God's appointed time, you will understand."

Then the angels faded away. Staring at nothing and still mystified by what just happened, a powerful wave knocked me over. Reality was back. I fought my way toward the boat against the tide as my sandals sunk into the sand. Another wave swept over my head. The undertow tried to pull me under. I wasn't sure I could get to the boat.

As I struggled to get beyond the breakers, a bright object streaked across the sky. Was it a rocket or a warhead? When it disappeared, a golden eagle soared into view. Gliding through the heavens, he cried out in a commanding voice, "Woe, woe, woe to the earth-dwellers."

I watched, mesmerized by his power and passion. He was more than a golden eagle.

CHAPTER 27

The salt water burned my eyes as I trudged through the waves. The drenched throbe made it almost impossible to swim, and I thought about disrobing. The undercurrent tugged at my legs, and another wave pounded me. I lost my sandals as I toppled backward. Regaining my balance, I braced for the next wave, jumping over it and getting beyond the breakers. I waved my hands to get the attention of the people in the boat.

Someone noticed me as the boat rocked like a see-saw. I was going to have to swim to the ship. They risked breaching if they came in any closer to shore.

I swam toward my rescuer with great difficulty, making sure I didn't let go of the weapon. At last, a wave pulled me out, and I headed toward the boat.

A shipmate threw a flotation device into the sea. I swam over and grabbed it, and he lowered the ladder and pulled me in. After a couple of failed attempts to clasp the bar, I held on.

Rough waves pounded against the ladder. Once I reached the top rung, I pulled myself up and crawled away from the ledge. Exhausted but relieved, I sat cross-legged in a pool of water as four men crowded around me.

"Are you all right?" one of them asked.

It took a moment to register who he was because he looked several years older. "Maurice?"

A puzzled looked crossed his face. "Daniel, is that you?"

Maurice was the smartest kid I knew and a long-time friend. I glanced back at the shoreline. Bavil was hidden. How would I explain how I got here?

"Yes, it's me."

The other shipmates' interest was piqued. One of them asked, "You know each other?"

Maurice laughed. "Yep. Daniel, this is E.J., Hatim, and Chris."

I would never have imagined I would run into Maurice here. He helped me with Calculus in high school, and we would hang out in the summers hiking and camping, and occasionally scuba diving. My friend handed me a towel. "You need dry clothes. E.J., can you get Daniel something from my bag?"

The youngest of the men took off to retrieve something.

Maurice stared. "You look the same as the last time I saw you in Hurva Square. Remember? When Lilly's father was injured." He stopped. "Daniel, I thought you disappeared in the purge."

I shook my head.

"Where have you been?"

I took in a deep breath. "I've been in Bavil, and before that the Sahara."

Maurice squinted and cocked his head as he peered across the waters to the coastline.

I knew what he was thinking. I pick you up in the ocean wearing a throbe—not even a wetsuit or trunks, and there are no hotels, public beaches, or people in sight. He let it slide for the moment. Without stating the obvious, he turned to another crew member who wore the label, "Divemaster Chris" on his shirt.

"Daniel is a long-time friend," Maurice said.

Chris tipped his hat. "Glad you made it onboard."

Maurice pointed to the guy standing next to him. "Hatim is the ship's captain."

Hatim's face remained expressionless. I sensed uneasiness on his part when I read his mind. He was concerned about safety. Could I blame him?

Hatim cleared his throat. "If you'll excuse me, I need to get us away from the shoreline."

I nodded "Thanks for picking me up."

Maurice and I watched as Hatim walked away. Stroking his chin, Maurice added, "The European Organization for Nuclear Research, otherwise known as CERN, rented his boat and services for the week to check out whale sightings and seismic activity. We even have a private chef to cook the meals."

The youngest crew member returned with a pair of shorts and a T-Shirt.

"E.J. is a friend of Chris, our Divemaster," Maurice said as I reached out to shake Chris's hand. Then I made eye contact with E.J. as he started to hand me the dry clothes, but I stopped him. "I'm too wet. Let me dry off for a minute. Just set them over there. Thanks."

When I stood the water collected on the deck floor. I apologized for making a mess, but no one cared. Maurice pointed to the upper deck. "That's Pierre. He came here with me from CERN."

I noticed he was elderly and looked like a scientist.

Maurice focused on me. "You look pretty wet and uncomfortable. Go ahead and get dried off. You can change in there. It's the closest head."

The engine revved up, and the live-aboard began moving. I glanced at the coastline. The desert provided no hint of a virtual city or an illusionary world that the angel called the City of Sin. I sensed it was still there, though, just hidden, and knew it represented the true reality beyond the veil of what we perceive as real.

I took the clothes and returned a couple of minutes later, hanging the drenched throbe and wet towel on the railing. A gentle breeze coming off the water would dry them.

A smile covered Maurice's face. "Let's go to the second deck where there're chairs, and we can talk."

We climbed up a level, and Maurice pulled a chair over next to his.

"I quit believing in coincidences long ago. Things happen for a reason."

I smiled. "That's an understatement."

Pierre walked over, and Maurice extended introductions. "Pierre, meet Daniel, a long-time friend."

The scientist pulled up a chair and eased beside us. After engaging in small talk that revealed a French accent, he focused on Maurice. "Have you looked at the latest readings?"

Maurice shook his head. "Not in the last few minutes. Any change?"

Pierre showed him a sheet of paper. "I think we need to head back to Eilat. The tremors are coming from there. Whatever we picked up here has disappeared."

Maurice crossed his arms. "I think God brought us here to pick up Daniel."

Pierre sighed. "I don't think that's very scientific."

"Probably not," Maurice admitted, "but we don't have to put that in the report."

Maurice turned to me. "CERN became aware of the increase in whale sightings in the Red Sea a couple of months ago. It seemed to correlate with an uptick in seismic activity—tremors in this area. There haven't been whales in the Red Sea for centuries until recently. They wanted to see if there was a correlation between the whales and the earthquake activity. A recent event was…disturbing, should I say."

Pierre gave Maurice the evil eye.

Maurice stretched out his arms on the sides of the chair. "That's about all we know right now."

I noticed the ship's captain, Hatim, watching me from the wheel. Even though I was Maurice's friend, to him I was a security concern. Perhaps I could find a way to reassure him.

CHAPTER 28

The three-tiered live-aboard was fancier than any dive boat I remembered. The view of the Red Sea from the bow reminded me of God's glory. Despite all the judgments and carnage, for those who searched, his majesty was still here.

The lowest deck extended out beyond the second and third decks, providing a spacious area for divers to suit up. Seeing the BC's, weight belts, and dive paraphernalia made me want to go diving again. I hadn't been to the top level, but I imagined it was for bubble watchers.

"Are there hidden cameras?"

"Nope. We told Hatim to remove them. CERN doesn't want the media to know we're here," Maurice said.

"Do you have a computer?"

Maurice wagged his head. "Daniel, I haven't seen you in years, and the first thing you want to do is get on a computer?"

"I want to know what's happened."

"Have you been hiding in a cave?" He threw up his hands. "Never mind. I'll get mine."

A couple of minutes later, he returned and handed me his. "I already entered the password."

I placed it on my lap, clicked on the search bar, and typed Prince

Adonikam. Millions of entries popped up. How much area did he control? I clicked on images and maps. His sphere of power was centered in Europe, Africa, Asia, and the Middle East. The United States still appeared free but was smaller in size. The West Coast was part of China, and part of Florida's peninsula was missing.

I was glad to see he didn't control China, Great Britain, a shrunken United States, and Australia. Some countries I couldn't tell. I typed in several more random words, but nothing helpful appeared.

I typed in revelation. The definition came up, followed by several generic entries. I typed Bible, book of Revelation. A 400 bad request error appeared on the screen.

I entered several other religious words, like rapture, tribulation, Yeshua, Jesus Christ, and Bible. Each time a 400 bad request error popped up.

I glanced at Maurice. "What's wrong with the internet? I can't find any entries for Bible."

He leaned over and studied the screen. "It's best not to search for religious stuff. I should delete it."

"Why would search engines remove all the entries that relate to the Bible?"

"You know Prince Adonikam burned all the Bibles. Religious books no longer exist—officially."

"Even in Israel?"

Maurice whispered. "There might be listening devices built into the software. Let me put the computer back in my room."

He took the laptop and returned a few minutes later. I glanced around the deck to make sure no one was around. "Maurice, can you give me a quick history lesson. What year is it?"

Concern crossed his face. "I know you were in a mental institution. Are you all right?"

I sighed. Some would always think I was crazy—like my mother, but Maurice and I had been close. "Trust me. I'm as sane as you are."

He leaned over and grabbed my chair. "That's good to know. I'm relieved. But seriously, anyone in their right mind would know what's happened unless he was dead or deranged."

"You left out a third scenario."

He cocked his head. "I did?"

"After we helped Lilly's father, Shale and I discovered that an antiquities dealer gave the scrolls we were looking for to my dad."

"And Shale is your girlfriend?"

I nodded. "Fiancée. She was with me that day, remember? We discovered the scrolls in an unmarked box my father mailed from Syria. We went to Nepal looking for him based on an email he sent. When we didn't find him, we returned to Israel. After rescuing a small child, the war started, so we went to Jacob, my brother. At that time, he controlled a stargate beneath the Old City in Jerusalem. We talked with my brother and decided in order to find my father we needed to talk to a man sent to the first century by a secret organization. We knew he had information. After a series of events, God brought me back here—except a few years into the future. Shale is still with Shira in the first century."

Maurice leaned back. "That time-travel stuff is a top-secret research project at CERN. It wouldn't surprise me if that was the organization. Few people know about it. I believe you."

Relieved, I took a deep breath. "So fill me in. What year is it?"

"Well," Maurice said, "according to the old calendar, nobody is sure. Prince Adonikam changed the times when the pole shift happened."

"What happened?"

"The rotation of the earth stopped, and the axis shifted. We've been circumnavigating the time-space continuum, so to speak. Time isn't moving forward," Maurice said.

"What year is this?"

"We're at three and a half years on this new calendar."

That sounded to me like the midpoint of the Day of the Lord. "Did the pole shift happen before or after the purge?"

Maurice took a deep breath. "Let me think for a second. The purge happened after the Ezekiel War. The government said the people who disappeared were taken by the Enki."

I remembered what Jonathan had told me. "And the Enki are aliens?"

Maurice kinked his head. "That's the official version, but I don't believe the official version."

"Tell me the official version and then what you believe."

"When the purge happened, the United Nations met. They decided we needed to unite together into a one-world government. They claimed aliens from a distant civilization attacked us. News broadcasts showed spaceships. It was all over the web, and many claimed to have seen them in person.

"After the purge, the United Nations claimed the aliens took the evil people away to save the planet. The New World Order said the Enki told them if we didn't quit fighting, they would come back and take more people. The United Nations allowed the NWO to form a one-world government to protect us if they returned.

"The U.N. divided the world into ten regions. Prince Adonikam replaced the United Nations with a ten-nation confederacy called the New World Order. The Prince made concessions to Israel, offering to protect them. That's how he got the Western nations onboard with this new one-world government. He confirmed a peace treaty. The Jews would've made a pact with the devil if they thought it would bring peace."

"What do you think happened?" I asked.

Maurice became subdued. "The rapture. It wasn't the Enki, a bunch of aliens that came and took away those millions. Yeshua took them."

"Do you believe Yeshua is the Messiah?"

Maurice steadied his eyes on me. "Well, Prince Adonikam isn't the Jewish Messiah. I want to believe Yeshua is the Messiah, but—how can I be sure?"

"Maurice, he died on the cross for everyone. The only way to heaven is through his death and resurrection."

Maurice rubbed his chin but remained quiet.

"The Bible says before the Messiah's return, there is a seven-year tribulation. If year one started with the purge—"

Maurice interrupted me. "No. Year one started with the pole shift when Prince Adonikam confirmed the seven-year agreement. The purge took place a couple of years before that."

"If that was three and a half years ago, Yeshua will return in about three and a half more years."

"I've been thinking about this," Maurice said, "but it's dangerous to talk about."

"How did you get involved with CERN?"

"You remember what Mr. Rushton, Lilly's father, told you in Hurva Square? When several bodies disappeared from the makeshift hospital inside the synagogue? He thought he was inside a tube and he heard French and English being spoken."

I nodded.

"That strange incident with Lilly's father piqued my interest in CERN. I've been doing an internship there while working on my Ph.D. in physics."

My thoughts drifted. "Maurice, were you the one who deciphered the Hebrew word 'Tekel' for the CERN scientists?"

He looked stunned. "Yes. That's why Pierre and I are here. That's when the anomalies began, the tremors."

"I heard your voice."

A blank look covered Maurice's face. "What do you mean?"

"When you deciphered 'Tekel' in Hebrew, it was your voice I heard."

Maurice's eyes bulged. "You know about that? A package came through. We didn't know what it was. The Hebrew made everyone uncomfortable."

I quipped, "I bet. Hebrew is the language of heaven."

He relaxed and changed the subject. "You've been gone a while and haven't aged a bit."

I gazed at the Red Sea that was as blue as the sky. "Why is the water red in some places and not in others?"

My friend crossed his arms. "We assume it's from the deaths of so many sea animals. It's widespread, but not everywhere. It's not just animal deaths. Millions have died following two nuclear exchanges. Famine spread beyond the poor, and there're new diseases doctors haven't heard of. Christians are being slaughtered if they don't convert to Chrislam."

Maurice's countenance dropped. "Lilly talked to me on several occasions about Yeshua, but I didn't know a single Jew who believed Yeshua was the Messiah. She disappeared in the purge, but she gave me a Jewish New Testament. I read it from cover to cover before turning it into the authorities. They burned all the Bibles."

"You don't believe Yeshua is the Messiah, even after reading the New Testament?"

Maurice hesitated. "I don't know. I'm still thinking about it."

"What happened after the Ezekiel War?"

"Damascus was obliterated. The Muslims weren't happy about it and invaded Israel. They discovered an abundant supply of oil and wanted it.

"God delivered us," Maurice emphasized. "He destroyed those invading nations—Iran, Turkey, Sudan, and Libya, but Prince Adonikam took credit. After the purge, he took over the media. Talk about rewriting history." Maurice waved his hand. "Adonikam took credit for everything. That's the way people remember things."

"You remember things differently?"

Maurice nodded. "Deception. Remember the book *1984*, two plus two equals five? This is worse than what George Orwell wrote."

CHAPTER 29

Maurice and I talked late into the evening. "How is your family," I asked.

He spoke in a whisper. "My mother died of leukemia last year."

I reflected on my mother dying in the seventh dimension and how devastating it was. "I'm sorry."

He took a sip of water. "The doctors said it was because of radiation exposure. If you look at cancer deaths in the past five years, they've increased, especially thyroid and lung cancers."

As much as I missed Shale and Shira, I was grateful they escaped the nuclear attacks. If half the population had died in the last three-plus years, probably one of them would have died. "So, what about your father?"

"My father is fine and my sister as well. She's serving in the Tzahal. Just four months left to finish."

"Did you complete your time?" I asked.

Maurice nodded.

I lamented. "I haven't even started yet."

"So you've been in the first century all this time?"

"Sort of—except I wasn't exactly back in time. I mean, I was and I wasn't. It's more like a parallel universe."

"What do you mean?"

I explained. "The seventh dimension is a spiritual dimension where time travel is possible. To learn about Yeshua, everybody must travel back in time. Once someone knows about the King's life, death, and resurrection, and believes that Yeshua is the Messiah, spiritual warfare erupts. Satan and his demons try to prevent the seeker of knowledge from believing Yeshua is the Messiah.

"As the seeker of truth uncovers the truth, Satan causes blindness, deception, and throws all sorts of cogs in the wheel, so to speak. In my case, God performed many miracles. It took a miracle for me to believe because I was convinced that Jesus was only for Christians and not Jews. I saw with my own eyes Yeshua die on the cross, and I witnessed his resurrection.

"I also met friends and family or their counterparts in the first century. I met Shale who was on her own spiritual journey. I met others who taught me about love, perseverance, patience, and wisdom."

Maurice half-smiled. "Did you meet me?"

I stopped to think. "No, but I did meet Lilly, my mother, my two sisters—"

Maurice interrupted me. "I thought you had just one sister."

"When you seek truth in the name of Yeshua Hamashiach, he reveals all truth."

"So you discovered another sister you didn't know about?"

"Yes." I didn't want to say more, and he didn't ask.

My friend stared out over the ocean. "Interesting. Physicists have long known there're multiple dimensions, and one of the purposes of CERN is to open doorways to other dimensions. I've never considered that one of those might be a spiritual dimension where you can time travel."

"Does it make you nervous, what you might discover?"

Maurice puckered his lips. "Recently, when the Hebrew words came through, God was talking to me."

"What do you think God was telling you?"

He lowered his voice. "Daniel, CERN is opening up wormholes. That's why they sent Pierre and me here. They believe a wormhole has opened up off the coast of Eilat because of the high level of seismic activity.

"What's a wormhole?"

"A tunnel—a tunnel that might connect to a different dimensions. They want access to other dimensions—shortcuts in the time/space continuum."

"Why? What are they looking for?"

His eyes bore into mine. "If they could deconstruct matter into its smallest particle and access other dimensions, they could create another universe in another dimension. That's why they're opening wormholes. That's why they smash particles in the collider."

"In other words, they would become as little gods?" I asked.

Maurice became quiet. "There is something wrong with that, isn't there."

I inhaled purposefully. "Do you think any scientist is wise enough to use that kind of knowledge only for good? And supposing one scientist, like you, was all good and loved God, and determined to use it only for good, how long would it take for that kind of power and knowledge to be used for evil by others who weren't all good and who didn't love God?"

My friend thought for a moment. "God was warning me, wasn't he?"

I nodded. "God is speaking to you—trying to get your attention." I could tell fear flooded his thoughts. I remembered Proverbs said fear was the beginning of wisdom. I didn't think he was far from the kingdom of heaven.

"The last time I spoke to your brother," Maurice said, "he talked about a mathematician—if I can remember his name—Saul Kullook. He was working on a thesis that claimed major events are predetermined related to Israel's borders and the axis of the planet."

I could imagine how that conversation went. "My brother was always—is more of a nerd than me."

"While it's a little complicated, it's also fascinating. Kullook believes the Jews have come back to Israel at fixed times following the forces of nature."

"God's appointed times. Of course, I doubt that most scientists would believe that."

My friend wasn't deterred. "I looked into it, and it was very compelling. According to Dr. Kullook's formula, the Ezekiel War happened according to dates as defined in the formula. Do you know what the chances of that are?"

I shook my head.

"Pretty slim. There're other parallels in history. Like the Babylonian exile. Kullook's formula matched the northern and southern borders of Jerusalem with the date of their exile and return. He predicted one more Aliyah back in 2018, and that happened."

"So you're saying it's possible to date specific events based on the borders of Israel and when the Jews have gone into exile and returned?"

Maurice nodded. "They're fixed times—written in the heavens, in the sun, moon, and stars. There is a correlation between the axial tilt of the earth and the geographical borders of Israel. We have no control over it. They're predefined algorithms."

If the formula was as accurate as Maurice believed, it was one more validation of Israel's importance to God. "That's fascinating," I said.

"I have to admit," Maurice said, "I've begun to wonder about Yeshua. Could he be who he said he was? I mean, the New Testament is as ethnocentric as the Old Testament."

I smiled. "While I like where you end up, I'm not sure I follow your reasoning."

"Look at it like this. Since we know how accurate the Torah is regarding Jewish history, the incursions into Israel, the chronologies of the rulers, the construction of the tabernacle and the Levitical Laws, then why wouldn't the prophecies be as accurate? Kullook's formula verifies the dates of the Jews' exiles and returns as they're recorded in the Bible.

"If Yeshua fulfills the Old Testament prophecies in the New Testament, shouldn't we take it seriously that he might be the Messiah? The Bible can't be accurate in one area and not in another. It's all or nothing. There is no middle ground."

I nodded. "I agree. No argument from me on that point." I studied the darkened sky above us. "One-third of the stars aren't shining."

"I know," Maurice replied. "Unfortunately, Kullook's formula can't be applied to the stars in reverse."

"Have you seen my brother since the purge?"

Maurice shook his head.

"Tell me more about what happened in the beginning. What was the first thing Prince Adonikam did when he came to power?"

"Seized control of the media. Does that remind you of someone from the past?"

I thought about World War II. "Hitler?"

Maurice nodded.

"You know," I added, "the book of Revelation says the dragon is given a mouth—in media terms, that's a platform."

"Well," Maurice said, "Hitler was a dragon, I mean, he killed six million Jews and probably more than eleven million if you include everyone, but I think Prince Adonikam is a worse dragon. He seized control of the internet within a month and removed the names of all those people who disappeared in the purge. According to current history, they never existed. Four billion people have died in the last four years."

"So—he began by taking over the media?"

Maurice waved his hand. "Before that, he implemented the Mandella Effect. He rewrote history—created a different past."

"Sort of like what the physicists want to do at CERN, create a different universe?"

Maurice nodded. "I hadn't thought about it like that, but you're right. After Adonikam destroyed all the Bibles and purged the internet, he closed museums and auctioned off the antiquities to the highest bidder. Then he deceived the buyers by not giving them the antiquities and made them pay more money, calling it a tax. The whole purpose of that was more purging—to kill those who wanted those antiquities. So he had all the money and all the antiquities and all the people who wanted the antiquities. While he was doing that, he seized control of Europe, the Middle East, Africa, Antarctica, and most of Asia."

Maurice gestured with his hands. "The media continues to pontificate his skills as a peacemaker and arbiter ad nauseam. Maurice crossed his arms. "He's not done."

"What do you mean?"

"He wants the Western nations. And he wants to control Israel. It was God who protected us—not him."

The unexplained darkness of the heavens seemed to expand as we talked. Leaning back, I clasped my fingers behind my neck. "I don't see how things could deteriorate so fast."

Maurice sighed. "The nuclear war killed many. People did whatever they could to survive. Damascus was destroyed. Those who became Christians after the purge have been persecuted, and many have died. The Minister of Truth, who I believe should be called the Minister of Untruth, Father Haman Urhammu, also known as Prophet Urhammu, came on the scene almost at the same time as Prince Adonikam. Under the broad powers given to him by the U.N., Urhammu made Chrislam the official religion. Those who refused to accept the ecumenical religion have been martyred. The process began with those who lived in Muslim countries in the Middle East and Africa. Europe is being razed now. The U.S. is next. They're a little behind Europe, but what you see happen in Europe follows in America —unless God raises up someone to fight it."

"What has Adonikam done to protect the Jews?"

"He's allowed the resumption of sacrifices in the rebuilt Temple and signed a treaty to protect them from invasion—including the Enka, but he has no political control over Israel. The number one thing to remember is Adonikam is a flatterer. People believe what he says because of the media. Those who oppose him are found dead or disappear. Israel was content to make a pact with the devil in return for peace, but I think Adonikam's ultimate goal is to own Israel."

I remembered what the prince said. Maurice was correct. "There aren't any more Bibles?"

"I don't know. I gave mine to the authorities. I have a photographic memory anyway, so it didn't matter to me. The stuff I wanted to make sure I didn't forget I memorized. Ask me anything you want."

Maurice sighed. "Israel has become very prosperous. For that, I'm thankful, but at what price? The Jews just wanted peace, but they paid too steep a price with Prince Adonikam."

The cabins of the shipmates were dark. Maurice stood. "We need to get some sleep. Let's hope we can figure out the cause of the increase in seismic readings CERN detected in Eilat tomorrow."

"I'd like to sleep out here."

"Are you sure?"

I nodded.

Maurice lingered for a moment longer and then headed toward his cabin. "I'll see you in the morning, then."

As he walked away, I looked up into the darkened heavens. The stars to the north reflected over the Red Sea as pinpoints of dazzling light. I hunted for the Big Dipper but couldn't find it. Perhaps it was to the south where a sinister blackness filled the celestial sky. In the days of Yeshua, the people asked for a sign. They missed the signs of the times. Now, powerful images from heaven spoke of another approaching time. As I gazed, a super bright light tracked across the sky.

CHAPTER 30

As the meteor fell, fiery fingers set off explosions before crashing into the Red Sea. An open door appeared in heaven, and I stumbled over a chair seeking shelter. I ran to the corner of the boat to hide, and when I looked once more, the door was gone. I tried to convince myself I imagined it—until I felt my body ascending.

A voice spoke. "Do not be afraid."

I recited Psalm 56:3, "כאשר אני מפחד, שמתי מבטחי בך. When I am afraid I will trust in you." As I neared the mountain of fire high above the Red Sea, a trumpet sounded, and the door reappeared.

The same voice spoke again. "Daniel, step through the narrow door."

I entered the Court of Heaven. King Yeshua stood before his throne in the assembly of the holy. An emerald rainbow surrounded him, and angels, redeemed saints, and heavenly creatures prostrated themselves before him. Precious stones of jasper and sardius, the first and last foundation stones, beatified the Holy Jerusalem, and seven lamps burned incense. The aroma was sweet compared to the bitter-sweetness of earth.

Flashes of lightning crisscrossed the holy gathering, and a trumpet sounded. A crystal river flowed from the throne room, and twenty-four elders, clothed in white robes and wearing crowns of gold, worshipped.

In the midst of the righteous were four-winged creatures. The worshippers cried out, "Holy, holy, holy, Lord God Almighty, who was and is and is to come. Only you are worthy to receive all glory and honor and power."

An angel said, "Daniel, join those dressed in white robes, and watch what is about to take place."

One of the shining redeemed urged me to sit beside him. I obliged. I now understood how Adam and Eve knew they were naked. Surrounded by light-covered beings that reflected Yeshua's glory, in my fallen state, I could not taste and see the goodness of the Lord as they could because they were perfect, and I was still a sinner. The light of God's glory had yet to be revealed in me.

A few minutes passed before I realized the white-robed humans were souls—the essence of what makes each of us who we are. The one who invited me to sit with him whispered, "We conquered death by the blood of the lamb."

I recognized his voice. "Jonathan?"

"Yes," he replied.

My friend who witnessed to the nomads with me was martyred? Tears filled my eyes. "What happened?"

"I was delivered into the hands of the authorities. I witnessed to my torturers before being beheaded. As a result of my testimony, one of them became a believer. He's now sharing the Gospel. Never again will I suffer fear or pain. Don't weep for me, but weep for those who will never see the face of God."

My heart burned within me.

Jonathan pointed. "Over there is someone you know."

I gazed at where he pointed. I didn't want to believe it was Shale's father. Brutus and I had been together less than a week earlier. I touched Jonathan's arm. "Excuse me. I'll be back."

He smiled. "No rush."

I edged over and crouched beside him. His soul was a perfect version of himself, and his white luminescent robe marked him as a martyr. While I knew he didn't have a head, he did have a head because I saw him as he really was—not what he had been in the flesh. Not that I totally understood, but it didn't matter.

"You never gave a hint you might be in danger when you were with me."

Brutus placed his hand on my shoulder. "I'm glad I can speak to you now as I wait to receive my resurrected body."

"Please tell me. I want to know what happened."

Brutus leaned back. "I'd been part of the Vatican elite for many years. At the top, it shared a secret community with the Illuminati. When Prince Adonikam ordered the destruction of the ancient writings stored in the Vatican, I became embittered. I'd spent a lifetime accumulating them.

"Some of the scrolls dated to the first and second centuries. I expected the Vatican to keep them safe for future generations. When Adonikam assumed control, he ordered even those burned, and the Vatican obliged. They were priceless. Overnight, all religious books were destroyed, and the internet was purged.

"Prophet Urhammu told the Vatican, 'We have an updated holy book that unites all the great religions, including, Christianity, Catholicism, Judaism, and Islam.' The New World Order was angry they didn't have Shale's missing scroll. They tried many different ways to retrieve it. The first time you went back in time, the scientists sent you. Unbeknownst to them, that was God's plan."

Brutus explained more. "Later, they sent others back in time, but they couldn't find the scroll. I was worried. If I went back to the first century and asked Shale for it, would she give it to me? We didn't have a good relationship. Of course, that was my fault. After I became a follower of Jesus, I asked Shale to forgive me, and she did. And that's why I'm here. Not because I honored God's word by collecting Bibles and other sacred writings, but because I believed, at last, what those words meant. I almost missed it, Daniel. I almost didn't make it here."

I nodded. "I understand. I haven't crossed into eternity as you have. Pray for me that I will be as faithful as you, even if it cost me my life." I choked up and couldn't say more, and Brutus squeezed my shoulder.

"I convinced CERN to let me try," Brutus said. "I found Shale in Caesarea and asked her for her diary. She promised she would give it to me if she could come with me, but I told her she shouldn't—not with Shira, and she wouldn't leave Shira behind. She made me promise to help you. I knew if I helped you, the chances of the Elite discovering my treason would be high, but I didn't tell her that."

"You mean helping me cost you your life?"

He nodded. "Everything happened the way God intended. I wouldn't change anything."

The trumpet sounded. The elders, the angels, the martyrs, and other heavenly creatures turned their focus to the King. A reptilian-like creature stood next to him. There was no luminescence emanating from the dragon, no beauty in his form, and I found it difficult to look at him because he was so evil. In stark contrast, King Yeshua was magnificent in all his glory.

Lucifer did not belong. His unusual appearance must have prompted Yeshua to call the assembly.

The King of kings addressed his listeners. "I am the Alpha and the Omega, who is, who was, and who is to come. The prophet Isaiah wrote in Isaiah 45:7, 'I form the light, and create darkness; I make peace, and create evil; I, the Lord, do all these things.'"

Yeshua bowed his head. "We knew from the beginning what Lucifer would do, but the angels didn't. They had never seen evil. They didn't understand the consequences of Satan's rebellion. They didn't know death, or hate, or war, or murder, or pain. They had to learn.

"Evil grew as one-third of the angels fought for possession of my kingdom. When the war ended, boundaries were set and order was restored—until the serpent deceived our most cherished creation. I forbade Adam and Eve to eat of the tree of the knowledge of good and evil, but the serpent beguiled Eve, and she ate. Adam listened to his wife and also ate.

"Once they ate, I opened their eyes. They lost their light-bearing covering, and shame became part of their existence. Evil destroyed their immortality, and death entered the world for the first time.

"Adam and Eve lost their fellowship with me and were banished from the garden. Soon their life became full of sorrow and regret. Thorns grew where blessings once abounded. Their hearts broke when Cain murdered Abel. Evil consumed the thoughts and ways of mankind every waking hour. Life was painful, burdensome, and hard.

"There was only one remedy—a secret that no one knew, a secret so profound once revealed it would turn creation on its head. The angels did not know what would be required to undo the evil Satan had caused. It was a mystery until the appointed time."

CHAPTER 31

An angel holding something in his hand approached the King, and the King took the object and held it up for all to see. Stirrings filtered through the gathering.

"We've never seen a clock in eternity," an angel whispered. "What must this mean?"

The King didn't answer. Instead, he set the round clock in a place of prominence where everyone could see the hour hand, minute hand, and second hand. The assembly focused on the timepiece. Gasps filled the Court of Heaven when the clock stopped, followed by the second hand reversing direction. Seconds passed in eternity that translated into thousands of years. The King's Book of Remembrance was opened.

An angel approached King Yeshua. His four wings meant he was one of the cherubim. Standing before Yeshua in radiant beauty, the cherub lifted his chin, pointed his finger, and declared, "I will ascend into heaven, I will establish my throne above the stars, I will sit upon the mount of the congregation, I will ascend above the heights of the clouds, and I will be like you, the Most High."

A war cry echoed through the chambers of heaven. Salutes and fist pumps filled the rarified air as millions of angels—too many to count—chimed in. They were ready to commit high treason against King Yeshua.

Once the clamor subsided, stone silence filled the chambers, and a deathly quietness settled over the assembly. What could Yeshua be thinking as he surveyed the warriors dressed for battle? Their scimitars shone brightly—their newly formed weapons of war. Never before did anyone challenge King Yeshua. To see mutiny before his throne, in his castle, above the clouds and above the stars was unprecedented. No one until now ever questioned the King's authority. Now they were committing high treason against their benevolent ruler.

King Yeshua bowed his head. Everything created was good. Mournful minutes passed. Then the King stood and faced his accuser. "Lucifer, this day iniquity has been found in you. There is no place for you in heaven, and you must leave. You must dwell in the shadows, in the depths, in the hollows, in the pits, in the darkness beyond the gates of heaven."

Lucifer's eyes fell on the King's throne—the throne his wings had protected since God created him. He sneered. "Am I not the most beautiful, the most intelligent, and the most beloved of all your creation?"

Yeshua shook his head. "No, Lucifer. No longer is that true. In the beginning, you were full of wisdom and perfect in beauty. You were covered in precious stones. You were the anointed cherub, and you walked upon the mountain of holiness, up and down in the midst of stones of fire. You were perfect in all your ways, but iniquity has been found in you.

"I must cast you out of the mountain of God because of your pride. You have chosen to reject my love. You've chosen to become evil. You must leave this assembly at once."

"Never," Lucifer shouted.

His followers held up their swords and saluted their new leader. "Lucifer."

Millions of angels who chose to remain faithful to Yeshua appeared by the King's side. Their scimitars shone just as brightly, if not more, and they stood ready to fight for their King.

We watched as a great war ensued. Satan was defeated and cast out of heaven. As the fallen angel roamed the earth, we saw the dragon set his sights on the apple of God's eye.

Yeshua closed the Book of Remembrance, sealed it, and reset the clock of heaven.

"I knew your ways from the beginning, Lucifer. I also knew the angelic host could not see evil until you became evil."

The King walked away from Lucifer to address the listeners. "We wanted to show the fruit of evil. To do that, we needed to allow evil to run its course. At the appointed time, we would save creation from death—and that day is here, known by many as the Day of the Lord.

"Free will had to be allowed—first to the angels and then to humans. Satan was jealous that man was created in our image. He wanted his own image imparted on those he could deceive. Some angels did an evil thing and went unto the daughters of men. A race of contaminated humans was born, and their wickedness threatened to destroy the earth. Their intermarriage with the daughters of men tainted humankind's DNA that bore the image of God.

"God wanted to destroy the world," Yeshua said, "but one righteous man remained. Noah walked with God, and for Noah's sake, God saved those in the ark, but every living creature was destroyed except the fish of the sea. God sent a rainbow as a sign he would never again destroy the earth with a flood.

"After the flood, Noah's family set out to repopulate the earth, but it wasn't long until another wicked man, Nimrod, began to build a tower—the Tower of Babel. Rebelliousness spread across the earth once more. If we didn't stop the building of the tower, one man could gain control of the planet within a few years. So God confounded their language."

Yeshua's countenance fell. "Again, we needed to allow sin to be shown for what it was. Who would have believed me if I'd said in the beginning what would happen, that evil would spread like cancer across the face of the earth? The angels and humans would have doubted my love. After evil exploded, then I could express my love—by way of the cross.

"To reverse the effects of sin requires a person to live a perfect life. The Torah as given to Moses showed man's inability to reach perfection. Perfection can be achieved by man through acceptance of my sacrificial love. I gave up my throne and humbled myself to live among men. I died on the cross for one reason—to save humanity. It began with a virgin who gave birth to a child—as foretold by the prophet Isaiah.

"Lucifer wasn't able to prevent my birth, but what if his image could be worshipped instead of mine? That would require my death prematurely, and so he sought a way to kill me. His first attempt was to provoke King Herod to murder the male babies up to two years old born in Bethlehem at the appointed time.

"To protect me, God spoke to Joseph in a dream. The young family fled to Egypt until the days of King Herod were over. Later, Satan tempted me in the wilderness. He offered to give me all the kingdoms of the world if I would bow down and worship him. I could have avoided the cross, but heaven would've been empty without humankind."

Yeshua held up his hands. His scars were seen across the heavenly Jerusalem; the second heaven made up of the stars, the planets, and the far-flung galaxies where celestial battles waged; and the first heaven, the abode of man.

Yeshua lifted his voice. "When I died on the cross, Lucifer thought he'd won, but my power is far deeper than his superficial magic. Two thousand years later, the adversary stands before us. The accuser wants to accuse your brethren, to send them to prison, and to slay them with the sword."

Yeshua turned his eyes to the martyrs. "Your hearts cry out for justice. You've waited all these years, all these centuries, all these millennia. In I Corinthians 6:3, it is written that the saints will judge the angels."

The King lifted his scarred hands in a gesture of love. "You are the most worthy of my followers. You have been given that privilege."

CHAPTER 32

Living fire crackled on the sea of glass as the winds of heaven stirred. Lucifer stood defiantly before the King, as if he still had the prerogative to strut on the stones of fire. One lightning bolt from the hand of King Yeshua would have vaporized him. Now I understood why God didn't do that in the beginning. Instead, God allowed Satan and the fallen angels to spread hatred across the planet—to cause division, strife, despair, and wars.

Horror covered the faces of those present. Memories grieved the angels who fought bravely for the Eternal King. Only Yeshua's love could redeem mankind from his disobedience and rebellion in the Garden of Eden.

The King turned to those listening. "What is your answer?"

Millions raised palm branches and prostrated themselves before Yeshua. "Cast him down," the voices cried. "Cast him down to the earth."

I saw Lucifer in Shambhala when Shale and I journeyed to Hades. Two thousand years later, he was even more horrid. I shook my head. Once the most esteemed of God's creation, how far he had fallen. He cowered before the mighty angels he once led, and with his clipped wings he seethed before the throne they once covered. Hissing and uttering profanities before the God he once served, he was hell-bent on defeating King Yeshua. Did he know he couldn't win? I didn't know, but I did know to lose even one person to this wicked creature pierced the Savior's heart—even more than the nails that pierced his hands and feet.

Lucifer's lot was cast and his destiny sealed, but even at this late hour, humans still could choose. It wasn't too late.

Satan stood naked before all, no longer clothed in God's radiant light. Horns protruded from his head, and blood-shot eyes spewed flames of hatred. He was such a monster I turned away. The goodness of God in me could not bear to look upon such evilness.

As the angels sang, the musicians played, and the heavenly-dwellers worshipped the King. The mighty angel Michael threw Lucifer and his followers out of heaven. The whole lot of them tumbled into the first heaven as a torrent of meteors lit up the sky. The trumpet sounded a long time as fire fell into the ocean. Smoke rose from its depths and darkened the heavens.

After such a dramatic event, a quiet satisfaction filled the throne room. Justice had been served, but we also mourned the suffering awaiting the earth-dwellers. Our only comfort was in knowing the Creator of Justice would shorten the days so some would survive.

As I lamented future events, an angel approached me. "The Lord has something to show you."

I followed the angel to an intersection of two tunnels.

"This is where the second heaven meets the third heaven. King Yeshua wants you to visit the world of demons and fallen angels. I'll go with you so you will not be alone," he said.

<h1 style="text-align:center">CHAPTER 33</h1>

“No one will be able to see us?”

"No," my angelic escort replied. "We're in the second heaven. Humans can't see you unless provision is made. No fallen angels or demons can penetrate Petra."

As we walked through the hot desert passing rocky cliffs, the sun appeared triple its normal size and growing. A fortified structure caught my attention. I recognized the famous façade, and as we neared, the entrance carved out of pink-tinted rocks became visible. In front of the guarded opening, an old man in a long, brown cloak greeted people.

The sculptured rock, carved hundreds of centuries ago, was well-preserved. I noted the photographs I'd seen didn't do the entombed structure justice. The long forgotten trading post was left abandoned for centuries when trade routes were no longer used. We entered through a door that opened into a renovated chamber. Men and women were breaking down boxes containing supplies of food and condiments.

I noticed security cameras in the cracks of the walls. A yellow emergency light was flashing as several workers ran up to a man wearing a white robe. "We've picked up something on radar."

The leader left and walked through a narrow tunnel until he came to a small room that functioned as a command center. He logged into a computer connected to one of several screens. The Colosseum in Rome flashed up, along with the Great Wall of China and St. Peter's Basilica. I didn't recognize the flag in front of the Vatican. Another screen showed the United Nations headquarters—but it wasn't in New York. It was in Babylon.

Transmitted images showed a skirmish near the temple. Crazy men wielding knives were trying to attack two prophets. Fire proceeded from their mouths when the hostile mob drew too close. The words of the prophets filled the airwaves. "Repent, the kingdom of God is near. Or else we'll shut up the heavens and smite your cities with plagues."

Someone knocked on the door, and the man opened it.

"Another shipment has arrived, and the room is full," the voice said. "Where should we put these boxes?"

"Is it more food?"

"I think so."

"Let's take it down to the next level. I'll be there in a few minutes. Arrivals are on the way."

"The time has come?"

The leader nodded. He shut the door, leaned against it, closed his eyes, and prayed.

My angelic escort elaborated. "Let me refresh your memory of something the King once said. He described the kingdom of heaven as being like ten bridesmaids. Five of the bridesmaids were wise. Along with their lamps, they took extra oil. However, the other five didn't take extra oil.

"The young virgins waited a long time for the bridegroom's arrival, but when he tarried, they all became sleepy and slumbered. At midnight, the call went out. 'The bridegroom cometh.'

"The ten virgins awakened. The five wise ones trimmed their lamps, but the five foolish bridesmaids ran out of oil. They went to the wise virgins and demanded, 'Share your oil with us.'

"The wise virgins admonished the foolish ones. 'Go purchase your own oil. If we share ours, we won't have enough for ourselves.'

"So the foolish virgins left to buy oil, and while they were gone, the bridegroom arrived. The five bridesmaids with oil went with the bridegroom to the wedding.

"Later, when the foolish bridesmaids returned, they stood outside the door. 'Lord, Lord, open the door for us.'

"But the bridegroom said, 'I don't know you.'"

The angel added, "Only half of the virgins went to the wedding even though they all had oil in the beginning. What does that tell you?"

"They weren't ready, they weren't prepared to meet him."

"You speak well," the angel said.

More scenes from various places around the world appeared on the screens. The angel waved his hand. "God prepared Petra for this moment, to provide a safe haven for the Jewish people during the time of Jacob's trouble.

"However, when the beast is unable to kill the remnant because they're protected, as you just saw, he will turn on the Christians. If a person doesn't have the mark on his right hand or forehead, he won't be able to buy food.

"Thousands will be martyred in the years to come, but it's better to be martyred for believing in Yeshua than to deny him and spend eternity in the lake of fire."

The angel's comments made me wonder about something. "If the Jews had received Yeshua when he came the first time, would Yeshua still have died on the cross?"

"He needed to die to fulfill the law and the prophets," the angel said. "Had they been ready, many more would have attended his wedding as guests. Those Jews and others who missed the marriage, however, are still invited to the feast. Sadly, Israel missed his first coming, and many Israelis will miss his second."

CHAPTER 34

Banging sounds on the door interrupted our conversation. The man in the white robe opened it, and two men who appeared frightened stood in the doorway. "We're picking up something on the radar," one of them said nervously.

The leader went back to the computer, and his fingers flew across the keyboard. Images of UFOs appeared on the overhead monitor—dozens of them.

"The Enki!"

The leader crossed his arms and shook his head. "Those, my friends, are demons."

The white spherical objects moved in formation at a high rate of speed.

"What should we do?"

"We'll pray at the assembly hall. Round up everybody."

"Come with me. You must see what is about to take place," my angelic escort said.

I followed him through the tunnel back to the entrance. Soon prayers and singing could be heard as the voices praised God.

"Follow me," the angel said.

We walked through the door, and I was jarred by thunder that peeled across the heavens. Lightning bolts split the sky in two, and I watched as UFOs poured through the torn veil.

"The demons think they can kill the Jews in Petra. The UFOs are part of the demonic army," the angel said.

I heard a shofar.

"The battle cry from heaven—the Day of the Lord is here."

I wanted to run back inside the mountain, but the angel prevented me. A nasty wind kicked up and blew sand in my face. I covered my eyes. Thunderous booms shook the ground.

"Look," the angel exclaimed. "What is about to take place is beyond anything ever seen or that will be seen again."

At the sound of his voice, weapons of war were unleashed from the flying saucers. Flashes of lightning crossed the sky like exploding firecrackers. UFOs descended from every direction.

The angel took me to a high mountain. I expected Petra to be engulfed in flames. Instead, the lightning bolts from the UFOs ricocheted off the mountains and shot back into the sky. Soon the UFOs were being struck, and they fell like balls of fire. Several disintegrated before slamming into the ground. Others were damaged and veered off, but most of them broke apart.

Once the UFOs realized their own weapons were being used against them, they changed tactics, but it didn't make any difference. After a dozen were shot down, the rest panicked. Their tight formation splintered into chaos. Several executed a sharp turn and self-destructed.

The ferocity with which the UFOs struck and their impotence to destroy anything but themselves dumbfounded me. The whole event lasted less than ten minutes. Fires burned where the UFOs fell, but Petra stood untouched.

"Look," the angel said.

In the desert sands, I saw desperate people. Some were so exhausted they collapsed while still a ways off. As they neared, anxiety filled their faces. Old men fell on their knees. Others cried out, "Have mercy on me, Yeshua. Have mercy on all of us."

A couple of women with infants wept. Sheer determination willed them to keep moving. How they made it, I didn't know. I wanted to rush over and help, but we were invisible.

The door to Petra flew wide open, and the man in the white robe appeared. He rushed down the steps followed by several others. After a quick appraisal, the leader shouted, "Quick. Go inside and get help. Bring out stretchers, and we'll carry those who can't walk."

I saw a middle-age woman who was very weak. A man rushed over to help. "When did you last eat?"

She sobbed. "I don't know." Her thin hands and sunken, pale eyes spoke louder than her words.

"Can I carry you?"

She nodded.

How many would wait too long to come?

The angel said, "The book of Revelation says the woman fled into the wilderness where a place was prepared for her by God, that she should be there one thousand two hundred and sixty days. More will come as they hear God's voice, but too many hearts will turn to stone.

"Even so, God will welcome souls into his everlasting kingdom until there is no more time. God is patient, not wishing anyone to die, but to come to repentance. To that end, even the days will be cut short. Otherwise, none would survive."

I thought about the parable the angel shared. Five foolish virgins missed the bridegroom's wedding, but even now, God wanted everyone to be at his wedding feast.

CHAPTER 35

By the end of the day, more than two hundred asylum seekers arrived. A few women were pregnant or carrying infants. Many needed medical care. Most were suffering from injuries, dehydration, and malnutrition. The stories tugged at my heart, and it didn't take long to realize the truth. The news media touted the lies it wanted people to believe. For the first time, survivors were discovering the devastation in other areas. The reports sounded like first-hand accounts straight out of the book of Revelation.

Hail scorched the countryside killing one-third of the trees and grass. The trees that didn't die in the beginning later died from nuclear fallout. A gigantic asteroid, known as Wormwood, fell and struck the oceans killing much of the aquatic life. Ships were reduced to ashes, including fishermen who earned their living on the waters.

Another asteroid fell, polluting the fresh waters and springs. The birds disappeared. The honeybees died. Reforested areas, the pride of Israel, became deserts. Many rivers turned blood red contaminating the fish and making food shortages worse.

The refugees talked about the abandoned cities now inhabited by looters. Weird-looking creatures with double heads appeared, hell-bent on killing what little wildlife remained. No one knew where they came from, but I surmised from scientific laboratories. I'd seen them in Shambhala and Bavil.

Reports of strange diseases surfaced. Some caused boils so painful people wanted to die. Gigantic worms appeared, boring through people's houses and eating human flesh while people slept. Depression and mental illness were rampant.

Rain hadn't fallen in months—except for acid rain the size of baseballs. Dust storms raged across the sky almost every day, blocking sunlight for hours. When the sun finally emerged, it cooked people with ionizing radiation.

People were forced to stay indoors or be fried like an egg. Cities along the coastline were invaded by sharks that could walk on land. Dead cattle littered the countryside. Chickens stopped laying eggs. Some saw strange-looking vehicles in the sky and feared the return of the Enki. The promises of Prince Adonikam did little to reassure people or make them feel safe.

My thoughts turned to my mother and sister. What about my father? Perhaps, as Nidal said, he had escaped from Perslea Castle. He would have returned to Jerusalem if he could. However, if things were as bad as the survivors said, perhaps he lingered in Syria.

I knew Syria was devastated by ISIS. I heard reports among several that Damascus was destroyed. Maurice told me the same thing. However, I took comfort in the words of Yeshua. He said my father was alive, and I would see him again.

Was the hidden complex underneath the Old City still intact? Could the stargate be used? I thought about possibilities. I wanted to go back to the first century. I wanted to make sure Shale remained safe. As I fretted over things I shouldn't have worried about—if I really trusted God—I was thankful Much-Afraid was with her.

After two days, I asked the angel, "Please let me be useful here." Apparently, I just needed to ask. The man in the white robe smiled when he saw me. "Welcome, Daniel. We can use your help."

The leader was an angel—in disguise. He even knew my name.

"Daniel, you've had experience in emergency situations before," he said. "We want the incoming arrivals triaged, and I'll put you in charge of the group most in need. Here's a list of doctors and nurses in the compound."

I wanted to assist in any way I could. Despite the physical needs of the survivors—and there were many—their spiritual and emotional wounds were greater. I could help by praying with them.

When night arrived, I sat beside a young man who wasn't much older than me. His face, arms, and legs were blistered from sunburn. He was stripped down to his underwear with a towel draped over him for modesty. He didn't want anything to touch his skin. His cracked, swollen lips made it difficult to speak. Every few minutes, I would touch his mouth with a cool, wet sponge. All we knew about the man was his name—Josi.

After a while, he opened his eyes.

I stood and leaned over him. "How are you feeling?"

"I'm lucky to be alive. Praising Yeshua Hamashiach."

"Are you from Jerusalem?"

Josi nodded. "Ramot."

"What made you leave?"

"God came to me in a dream. He said I needed to leave Ramot. I told my friends they should leave, too, but they didn't listen. They said as long as Prince Adonikam allowed the Jews access to the temple and the offering of daily sacrifices, they would trust him."

As he talked, his sentences became more incoherent. Then he went into a trance, flailing his arms. "Get away from me, get away."

What was he seeing? I touched him on the shoulder. "There is no one here but me."

He dropped his arms, and his eyes met mine. "I'm sorry. They try to eat you."

I blinked. "What tried to eat you?"

The man's eyes teared, and his voice cracked. "They're monsters. They'll kill you for food." He sobbed. "I'm sorry, Yeshua, forgive me."

I couldn't get him to calm down, and a nurse came over to help. I told her what Josi said.

"I'll give him a sedative," the nurse said. "He must rest."

Several minutes later, his sobbing stopped and he dozed. Among his belongings was an old, worn-out Bible, the first one I'd seen since returning to this century. I flipped through the tattered pages. How had he managed to keep it?

He grabbed my arm, startling me.

"Can you read Joel 2:27-32 to me?"

It was the King James Version, and I flipped to the book of Joel in the Old Testament.

And ye shall know that I am in the midst of Israel,
    And that I am the Lord your God,
    And none else;
    And my people shall never be ashamed.
    And it shall come to pass afterward,
    That I will pour out my spirit upon all flesh;
    And your sons and your daughters shall prophesy,
    Your old men shall dream dreams,
    Your young men shall see visions.
    And also upon the servants and upon the handmaids in those days
    Will I pour out my spirit.
    And I will shew wonders in the heavens
    And in the earth,
    Blood, and fire, and pillars of smoke.
    The sun shall be turned into darkness,
    And the moon into blood,
    Before the great and the terrible day of the Lord to come.
    And it shall come to pass,
    That whosoever shall call on the name of the Lord shall be
delivered;
    For in Mount Zion and in Jerusalem shall be deliverance,
    As the Lord hath said, and in the remnant whom the Lord shall call.

· · ·

Josi's eyes focused on mine. "I see my Lord. He has come to take me home. Yeshua says you must go to Jerusalem."

The man stopped speaking, and a quiet peace covered his face. I called for the nurse, but I knew he was no longer with us.

CHAPTER 36

Two Days Later

Singing filled the hollows of the hidden world. People arrived at all hours, and those musically gifted welcomed the Messiah seekers with song and dance. Noticeably absent were children, although a few young mothers came with infants.

I heard someone approaching and turned to see who it was.

"We must leave," the angel said. "The Lord needs you elsewhere. I'll see you at the entrance in a few minutes."

I told one of my coworkers I was put on another assignment. After climbing the steps, I hurried through the tunnel toward the entrance. When I stepped outside Petra, the angel was waiting.

The view from above flying as a bird over the desert revealed the depths of scorched earth below. The white rock and limestone formations looked like blackened catacombs. The air smelled of spent fire-crackers. At least the jet currents kept us cool despite the heat. I relished the speed at which we traveled. We would get to Jerusalem quickly if that's where we were headed.

As we approached a patch of mountains, a thick swarm of bats flew out of the mouth of a cave and headed straight toward us. I hated those creatures. As a kid, one bit me on a camping trip. I could hear their squeaks even before they were close. Outnumbered because there were thousands, I imagined them attacking us and sucking all the blood out of me—I didn't know if angels had blood—and I'd be left as a blood-less corpse.

"Those are vampire demons," the angel said to me through mind-speak. "They come out of the second heaven and invade the first heaven at will. They can't harm us, but the possessed ones torment earth-dwellers, especially now that the veil is torn."

When the lead vampire saw the angel, he veered off leading his followers away from us.

Through mind-speak again, the angel said, "We're away from the protection of Petra, out in the desert where demons hang out in search of prey. They stay in the caves until dark. The possessed bats are looking for a pagan sacrifice."

My mind conjured up the worst thing possible. "What kind of pagan sacrifice?"

"Child sacrifice, animal sacrifice, ritualistic idolatrous offerings, to name a few. The life of the flesh is in the blood. Demons feed off the blood. It's getting toward nighttime, and they're hunting."

As I watched them disappear in the distance, I became aware of strange vibrations. How could we feel anything but the air around us? "What's that pulsating?"

"The planet is breathing," the angel said. "It's out of sync—abnor-mal, indicating the planet is in great distress. The seasons are reversed because of the pole shift. The earth and the sun are vexed because of the seal and trumpet judgments. Even the oceans are perplexed. They're roaring, lashing out as inward sickness overwhelms them.

"Their lifeblood is being sucked out as sea creatures die and pollute the waters, as volcanos erupt and spew out liquid fire, as the rivers and springs reek of death. The trees, plants, and grass can no longer breathe.

"You feel the vibrations now because you're in a different element. In your ordinary world, you would feel it in negative ways—unless you prayed and ask for God's help and the Holy Spirit to intercede."

"What do you mean?" I asked.

"Have you ever been depressed?"

"Yes." I thought for a moment. "You must know all about me—my struggle with depression and my aversion to bats."

The angel smiled. "Daniel, have you ever read Psalm 91:11?"

"What does it say?"

"It says, 'He shall give his angels charge over you, to keep you in all your ways.'"

"What about the earth-dwellers? Do they have angels guarding them?"

His answer was not what I expected. "Fallen angels transform themselves into angels of light in the Day of the Lord. Because of the hardened hearts of the earth-dwellers, they will be fooled by these angels of light and follow them—as you shall see."

CHAPTER 37

After arriving in Jerusalem, we saw loiterers drinking beer, shooting firecrackers, and sharing smokes. As we walked over to them, a medical van pulled up. Two men and a woman exited the vehicle and approached the malcontents.

"Remember," the angel said to me, "I'm in the second heaven and can't be seen, but special provision has been made to make you visible."

I moved in closer to hear the voices. The three men and two women were rough looking and covered in tattoos. Life had not been kind to them. As I watched, I noticed strange creatures hanging out nearby. At first, I thought they were other loiterers, but when my eyes were opened, I saw they were different. They stood upright like humans, but they had cloven hoofs and ape-like hands. There were more of them than there were loiterers.

The angel spoke to me. "Those are chimera—half-human and half-demonic. They're using mind-control over the humans. If you call on the name of Jesus, they'll flee."

The medics walked toward the human slaves of the chimera.

The angel spoke to me again. "The medics can't see the demons because they can't see into the second heaven."

The woman medic held up three bottles of water and offered them. Two turned them down, but three accepted the water.

"We have more in the van," she said.

One of the malcontents who declined water at first changed his mind. "Can I have some?"

A medic went to get more.

Supernatural boldness came over me, and I swaggered up to the chimera. "In the name of Yeshua, flee."

Immediately, they obeyed. They blasted toward the desert, but before they got very far, the angel slew them. Their screams pierced my ears like fingernails on a blackboard. The ground opened and swallowed them up.

"Earthquake," someone shouted.

I hurried over. "Fear not, for God is fighting for us."

"We're Christians," the woman medic said. "We're seeking the lost who need medical attention."

The medic returned with more bottled water and handed them to the other two loiterers who were about my age.

"Can I help?" I asked.

A woman held out her blistered hands. "Get these off of me."

I looked at her hands. What did she mean?

The vampire bats appeared overhead making squeaky noises. I knew they just wanted to annoy me.

The angel spoke in mind-speak again. "The lost are under the delusion their hands are bound."

I read the woman's mind. "I can't remove your chains, but Yeshua can. Believe in Yeshua, and he will set you free."

A medic added, "Your chains will fall off, and you will no longer be in bondage, taunted, and controlled by evil."

His intercession amazed me. He couldn't see into the second dimension, he couldn't read minds, and an angel wasn't mind-speaking to him. The Holy Spirit gave him a word of knowledge.

Five pairs of hollow eyes stared back. The women shook their heads. One of the men shouted, "Never." He raised his invisible shackled hands and pointed to the sky. "This is God's fault."

The vampire bats laughed, and one spit in the man's face.

He became angry and uttered profanities. He couldn't see anything, but he was reacting to the spiritual attack on him.

A bat laughed again in that squeaky voice I hated.

I shouted at the demons. "In the name of Jesus, I command you to leave."

Within seconds, they disappeared.

One of the women stared at me. "What are you trying to say, that I have demons?"

I pointed at the burial site of the chimera. "If you knew how God just protected you, you would be thankful. Even now the evil one has bound you in chains that you can't see."

One of the women rolled her eyes and sneered, "It's a trick. You're speaking like that to frighten us."

A medic interrupted. "We can't set you free, but God can."

"Thank you for the water," one of the men said.

The other four became hostile.

"Repent and be saved," the woman medic urged. "I was once lost like you, but God set me free, and he can set you free, too."

Lifeless eyes peered out of hollow brains, but the one who said thank you hesitated. I knew the taunts of the others held him back.

I pointed to him. "What's your name?"

"Thomas."

"Do you have a family?"

He shook his head. "They all died."

Another man spoke. "Don't you know four billion people are dead? Would a loving God kill half the population on the planet? You expect us to believe in that kind of God?" The man followed up his outburst with blasphemous words.

"Thomas," I said, ignoring the comments of the blasphemer, "what would it take for you to believe Yeshua died for you?"

He slumped over. "Not to see any more death, for this nightmare to end."

The other four captives laughed. "There is no God. Accept your fate and die."

"I can't die," the man said. "I've already tried, but all I can do is suffer. I think I'm doomed to suffer forever."

I shook my head. "No, that's a lie. Yeshua will set you free if you confess your sins and turn to him for salvation."

One of the women kicked rocks toward us. "If you say that name again in my presence, I'll puke on you." Then she stormed off. Three followed her.

I clasped the shoulder of Thomas. "Believe," I urged, "while you still can. Today is your day of salvation."

The man was torn as he watched his friends walk away.

One of them shouted back, "Are you coming with us or not?"

His eyes darted.

"What else are you thankful for?" I asked. "Anything?"

Tears came to his eyes. "I'm thankful you're here. I want to believe in Yeshua, but I don't know how."

The four of us spent the next few minutes sharing with Thomas God's love. We explained to him that all the pain and suffering now upon the earth was God's final attempt to bring salvation to anyone who would listen.

While we spoke, the others disappeared into the desert, perhaps never to be seen again. Their minds were already too infected with hate to receive love. I could see them wandering in arid, dry places where sordid creatures roamed. And when physical death claimed their lives, eternal death awaited them on the other side.

<h1 style="text-align:center">CHAPTER 38</h1>

As Thomas listened, light entered his pale eyes. He prayed, "Lord, if you are real, please show yourself."

I saw the demons flee and heard the invisible chains fall off his hands.

"Forgive me, Lord," he prayed.

After exchanging hugs, Thomas went with the others. One of the medics stopped and asked me, "Where is your car?"

I glanced at the angel, but the medic couldn't see him. "I'm here with a friend."

His focus was on the new believer, so he nodded and continued walking with the others.

As the van was leaving, I waved my hand to get the driver's attention. He stopped and rolled down the window. "Things will get worse," I warned him. "The safest place for believers is Petra."

The medic nodded. "I know, but we want to reach as many here as we can."

I watched as they drove away, and the angel came alongside me. "It's getting dark, but we have more people to witness to before we return."

I started to ask him what he meant, but no sooner did he speak than we heard footsteps.

A man called out to me, "We're headed to Petra to flee from the wrath to come. We thought Prince Adonikam was the Messiah. Now we know Yeshua is the Messiah. We've been pursued by enemies—even a swarm of bats attacked us. We escaped by the grace of God."

"I'll be returning to Petra soon," I said. "If you want, we can travel together for safety."

Several men and women came out of hiding. As we walked, we stumbled upon others making the same pilgrimage. While I agonized over the long distance, I wasn't prepared for what happened next.

The angel spoke to me in mind-speak. "God gave up the title deed to the earth. That means the sea, the land, the fowl, the animals, and every living creature has suffered. It's not Yeshua's desire that anyone should perish. However, love that tolerated evil would be cheap and worthless if not for judgment. The love of God must be just to be perfect."

As we walked in the twilight of neither light nor darkness, I felt the weight of those following me. I could read their minds. Most were new followers of Yeshua, coming to faith in recent days. Many had lost family members.

Now I understood. I didn't need to see the second heaven to know it was there. Everything we needed to know about spiritual warfare was in the Bible. I just needed to believe by faith.

As we traveled, we sang.

"Amazing Grace,
How sweet the sound,
That saved a wretch like me.
I once was lost,
But now I'm found,
Was blind,

But now I see."

In the darkness, we came to an area of destruction. Among the ruins, several figures hid in the shadows. We stopped singing. Above us, I saw several large-winged creatures. Straight ahead something was happening. As we neared, two individuals came into view. When those behind me saw what was happening, fear seized them, and they hid behind the rocks.

The perpetrator stood his ground and guarded his prize. Blood oozed from his mouth and saturated the ground as he ate the victim. I couldn't see well enough in the darkness to know if the person was alive.

I'd heard these terrible stories from the survivors at Petra, but it was hard to imagine in the twenty-first century—cannibalism.

A person wept. "Zechariah 11:9: 'Let those that are left eat each other's flesh.'"

I cried out, "In the name of Yeshua, depart from us."

The demons fled, and the giant, who I perceived to be a Nephilim, took off. He was taller than a human, and when I tried to read his mind, I couldn't.

Was it too late for the man lying in his own blood? I rushed over, and a man among those hiding joined me. "I'm a doctor," he said. He pulled out a tourniquet and began to work on the victim.

I rushed back to the others. "Please pray for God to spare the man's life."

The believers prayed. After several minutes, the doctor said, "His blood pressure is improving, but he needs more help than I can provide here."

I returned to the prayer warriors to give them an update. No sooner did I do so than the gang I'd seen in the shadows returned. Now there were twice as many. They were dressed in cavemen-like clothing sporting full beards and disgustingly long hair. They were too tall to be human, and they looked too human to be Chimera. Maybe they were another kind of Nephilim, or perhaps they were demons.

CHAPTER 39

The cannibals were a stone's throw away. The doctor continued to work on the man, distressed that the creatures were so close.

I encouraged him. "God is on our side, and I have a weapon." Still, I was nervous. I had never used it, and the angel who brought me seemed to have disappeared.

The eyes of the monsters glared at us in the darkness. The putrid smell of road kill emanated from their direction, like a dead animal's rotting flesh being feasted on by buzzing flies. I breathed through my mouth to avoid the noxious odor.

The aggressive one stepped closer while the others ogled us.

I held up my hand. Could they tell it was shaking? "Don't come any closer."

The leader ignored me.

"Leave us," I said once more.

Laughter followed—that kind of laughter peculiar to demons.

The pack leader snickered, and I pulled out the weapon.

He ignored my final warning and lunged toward me. I activated the laser, and fire consumed him. One second he was there; the next second he was gone.

The others scattered. They belonged to the devil, and nothing could save them. God's righteousness meant they must die.

With the cannibals gone, I returned to the victim, an older gentleman that could have been somebody's grandfather. The cannibals had taken advantage of his frail condition.

The man asked, "Yeshua saved me?"

The doctor nodded. "Yes."

He smiled.

I heard sounds overhead. Fortunately, my trepidation was short-lived. I saw a plane, and the angel spoke to me. "I needed to fight demons in the second heaven to bring the mercy plane here from Petra."

When the plane became visible, praise left the lips of the exhausted followers. Once it landed, I went inside and was pleased that it was well-stocked with food, water, and medicine.

"You know, you never told me your name," I said to the angel sitting in the pilot's seat.

"You know my name," he said.

"I do?"

"I was in the garden."

"Mr. Clover?"

"That's me." The angel chuckled.

"So you know how to drive trains and fly planes."

The angel laughed. "That's right. Let's get back to Petra. We need to go farther to be under God's protection."

I exited the plane and spoke to the others. "We need to get the injured man in first. Can someone help me?"

A strong man came over, and between the two of us, we placed the patient onto the cot and into the plane. Everyone was lining up to board when the heavens opened. I saw though the broken veil into the second heaven—again. Satan was not going to give up.

A red dragon with seven heads and ten horns materialized in the heavens, and on each head was a crown. The devil swiped his powerful tail across the night sky, casting one-third of the lights to earth. As they descended, I became aware of lights in the shadows—lights that looked like eyes.

To know what is unknown and to see what is unseen is a heavy burden that God didn't mean for us to bear. Ignorance would have been bliss. I'd prefer to imagine hyenas or wolves watching us. How many times did God rescue me from not only the dangers I saw but the ones I didn't see?

The stalkers watched as we boarded the plane, and I prayed for God's deliverance. The devil knew his time was short, and we needed to hurry.

I felt the ground rumbling beneath us.

"Earthquake!" someone shouted.

A chasm opened between the supernatural beings and God's army. To be buried alive seemed worse than being attacked by demons. We backed away from the crevasse, and I heard water rising up from the deep. It flooded the ground on the other side. The eyes in the dark disappeared, and within seconds, the ground swallowed them up. As quickly as it happened, the desert quietness returned.

"Is everyone all right?" I asked.

Relief flooded through those still waiting to board. We watched as the watery graveyard disappeared.

The Eagle, as I nicknamed the plane, flexed her wings. The navigator revved up the engines, and the rest of us, awed at God's provision, boarded. Once inside, I closed the door, and we prepared for takeoff.

Satan shouted in the second heaven, "I'll make war against the Christians and all of those who have the testimony of Jesus Christ."

With that proclamation, I bowed my head and prayed. I prayed for those who would come after us and for as many of those as possible to make it to Petra.

After landing, when everyone disembarked, I realized I'd seen more in the second dimension than I could have imagined. "It's time, isn't it?"

Mr. Clover pulled out that well-used cloth I'd seen him use when he was the train conductor in the garden. He wiped his hands and smiled. "When I take you back to the boat to be with your friend, Maurice, treasure these lessons. They are meant to build up your faith for the trials and tribulations in the future."

CHAPTER 40

The next morning when I awoke on the deck of the boat, the sky was still dark. As I remembered Petra, the events of the past several days flooded my mind. The concept of multiple realities existing at the same time seemed perfectly natural now. God being omniscient, existed everywhere at all times, while, experientially, I could only be in one place at one time How reassuring it was to know, no matter where I was, God was with me.

Try as Lucifer might, there were some things he would not be able to emulate, like omniscience and infallibility. Satan had underestimated God's love and overestimated his own worth—all given to him by God. Pride comes before a fall, and he would fall hard on earth just as he had fallen hard from heaven.

I peered out over the ocean and didn't see any lights from other boats or the shoreline. While I wanted to understand everything God had shown me, I wasn't sure if sleeping a little longer wouldn't be a better choice. The more I thought, the harder it would be to go back to sleep.

I still found it hard to believe Brutus and Jonathan were in eternity. In some ways I envied them. They had conquered death, but my race wasn't finished—just as Michael, the archangel, told me following the chariot race. While my mind was revved up to solve all the problems of the world, I force myself to close my eyes, determined to rest a while longer.

When I awoke again, the pink horizon painted an eye-catching backdrop against the blue, tranquil waters. Squawking seagulls flew by. I arose and walked over to the railing. As I leaned against it, my mind drifted to Shale as memories from the last several days lingered. I longed to share with her what I'd experienced as she would understand without me having to explain everything. How I missed her and wanted to be with her.

Vapors hovered over the water, and a giant sea creature glided underneath the surface. Suddenly it shot up like a cannon, twisting its torso in a spectacular breach. When it fell back, water sprayed in all directions.

So whales had returned to the Red Sea. I watched for a while until it moseyed off, and Maurice walked out on the deck with a cup of coffee.

"Guess what I saw?"

He puckered his lips. "A whale."

"How'd you know?"

"That's one of the things we were sent here to study. The first one in hundreds of years was spotted in 2018. Dozens have been seen since. A shark was also recently seen. The unusual seismographic readings happened at the same time as the whale population dramatically increased."

I pointed to the lingering haze above the water. "Do you think there is a heat vent down there?"

Maurice cocked his head. "I saw that haze when we first arrived. We'll check it out on the dive."

Chris was at the back of the boat with E.J. setting up tanks and diving equipment.

Maurice changed the subject. "Do you know what time it is?"

"No."

"It's eleven in the morning."

"And the sun is just rising—that doesn't make sense."

Maurice tapped the railing. "No, it doesn't, and while it's a beautiful sunrise, it's not as bright as you'd expect."

"Now that you mention it…" I thought about Bavil where it was too bright. The balance of nature was out of kilter. "Why is that?"

Maurice's eyes panned the horizon. "I'm not sure." He leaned on the railing. "Our days are shorter."

I remembered what one of the angels said when they rushed me out of Bavil and brought me to the Red Sea. The days are shorter today than they were yesterday. "Perhaps the tilt of the earth has changed again—like after the polar shift."

Maurice shrugged. "I don't know."

"With less sun you also have cooler temperatures."

"How long has it been since you went diving?" Maurice asked.

"Scuba diving? I haven't been since we went in high school."

Maurice cocked his head. "That was a long time ago. Do you remember all the hand signals?"

"I remember the important ones. And it hasn't been as long as it seems."

"Yeah, that's true in your case. Well, diving isn't something Pierre enjoys, and he's happy to let you do the videotaping. Do you want to go?"

"Sure. Maybe I can video that whale if he hangs around."

"Let's do a quick review of the signals." Maurice held up his hand, palm forward, like a traffic cop.

"Stop."

He pointed to his ear.

"Equalization problem."

He put his thumb and index finger together, making a circle, fanning out his third, fourth and fifth fingers.

"I'm okay."

Then he flattened his hand and rotated it side to side.

"Something's not right."

"Okay sign above the surface?"

I joined my hands together over my head to make a ring.

"Can you do it with one hand?"

I touched the top of my head with my index finger.

"Great. That's good. How about this one?" He pounded on his chest with his fist.

"Low on air."

He pointed with his thumb down.

"Descend."

He pointed to his eyes.

"Watch me."

"Last one." He swiped his hand in front of his neck.

"Out of air."

"Good." Maurice put his two index fingers side by side.

"Stay with your buddy."

Then he pointed with his index finger at his other flattened hand.

"You want the slate."

He pumped his fist. "Great. Make sure you grab one and put it in the pocket of your BC. Find a mask you like. Do you remember how much weight you need?"

"No."

We walked to the back of the boat where Chris was filling up the tanks. "Daniel is going to be my dive buddy instead of Pierre."

"Do you have your Certification card?" he asked.

I shook my head. "It's been a few years, but I've done a fair number of dives with Maurice."

"As long as he vouches for you."

I went through the equipment—buoyancy control device, regulator, octopus, snorkel, facemask, gloves, and fins. The salty smell brought back memories. "We're looking for a possible heat vent. Anything else?"

Maurice cocked his head. "Mostly we're documenting what we see because of the increased seismic activity—and if we see any whales, sharks, or other fish not typically seen here."

Chris folded up the dive map. "Heat vents could be related to seismic activity. Eilat is considered a high-risk zone."

Maurice pulled the video camera out of a freshwater bucket and showed me how to use it. "Think you can do it?"

I nodded. "Sure."

"Any ear problems?" Chris asked.

"Nope. I'm good." I put the camera back into the bucket.

Maurice slapped me on the shoulder. "Let's eat. Di, the cook, should have breakfast ready by now."

CHAPTER 41

"The anchor is secure," Hatim shouted from the bow. E.J., Maurice, and I were at the stern suiting up. I attached the baton to my dive belt. Seven kilograms might be too much, but better to have too much weight than not enough. Otherwise, I'd spend the whole dive floating upward. Chris already secured the BCs onto the filled tanks. They sat securely in the bucket holes along the wooden plank. The octopuses and regulators dangled like sea creatures with too many limbs, and as Maurice asked me to do, I put a slate and pencil inside the BC pocket.

I purged the regulator and checked the air pressure. Thirty-one hundred psi was acceptable. Once I felt like everything was ready, I pulled the buoyancy control device over my shoulders and strapped on the tank. With gloves and flippers in place, we'd have to sit and wait, like a fish out of water, until Chris gave us more instructions.

"Everyone ready?" he asked.

We nodded.

He went down his checklist. "We'll enter with the back roll. Is everybody familiar with that?" He looked at me.

I nodded.

As if not convinced I knew, he explained briefly. "Sit at the edge of the gunwale with your tank toward the water. Tuck in your chin, and holding your mask and regulator in place, do a backward roll into the water. Once you're upright, inflate your BC. We'll go down together once we know everyone is ready. Maurice, you and Daniel go in first."

We wobbled out to the gunwale like penguins. I pulled my mask down. Maurice was ready before me, so he went first. He back-somersaulted in, resurfacing with a one-handed okay sign, and floated backward to give me room.

I inhaled.

"Ready?" Chris asked.

I nodded.

He shoved me in. I heard the muffled splash as the water closed over me and bubbles floated up in front of my facemask. I gulped in some air through the regulator which was reassuring. Then I flipped upright and popped up to the surface. Feeling a little heavy, I released some air from my BC. Chris handed me the camera.

Maurice swam over. "CERN just wants to get a look at the fish, see the condition of the coral, if there're any thermal spots, that kind of thing. You don't need to start videotaping until we get to the bottom."

I slipped the camera cord on my wrist as the water lapped at the surface. I didn't anticipate it being rough underneath us where there was less wave action, but securing the camera cord around my wrist would make sure I didn't lose it.

Maurice and I drifted back so Chris and E.J. could roll in. Once everybody gave the okay sign, Hatim waved. Even the cook, a short little man with jovial eyes, came on the deck to see us off.

"I'll be watching your bubbles," Di teased.

Maurice told me earlier Pierre would be tracking us with the computer and would be able to pinpoint where we were. The compasses on the regulators would guide us below the surface.

Chris gave us final instructions. "We'll be at about eighteen meters. That gives you about an hour. Keep an eye on your psi. At forty-five minutes, do a check and see how far you are from the boat. You need to have no less than 500 psi when you return. If you hit 1000 psi before forty-five minutes, come back sooner. Maurice and Daniel, you stay together. E.J. and I will be hanging around."

We nodded.

"Any questions?"

No one said anything.

"Great. Let's go."

I pushed the button on my BC to let out some air and descended, holding my nose with my fingers and breathing out to equalize. The underwater shelf made it easy to track our progress. The visibility was good. Conditions were about as perfect as they could be. Time beat at a slower pace here as shy creatures lurked in hidden crevasses among the coral.

When we reached the bottom, as Chris said, we were at seventeen meters.

He pointed at Maurice and me with his index fingers side by side, and then he and E.J. took off. Maurice reached over and turned on the camera. I aimed the lens at the bottom where eels, pretending to be plants, created an underwater garden that swayed back and forth. A couple of lionfish swam close enough to check out the video camera, and a school of blue angelfish darted within a few meters of us. Clownfish hovered around the fire coral. I got so wrapped up in the videotaping I forgot about Maurice.

He tapped me on the shoulder. Then he pointed at his compass and pointed.

CHAPTER 42

I followed Maurice along the colorful shelf where clownfish darted in and out of sea anemones. From the shimmering schools of fish to the tiny, shy creatures lurking under overhanging crevasses, God spoke to me, even if that voice was only to evoke in me a longing for more. Of what, I wasn't sure. Whether in the Court of Heaven or in the ocean's depths, Yeshua was with me.

How could I fathom the depths of God's handiwork in the window of the deep? How could I know the inner workings of the tiny seahorse or understand the symbiosis between the known and the unknown? I wondered about this and more as I recorded the extraordinary beauty.

I marveled how the masterful artist spoke this world into being before he created man. Extravagant love blessed these waters and said it was good. Who could deny it came from a stroke of genius except for someone who didn't want to believe in God?

We hadn't gone far when our surroundings changed. The protective wall was a death trap. Heaped upon the sandy bottom were skeletons of decomposed fish. I heard a muffled grating noise. Did death have a voice? Perhaps it was there all along, drowned out by our regulators and the rhythmic heartbeat of the sea.

I recorded in all directions to capture the disturbing changes. The euphoria of being beneath the waters after such a long absence evaporated. The rainbow world of the deep had become a morbid cemetery. The vibrant colors of living coral were nothing more than whitewashed tombstones. Devoid of life, this part of the Red Sea was now a ghost town. Maurice and I exchanged glances. Something polluted the ecosystem—but what?

The water became warmer as we glided along the shelf. Maurice wrote something on his slate and held it up—water temp?

I took his slate and wrote, "global warming?"

He shook his head, putting the slate back in his pocket. We followed the shelf until it leveled off, and we came to a white sandy bottom. I checked the depth gauge—eighteen meters.

Maurice wandered away a short distance and swam back, signaling me to follow him. His eyes were as big as bowling balls.

I made sure the camera was on, and after swimming a little way, I saw a large, shimmering creature that held a sword. He stood upright using no breathing apparatus or diving gear.

I could tell Maurice was hyperventilating by the number of air bubbles surrounding him. He pointed at the camera. I nodded. I edged in closer, much to Maurice's chagrin. When I was as close as I dared, I could see on the sandy floor a deteriorating grated door. Could it be from a boat or tank that sunk long ago? If that's what it was, why was the shimmering creature guarding it?

The water pouring out of the opening was bubbling so it couldn't be a sunken relic. A wormhole, perhaps? Suppose CERN created this tunnel with their experiments? Why would a geyser be streaming out of a chasm covered by a heavy grate?

Suddenly, the shimmering giant struck the opening. Liquid fire shot up and lingered over the hole. I heard a muffled piercing sound followed by an explosion. The chasm doubled in size and fire traveled along the water currents in all directions. I dropped back to where Maurice was, hidden behind whitewashed coral. More water torpedoed out, and the hole tripled in size.

Smoke and lava bombs shot out of the chasm with increasing intensity. Maurice grabbed my shoulder. He wanted to leave, but I wanted to videotape.

Out of the smoke poured thousands of creatures. They reminded me of locusts because of their wings, but their size was too big. The horrific memory of seeing them in Shambhala made me panic. Now the spiritual was no longer invisible.

The strange creatures had crowns on their heads, and their mouths were large, revealing teeth like a lion. Even through the water, their anthropomorphic wings sounded like horses running into battle. They slowly swam to the surface. Transfixed, I stared at them with the video camera running.

I finally tore my eyes away to see Maurice swimming back to the boat. When the first swarm reached the surface, I breathed easier. They weren't coming after me. I continued to record the locust-like super-insects as they ascended. Then something more horrifying came up from the hole. I saw a dinosaur with useless wings and hippo limbs. He was fierce and full of bravado. With the flip of his tongue, the king of the locusts herded the lingering wayward monster insects upward. Natural grasshoppers didn't have kings—but these creatures did. Could that hole descend to the bottomless pit?

When they were almost to the surface, I started to return to the boat. Before I could move, however, another terrifying creature appeared out of the smoke. This one was worse than the others. Fine scales covered his long slender body, and seven heads dangled off his reptilian torso. The crocodile-like heads displayed razor-sharp teeth. The eyes of the seven-headed monster were yellow and slanted like a snake's. The serpent writhed in twisted contorted meanderings. Each head bopped in mini-circles with eyes flickering, hunting for unsuspecting prey.

As I watched, terror-stricken, yet another creature appeared out of nowhere. I couldn't describe this beast. He was black, so black I couldn't see his form. He was shapeless, and he edged over to the seven-headed creature and subdued it—or absorbed it. They became one retaining characteristics of both.

The monstrosity turned his eyes toward me. The thought that he might absorb me into himself sent me over the edge. Everything I ate for breakfast came up. I expected to choke on my vomit, but the regulator dispersed it into the water. Now I was surrounded by regurgitated food that floated within inches of my face. The dry heaves continued. I tried to pull out the baton the angel gave me, but I was too panicky.

As the monster neared, I was sure I was going to die. Suddenly the guardian of the hole lifted his sword and struck the reptilian seven-headed creature. One of the bobbing heads fell off. The decapitated animal cried out in hate-filled rage. I froze.

A voice spoke in my mind. "L-e-a-v-e."

I started to leave, I wanted to leave, but I was paralyzed by fear. It took me a few seconds, and then I high tailed it back. I thought I'd escaped when the chopped-off head shot up beside me. I would have screamed if I could, but sound doesn't travel very well underwater, and no one was around to hear me anyway.

I tried to get the baton out and accidentally dropped the camera. Thank goodness it was attached to my wrist, even though it was now cumbersome and weighty hanging off my arm. I was even more terrified when I realized the chopped head was still alive. His fiery eyes toyed with me, and his clown-like face smiled. I averted my eyes. I'd never look at a clown the same way again. Stride for stride, it mimicked me. Suddenly, one of the eyes popped out and tried to peck my face like a bird.

I fumbled with my belt to dislodge the baton to no avail. I almost gave up, offering up a prayer when the baton began to glow. Now I was able to detach it, and I slammed the baton at the floating orb. The detached eye pecked at my mask, and the mask slipped sideways. Saltwater seeped through my facemask burning my eyes. I clenched them shut, making it impossible to see. Water began to accumulate at the bottom of the mask, an uncomfortable sensation. I waved the baton and willed my stinging eyes to open.

A stream of fire shot out from my weapon and latched onto the orb. I invoked the name of Yeshua, and before I knew what happened, the head turned into a ball of blue fire. The decapitated appendage spewed blue blood in all directions as it swirled around and sunk to the ocean floor. I watched, briefly mesmerized, and then glanced back to make sure there were no more surprises. Reassured I was out of danger, I followed the shelf back to within sight of the boat bottom.

For the first time, I remembered to check my air pressure. I'd used more than I realized but I had enough to get to the surface. I drifted up slowly to decompress.

What did the creature that saved my life loose beneath the ocean? Was it Leviathan, the monster that arose from the sea, or Abaddon in the book of Revelation? I was convinced the creature guarding the hole was an angel. He had saved my life, and those creatures let loose had to be tied into Lucifer's fall from heaven. While timing on a human level might seem coincidental, with God, they were always appointed times.

I also knew these seemingly unrelated things were related—the world of Bavil, my visit to the throne room, and my journey to the second heaven. I also knew I'd see those locusts in the future.

I reattached the laser to my weight belt, pulled up the dangling camera, and ascended. As I neared the surface, I looked beneath me for E.J. and Chris, but I didn't see them. When I popped above the water, I took a minute to compose myself. No one was at the ladder to help me, so I had to pull myself up. Once I reached the top, I collapsed on the deck.

As I caught my breath, I heard groans from the bow. Maurice was sitting a short distance from me in a state of shock. His mask was off, but he was still wearing his BC and octopus.

I glanced up at the sky. "Where did the locusts go?"

Maurice didn't answer, and I needed to check on the others.

CHAPTER 43

I dumped the video camera into a bucket of freshwater, unclipped my BC, and dropped the tank into the rack. Then I rushed over to Maurice. "Say something to me."

"I'm okay," he said.

"Here, let's get the tank off." After pulling it off his shoulders, I put his tank in the rack next to mine. I could still hear moaning from the bow. I was conflicted because Maurice was not okay despite his reassurance.

His eyes met mine. "Go check on the others. I'm okay."

I climbed the ladder and ran along the outside of the boat to the front. I didn't see anyone at first. Then I heard groaning and spotted Hatim sprawled out on a chaise lounge. Nearby, Pierre was sitting on the deck floor.

I briefly looked at the ship's captain, but I didn't see a visible injury. "Where do you hurt?"

He lifted his head, and his darkened face concerned me.

"My lower back," he said.

"Which side?"

"Left. Don't touch it."

"I promise I won't touch it."

"The pain is horrible."

"What happened?"

Hatim's teeth chattered. "I don't know. At first, I heard a swishing sound. Then I felt pain in my back. Right after that, I heard Pierre screaming. Di ran out and ran back inside. I think he was stung when he came out."

I hated to think it might be those locusts from underneath the ocean, but a sinking feeling in my gut told me it must be. "When you say stung, did you see insects?"

"I guess the swishing sound I heard reminded me of insects, now that I think about it."

I heard groans from Pierre. Maybe he saw more than Hatim did. "Let me check on Pierre."

When I rushed over to Pierre, I heard Chris, E.J., and Maurice on the lower deck. They seemed to be okay as I didn't hear any of them groaning, probably because they were underwater like Maurice and I were when the attack happened.

Pierre was an older man, well along in years, and no doubt better suited for intellectual challenges than physical ones. His face was darker than Hatim's.

"Where are you injured?"

He pointed to his thigh. "I was stung."

"What stung you? Did you see it?"

"I caught a glimpse of huge flying insects, and one of them stung me. The sting felt like a scorpion."

"What makes you say that?"

"I was stung by one a long time ago."

I was convinced it was the locusts I saw fly out of the pit. I helped Pierre off the decking and directed him to a chair that I'd pulled up for him.

"I'll be right back, but I want to check on Di."

"He was stung too," Pierre said. "He ran inside."

I looked up and saw the locust swarm I'd seen underneath the ocean. It was so thick, I couldn't see the sun. Then, as quickly as the shadow appeared, it disappeared. I stared, waiting to see if the shadow came back. When it didn't, I was convinced the locusts were traveling in and out of dimensions—and that would enable them to reach people all over the world in a matter of hours.

I ran inside to find the cook. Di sat on a stool with his back to me, and I edged in front of him. His head hung down to his chest. As bad as the others were, he seemed worse.

I crouched before him. "Di, where were you stung?"

He held up his swollen hand. His face horrified me more than his hand.

"Did you see what stung you?"

"No. None of us saw what it was."

Apparently Pierre didn't tell Di he saw locusts.

Di reached over with his other hand. "Daniel, will you pray for me? Please ask God to take away the pain. I overheard you last night talking to Maurice. I'm a wicked man, but you are holy. If you pray, God will listen to you. I'm afraid I'm going to die."

I held his hand in mine. "Di, you won't die. You will suffer for five months, and then it will go away."

He shook his head. "I don't want to live that long in this pain."

"I can pray for healing, but God is the one who heals."

"Help me, Daniel. Ask God to take away the pain."

"You acknowledged you're a sinful man. If you confess with your mouth that Jesus is Lord and believe he died for you on the cross, God might heal you right now."

Di wailed. "I do. I do believe in Jesus. I do believe in Jesus."

I placed my hand on his thigh. "Yeshua, you said you give believers authority over snakes and serpents. I pray that you remove this vile curse from Di and take away his pain."

I prayed for a couple of minutes, allowing my words to sink in for Di's edification, although I knew God heard me the first time. When I finished, his hand remained swollen, and his face was still dark. Initial disappointment upset me, but Di's words lifted my spirits.

"The pain seems to be less," he said as he moved his fingers. "God is healing me."

Goosebumps covered my body.

"I need a Bible, Daniel. I need to learn about Jesus."

"I don't know if there're any more Bibles except in Petra."

"I must find one."

"We'll try, but first, Pierre and Hatim were also stung. Can you tell them that Jesus is healing you?

He stood. "Yes, right now."

As we approached the door, sunlight hit Di's face, and the black curse was gone.

CHAPTER 44

We walked over to Hatim and Pierre.

"Your faces..." Di said.

Pierre ran his hand along his cheek. "What's happening to me?"

A deep shadow hung over Hatim. "This is your fault, Daniel. Our luck turned bad when we rescued you."

Di held up his hand. "No, Hatim. It's not Daniel's fault."

The ship's captain turned to him. "Weren't you stung, too?"

"I was," Di replied, "but God healed me."

Hatim shook his head. "Don't give me that God stuff."

"Excuse me. I need to talk to Maurice," I said.

I climbed down the steps as my dive buddy was taking the video camera out of the waterproof container. Chris, the Divemaster, stood next to the ladder. "Be careful, it's slippery," he cautioned.

When I stepped on the lower deck, Chris seemed relieved to see me. "Is everything okay up there?"

"Hatim, Pierre, and Di were stung by something while we were on the dive."

"I'll see if they need help. I'm also a United Hatzalah volunteer."

E.J., who was with Chris, didn't say anything but his eyes looked bewildered. He followed Chris up the ladder. I read E.J.'s mind—he was freaking terrified by what Maurice told them.

I put my hand on Maurice's shoulder. "Are you really okay?"

Maurice averted his eyes and stared at the ground. "I owe you an apology."

I tried to cut him off, but he held up his hand. "I owe you an apology. I left you and went back to the boat because I was a coward. I hope you'll forgive me."

I took in a deep breath. "I was terrified, too. I understand. Perhaps if I didn't want to videotape it, I would have left with you. I should have. You were in charge."

Maurice walked over and sat in a chair as he held the camera. "I want to see what's on the card."

I leaned over and looked into Maurice's eyes. "You said you read the Bible once?"

Maurice nodded.

"Then you know what's happening here is in the book of Revelation."

Maurice's eyes flitted around the deck as consternation filled his face.

"Maurice, don't wait," I said. "We don't know how much time we have."

He bit his lip. "I know."

What else could I say? He probably knew the Scriptures better than I did with his photographic memory.

"Let's see what's on this card," Maurice said, "before darkness comes. I also need to talk to Pierre."

We climbed the steps to the second deck where the others were seated in a semicircle. Di was leading E.J. to Christ. The cook was saved less than thirty minutes, and he was already sharing Jesus with the young lad.

We waited until he finished, and E.J. hugged Di like he was his father.

"Why is it so easy for him and so hard for me?" Maurice murmured.

"You have to become like a child and be born again. Jews think they're under the law, but when Yeshua came, he fulfilled the law."

Maurice didn't respond and turned his attention to the others. "Does anybody want to watch the video?"

A few minutes later, we all congregated in Maurice's room. We helped Pierre and Hatim inside and put them on Maurice's bed. The rest of us took chairs from the deck.

Maurice put the card into the computer. Everything looked normal for the first minute. Then the scene abruptly changed, revealing skeletons on the sandy bottom, white bleached coral, and a sea devoid of fish.

In the colorless distance, a shimmering giant creature stood. The camera lens captured more than I saw through the mask. Light emanated from the giant as well as his sword.

"What is that?" Chris asked.

The guarder of the wormhole slashed the chain and grate. He stepped away from the opening as the cover blew off, and an explosion thrust streams of fire into the seawater. Within seconds, the opening tripled in size. Once the spigot stopped, a ballooning fountain of horse-like locusts poured out of the wormhole.

Maurice brought the lens into better focus.

"What are those things?" Chris asked. "I've never seen any underwater creatures like that, and I've done several hundred dives."

"Just what I thought," Maurice said.

I didn't know what he meant.

"They look like horses," Chris said.

Maurice focused the lens on one of the creatures. "They're locusts."

Pierre covered his eyes.

In the close-up, the insects looked like grasshoppers. Their faces were like the face of a man. Their long hair, like that of a woman, rippled through the water, and their teeth looked like the teeth of a lion.

"They are—demonic," Di said. "That's no fish."

Iron breastplates covered the locust-horses. Di was right; they were demonic. On the end of their scorpion's tail was a stinger.

Maurice broke the stunned silence. "And their power was to hurt men five months. They had a king over them, the angel of the bottomless pit, whose name in the Hebrew tongue is Abaddon. One woe is past, and behold, there come two more hereafter."

"There're two more woes?" E.J. asked.

"That's what stung us," Di said hoarsely. "We were stung by locusts."

Maurice restarted the video. Once the locusts reached the surface, the video switched back to the wormhole, and a large reptilian creature covered in scales emerged from the growing chasm. It had seven heads gyrating off long necks as they bobbed in the water.

As horrid as he was, I knew the last beast was even more terrifying. Then the video stopped.

Silence filled the room.

"I guess that's when I quit recording."

Maurice turned to Hatim and glanced at Pierre. "I need to send this video to CERN and discuss what they want us to do. Pierre needs medical attention as well as you."

"Can you take us into port?" I asked.

Hatim's murderous eyes spoke louder than his words. "Who put you in charge, Mr. Troublemaker?"

CHAPTER 45

Di cut through the tension. "We're all hungry and…upset. Hatim, you need to eat. I'll cook a light meal."

I took Pierre to his cabin, and Chris and E.J. took Hatim to the helm.

When I got Pierre to his quarters, he wanted to sit in a chair even though I encouraged him to lie down. He was a distinguished-looking man, but his blackened face made him look much older.

"Can you stay for a minute?" he asked.

I sat beside him.

"You and Maurice are long-time friends?"

I nodded. "We went to school together and spent summers hiking and camping…and diving when we turned sixteen. I guess we did about a dozen dives here in Eilat."

"Sounds like good times."

Those good times seemed long ago, I mused silently. "Maurice helped me with Calculus in high school. I don't know what possessed me to take it, except I wanted to go to medical school, and I knew Calculus was a prerequisite."

"Do you still plan to go to medical school?"

My priorities were so different now I wasn't sure how to respond. "I think…I want to be a rabbi."

"How can you be a rabbi and believe Jesus is the Messiah?"

How did Pierre know I was a Jewish believer? Perhaps he overheard Maurice and me talking, or Di told him. I couldn't remember what I'd said, or maybe he knew about me from CERN. "Do you know Nidal and Tariq?"

Pierre shook his head. "Should I?"

I shrugged. "I just thought you might since you work for CERN."

Pierre winced. "It's very compartmentalized for security reasons."

"Well, to answer your question, Saul, known also by his Roman name, Paul, was a Jewish rabbi who became a follower of Jesus after meeting him on the road to Damascus. So yes, it's possible to believe Jesus is the Messiah and also be a rabbi."

"Interesting." Pierre said. "Jesus must have healed Di, but I'm an atheist. I don't believe in God."

"Do you believe in demons?"

Pierre shifted uncomfortably. "Enough to know they inflict terrible pain. I never thought about it until now. Locusts don't wear crowns."

"If you can believe in demons that inflict pain, is it a stretch to also believe in God?"

Pierre stared at me, grimacing as he touched his thigh. "Maurice said the suffering would last five months. I'd rather die than suffer like this for five months."

"You do have another choice."

"I'll think about it," Pierre said.

I shuffled to the door. "I need to get back to Maurice."

"You don't by any chance have a Bible, do you?"

I shook my head. "I don't."

I walked back over to Pierre and lingered. "There is a verse I want to give you. See if you can memorize it. Better yet, I'll jot it down for you on a sheet of paper."

Pierre handed me paper and pen. I wrote the verse and handed it to him.

He read my words. "John 3:16: 'For God so loved the world that he gave his only begotten son so that whosoever believeth in him should not perish but have eternal life.'"

I edged closer to the door. "Memorize it and then destroy the paper. Leave no trace of it anywhere. Write it on your heart." I looked at his swollen thigh. "God can heal you as he healed Di."

Pierre nodded. "Thanks."

As I returned to Maurice's cabin, I felt the boat moving. We would dock soon. As I sat in a chair in Maurice's cabin, I overheard him on the phone.

"How soon do you want me to go? Sounds good. I'll let you know when I get there."

When he finished the call, he looked at me. "Do you think Pierre is up to driving?"

"He was stung on the left thigh, so his right leg should be okay. I guess it depends on his pain tolerance."

Maurice looked away and became very quiet.

Curiosity got the best of me. "What did CERN say?"

Maurice returned my gaze. "We need to rent a car. They want Pierre to take me to Jerusalem for a meeting with some dignitary. Then Pierre will continue to Tel Aviv and return to France. CERN wants him to be seen by one of their doctors."

"Have they looked at your video?"

"I doubt they've had time."

"Where in Jerusalem?"

Maurice half-shrugged. "Somewhere near the temple, they want me there as soon as possible."

I was tempted to read his mind to find out more but refrained. "Does it have something to do with Prince Adonikam?"

Maurice hesitated. "Maybe."

"I need to go to Jerusalem. Do you think I can hitch a ride with you and Pierre?"

"Sure, I guess. CERN pays for the car. Pierre needs to make a booking. I just don't know if he's up to driving. I mean, I can drive us to Jerusalem, but what about to Tel Aviv?" Maurice stood and gazed out the window.

I waited for him to say something, but all I could hear was the wind blowing and the door beating against the doorframe. "Something is bothering you. What is it?"

He turned to face me. "What must I do?"

"To be saved?"

Maurice nodded. "I'm not leaving this cabin until I know I'm a believer. I mean, I know what CERN's intentions are, but I don't think God is happy about it."

"What are their intentions?"

Maurice hesitated. "Well, the scientists at CERN aren't typical scientists. They're brilliant, but I don't think it's because of their I.Q. I've known for a long time their quest went beyond the frontiers of science. I'll just say it like it is, Daniel. They want to be gods themselves."

If Maurice could believe, what could God do through him? His words were so precise, I imagined he had been bothered by things for a while but didn't know anyone he could confide in that would understand his concerns.

"I'm sure you've heard about all the strange things associated with CERN—I mean, even their emblem looks like 6-6-6," Maurice said.

"I don't know very much at all about CERN."

"Well, if you put science, spirituality, and humanism together without God, you end up with an occult form of worship. They've a grandiose desire to transform the universe—to deconstruct and recreate it. With unlimited funds to accomplish their dream, what will stop them? You wouldn't think Hinduism and humanism would have anything in common, but that Shiva statue in front of the complex is the Hindu god of destruction."

It was easy for me to make the connections—Satan's desire was to destroy everything that God created, so why not symbolize CERN's quest to deconstruct the universe with Shiva, the Hindu God of destruction?

"The CERN community is very compartmentalized," Maurice said, "and I was the only one there that day who could read Hebrew when the writing appeared in the collider. Doesn't it seem strange God would write that warning in Hebrew?"

"He wrote it because you were there to interpret it…and understand its significance."

Maurice crossed his arms. "CERN created the World Wide Web. W stands for Vav in Hebrew, which has a numeric value of six."

I finished Maurice's point. "That means the symbol for the World Wide Web in Hebrew is 6-6-6. Could the World Wide Web be part of the mark of the beast?"

"The more I think about it," Maurice said, "the more I think we are living inside a matrix that is a beast system."

My mind froze. "Like Bavil," I whispered.

CHAPTER 46

My question stirred Maurice more than I realized.

"Daniel, someone else needs to know about something that's going to happen besides me."

"Like what?"

Maurice paced the room with his head down, wrapping his arms in front of him. "Things have been coming through the Hadron Collider."

"What kinds of things?"

"You know about the Hebrew writing?"

I nodded. "Yes, I heard that...in another place."

Maurice stroked his chin. "God isn't pleased with what we're doing. Something came through the tunnel—something very significant."

I couldn't imagine what came through.

My friend became quiet for a moment. His eyes searched the room, and then he wrote on a sheet of paper the phrase, "listening devices."

I brushed my hair with hand thinking where to look first—the bathroom. I searched there and other places, but didn't turn up anything. "Why are you so concerned now?"

"Because of Hatim's reaction. If he's on the side of evil, of course he wouldn't want you on his boat."

"Hatim blames me for all his bad luck, including getting stung," I said.

After a thorough search, Maurice seemed relieved. "I think Hatim might be a victim, but certainly it's his choice what he believes. Maybe he's just a paranoid individual."

I shrugged. "He just doesn't like me, like I'm bad karma."

"Well," Maurice said, "we've got to move on. I need to tell you some things I want you to know in case something happens to me."

"I'm listening," I said. "However, I don't think anything is going to happen to you."

Maurice looked out the cabin window. "I know Yeshua is the long-awaited Jewish Messiah. The Jews missed his arrival the first time, and many have already accepted another who has come in his own name."

He pumped his first in his hand. "I won't miss him this time, Daniel. You are my witness. Yeshua died for my sins. His shed blood made atonement for me. The animal sacrifices were a foreshadowing that pointed to Yeshua as the sacrificial lamb. I accept Jesus, God's Son, as my Lord and Savior."

He turned to me. "Did I leave anything out?"

I smiled. "I don't think so." I walked over and slapped Maurice on the back.

He raised his hands triumphantly as God's spirit filled the room. After several emotional minutes, I broached the trip. "Tell me the plan."

Maurice stretched his back. "First I need to tell you what has been hanging over me."

I nodded. "Okay."

"Daniel, in the book of Zechariah 5:8, Zechariah sees a flying scroll. I think a better translation in Hebrew is roll. The angel tells him it's a curse that goes forth over the whole earth. God says he will bring the roll into the house of the thief."

Maurice paused. "Could the house of the thief be the Third Temple?"

I shook my head. "I don't know. I'd have to see it in context. I mean, I don't have a photographic memory like you, and I never really understood that passage. I never looked at the words in that way."

Maurice nodded. "It's fine. I'm just speculating. Zechariah says in the seventh verse, 'Behold, there was lifted up a talent of lead, and this is a woman that sitteth in the midst of the ephah. And he said, this is wickedness. And he cast it into the midst of the ephah; and he cast the weight of lead upon the mouth thereof.'

"Are you with me so far?" Maurice asked?

I nodded. "I think so."

"Then Zechariah said, 'There came out two women, and the wind was in their wings; for they had wings like the wings of a stork, and they lifted up the ephah between the earth and the heaven.'"

Maurice paused. "What does that remind you of?"

"A cruise missile. They have wings," I said.

"And an ephah is a measure… missiles are measured by their thrust in terms of pounds or kilograms."

"You never cease to amaze me with your brilliance, Maurice, to make that correlation."

Maurice continued, "Right after that, Zechariah asked the angel, 'Whither do these bear the ephah?' And the angel replied, 'To build it a house in the land of Shinar, and it shall be established, and set there upon her own base.'"

As usual, Maurice was a little ahead of me. "Now, what does that have to do with CERN?"

Maurice sat on the edge of the bed bracing himself with his arms. "I think there is a better interpretation for woman in that passage. I think it should be fire. The two words are spelled so similarly in Hebrew… there were two fires in the container, not two women."

"You mean there were two fires in a roll sealed by a disc of lead?" I asked.

"Why else would it be called evil and sealed by lead?"

"It sure sounds like Zechariah is referring to a missile, doesn't it? But how does that relate to CERN?"

"CERN is bringing a package to the Third Temple." Maurice shook his head. "The Jews won't allow it to stay. Even some of the Muslims won't like it. They've got their own holy places on the Mount. I think God will remove the silos after a war, and they will be taken to Babylon. There the Antichrist will build it a third home in Babylon that will be destroyed at the Lord's appearing. That's why that land isn't inhabitable in the millennium."

"So what's the first and second home?"

"The second home is in the Third Temple," Maurice replied.

"So where is the roll now?"

He hesitated. "Promise you won't repeat this?"

I nodded. "I don't know anyone who would even care, except for Shale, and I don't know when I'll see her again."

"I think this is what's going to happen," Maurice said. "CERN will transport the Kaaba Black Stone from Mecca to the Third Temple in Jerusalem, and they will place dark matter from the Hadron Collider inside the Third Temple—perhaps in a statue of some sort."

I stared at Maurice. "Why would they do that?"

"The Kaaba Black Stone is the stone that fell from the sky. It might even be the same meteorite that was worshipped in Ephesus at the Temple of Diana. Of course, the stone can't speak, but suppose it could?"

"So how is dark matter related to the Black Stone?" I asked.

Maurice was quiet for a moment. "First, they both come from the other side. We know the Black Stone is a meteorite, and we know Satan fell from heaven. Why would anybody worship a meteorite unless it had a religious significance? I think there is a correlation. We know dark matter is antimatter, the opposite of matter, and highly, highly flammable—and evil. That's why CERN will transport it in a container sealed with a lead disc. To receive that much dark matter from another dimension—it could destroy the entire universe."

I was stunned by Maurice's thoughts. He was brilliant—like all the scientists at CERN, but he worshipped God and not science.

Maurice rubbed the tips of his fingers together as he spoke. "A statue of Shiva, the god of destruction, stands in front of CERN. And isn't that what Abaddon means, the angel of death, that is mentioned in the book of Revelation?"

"What about speaking?" I asked. "The image speaks."

"CERN has opened the portal," Maurice said, "and the book of Revelation says the beast is given a voice."

We both remained silent reflecting on what we'd witnessed.

"I believe Prince Adonikam is the Antichrist," Maurice said, "and I think on the dive, Abaddon was let loose by God's angel to be king over the demonic locusts."

Maurice took in an intentional breath and exhaled. "I believe Prince Adonikam is the predicted Mahdi, and the world has been duped."

"You mean he's the Antichrist?"

Maurice nodded.

"I think God plans on keeping you around, Maurice—seriously." I voiced it as much for my benefit as for his.

Even though we were both tired, we needed to make plans. Maurice finally said, "Logistically, darkness is approaching. I'll tell Pierre CERN wants him to rent a car."

As we were talking, someone knocked on the door.

Maurice opened it as Pierre leaned against the doorframe. "CERN has reserved a rental car. Hatim just docked, and Hertz is on the way to pick us up. Once I get things sorted, I'll come and get you. That'll give you time to pack."

"How are you feeling?" Maurice asked.

Pierre's face twitched. "Terrible. I'll get the car, but you might have to drive. CERN is sending a package they want you to receive, and there is a VIP person they want you to meet, but they didn't say more than that. They'll tell you when you get to Jerusalem."

"They already told me," Maurice said.

Pierre raised his eyebrow. "I didn't know you talked to them. After I drop you off, I'll drive to Tel Aviv and take a plane back to France. I'm sure they can give me some pain medication. The Tylenol isn't helping much."

"Daniel wants to come so he can visit his family."

Pierre nodded. "That's fine. I'll be back in about an hour with the car."

Di prepared some food even though I wasn't hungry. However, I wasn't one to turn down a meal when someone fixed it, so I ate some fish and stuffed the pistachio nuts in my pocket.

The sky was a never-ending twilight—not light and not dark, just shades of gray. The sun and the moon were visible—but the moon was red, and the sun was black. No wonder everything green was dying. Next on the list of climate change agenda fixes would be oxygen depletion. Life couldn't exist without oxygen, but without sunlight, plants and trees couldn't exist either.

We took Route 90 north toward Jerusalem, and I settled in for the four-hour drive. I closed my eyes as the vibration of the car made me sleepy, drifting off against my will, but I was awakened when we approached a security checkpoint. Three men traveling in a vehicle would raise more concern than a man and woman, but when we showed our I.D.s, because two of us were Israeli, they waved us through.

That awoke me, and I sat up to look out the window. On the other side of the road was a group of misfits dressed in rags holding up signs. "Prepare to meet thy God, O Israel. Seek good and not evil that ye may live. Woe to them that are at ease in Zion," and other similar sayings. Would anybody believe them?

As we traveled, more people filled the streets. Many were beggars carrying similar signs as the others. "The end of the world is near" seemed to be the prevailing theme.

We passed by the Dead Sea. To my astonishment, I saw several fishing boats. "When did people start fishing in the Dead Sea?"

Maurice glanced out the window. "A couple of years ago, people started seeing fish. There is now a growing fish industry here. Of course, a third of marine life in the oceans has died, so it's been an unexpected blessing."

We didn't go much farther when Pierre pulled off to the side of the road and stopped. "I want to scream," he exclaimed. "I can't drive any longer. I can't take the pain."

I looked at Maurice.

"I can drive," he said.

We switched to the front seat so Pierre could stretch out in the back. I turned on the radio to get some news and caught the tail end of a report. "Prince Adonikam meets with leaders on the southern front. Talks have been cut short by alarming news from the North. We understand he's on his way back to Jerusalem."

Static filled the airwaves so I couldn't hear any more. I turned the dial looking for something else but without success. I turned off the radio. Darkness was slowing taking over the gray skies. The clock said four. How could it be this dark this early?

As we sat in silence, groans from the back reached our ears. I leaned over to see if Pierre was okay. I wasn't sure he'd even make it to Jerusalem.

"What should we do for him?" I asked.

Maurice shook his head. "I don't think there is anything we can do."

My edginess increased as we drove. Few cars were on the road, and my spirit felt burdened. Maybe it was Pierre's howling in the back— his pain, his unwillingness to call on the Lord. Perhaps it was what Maurice shared—or both.

"Look," Maurice said. "What is that?"

Coming up over the desert were lights flying in formation, but they weren't airplanes. The objects were cylindrical. There must have been a dozen of them. Maurice slowed the car down to watch as they passed overhead.

Maurice and I exchanged glances. "UFOs," Maurice said.

"They're demons," I said. "What is happening?"

Soon more appeared and followed the same course as the others, disappearing over the horizon.

"They're going in the same direction as us."

"Jerusalem."

The groans from the back bothered me more than I wanted to admit.

We traveled for another hour without talking much, until we neared columns of fire that lit up the sky in the distance. As we approached, I could see the roadway was impassable. A vast chasm had opened, and smoke was seeping up from the ground.

We stopped, and Pierre straight sat up. His cries had worsened over the last hour, and when he saw the chasm, he became more recalcitrant. I rolled down the window, but it didn't help.

"I've got to get out, Maurice," I said. "I need a break."

Maurice stopped the car, and I opened the door. No sooner did I exit than Pierre scrambled past me. He shouted, "I want to die," and ran off.

I turned to Maurice. "What should we do?"

"You stay here with the car. I'll go get him. CERN needs his expertise."

Maurice took off, and I turned my eyes to the road in front of us. Smoke rose from the chasm, and I imagined it was a bottomless pit.

CHAPTER 47

I watched as Maurice chased Pierre into darkness. I despaired. I should have gone with Maurice. The fire crept closer as it circled around from behind. I should move the car. I got back in and pressed on the accelerator, but the car stalled out after starting. I tried again, but as soon as it started, it would turn off. Perhaps the smoke had done something to the engine. If I abandoned the car, how would Maurice and Pierre find me when they returned? They wouldn't, but I didn't have any choice but to leave it. As the fire consumed other abandoned cars, in the glowing light, I saw people walking. Until now, I hadn't noticed them.

I wanted to look for Maurice and Pierre, but now molten lava was between us. I'd be swallowed up. I glanced behind me, dismayed that the lava was creeping closer. As I stood on an elevated berm, I watched as our car sank into the fire like the others. What would we do now?

Someone screamed and started toward me. I couldn't tell who it was, but the voice sounded like Pierre. It took me a moment to make him out in the darkness. I looked down at his feet, and he was walking on fire—how could he still be alive?

"Where is Maurice?" I shouted.

"He chased me into the hole," Pierre replied. "I tried to die, Daniel, but I can't. Help me to die." He walked in and out of the flames. I was so terrified I almost fainted. I couldn't breathe. Maurice must be dead by now, but suppose he wasn't? Suppose he was still alive?

"Maurice," I shouted. My eyes couldn't get past Pierre who stood in the howling flames.

"I want to die. Somebody kill me," he cried out.

"Call on the name of the Lord Jesus Christ," I shouted. "Remember John 3:16, 'For God so loved the world…'" but it was too late. He couldn't hear me.

I shot one last glance in the direction where I saw Maurice chasing Pierre. I didn't want to remember our last conversation in the boat. I couldn't deny the foreboding I felt when he said he might die. Emotionally, I didn't want to let go. I sobbed. "Maurice, I'm sorry."

A hot wind pushed me forward. I couldn't go back—nothing was there. I walked, forcing myself to put one foot in front of the other. I couldn't focus on anything. All I had the strength to do was walk. Soon I became aware of others around me, but I couldn't see them.

Flying bats came out of the abyss, and I swatted at them. "Get away from me." Why had God created such vile creatures?

Then I heard a gentle voice, "In the name of Jesus, leave."

Immediately the bats left. I looked around to see who spoke, but I didn't see anyone—except an injured bat lying in the dirt. I never wanted to see another one of those things again; yet, a strange pity for the helpless beast came over me. His wing was torn.

I reached down and picked him up. Oh, how ugly he was, and how I hated bats. I wanted to step on him, but I couldn't. I saw his pain, and something about that made us comrades. If I carried him to safety, I knew God would help me to get to the other side. I knew God would anyway, but to take pity on a creature that I hated made the depths of God's love more profound. I did not deserve God's mercy, and neither did this bat deserve mine.

I wanted to stuff my ears so I couldn't hear any more weeping, including my own, and then, through all the words of despair, I heard someone reciting the Twenty-Third Psalm. "Though I walk through the valley of the shadow of death, I will fear no evil; for thou art with me. Thy rod and thy staff, they comfort me..."

Tears came to my eyes. They were the most beautiful words I'd heard in a long time.

CHAPTER 48

Heat from the fiery pit scorched the hopeful words until I no longer believed them. I was convinced I was going to die. I choked on the flames, and the white embers snaked around me like hungry demons—as if the fires of hell couldn't wait to consume me.

The plants, animals, trees, and birds were just collateral damage in Satan's quest to eliminate humankind. He hated God's image bearers. I gazed across the flaming desert. The cascading layers of smoke, the embers falling like feathers, and the crackling lava bombs in the fiery river held an evil enchantment—until I witnessed the souls of men— grotesque faces, gnashing of teeth, and wails of remorse. Stunned, my knees buckled, and I fell to the ground.

The scroll of heaven rolled up and revealed a vision in virtual reality. I saw a fortress protected by thick walls lined with gun turrets on a steep mountaintop. My enhanced vision allowed me to see through the fortified walls, and an impressive vestibule came into focus that led to a large atrium. The vaulted ceiling reached up into the heavens, and crystal chandeliers swayed in dignified grace. Marble arched columns reminded me of Roman decor. Natural light shone through prisms of etched glass.

I watched as a coronation was in progress. A holy man in white vestments was placing a crown on Prince Adonikam's head. Ten distinguished dignitaries stood in attendance. When the ceremony finished, applause followed, and the crowned prince held up his hands. Those present bowed before him.

The scene pushed forward, and I saw myself dressed in a white robe hiding behind the vestibule door. I held a shiny sword in my hand that I whipped through the air. My eyes dripped with murderous intent. I stared at my nemesis.

The proceedings ended with celebratory music, and the newly crowned prince walked toward the vestibule. I was huddled in the corner out of sight. I heard my labored breathing as I lay in wait. I wanted to cover my eyes.

As Prince Adonikam entered the hallway, I jumped out and slashed him with my sword. Blood oozed from his head, and he collapsed. I saw myself looking at the fallen prince without a shred of remorse, like a sick psychopath.

Before anyone could reach me, I dropped the murder weapon and ran out of the fortress. Chaos ensued as gunfire erupted and sirens blazed. I watched as I eluded capture and disappeared into the darkness.

The scene switched to news feeds. Networks were broadcasting raw footage. "Prince Adonikam has been assassinated at his palace in Samaria following his coronation. It has been confirmed the assailant is Daniel Sperling, a Jewish man from Jerusalem..."

Soon helicopters hovered over the fortress. I saw dozens of militia scouring the mountain searching for me. Was this my future? I prayed to God it wouldn't be. "Even if he's my alter-ego, I don't want my name associated with the assassination of Prince Adonikam, Antichrist or not."

God revealed the wickedness of my heart—my pride didn't want it. Could God not use me how he chose? God allowed Yeshua to hang cursed on a tree so he could rescue us from the fires of hell. Could I not allow God to use any part of me however he wished?

The lava edged closer as I argued. I poured out my conflicted feelings. "I'd rather die than commit this heinous crime. Vengeance is yours, not mine. Forgive me for all my sins, even those I've yet to commit." And then I added, "But your will be done, not mine. If this is how I am to glorify you, let it be so."

The smell of sulfur burned my nostrils. I sunk so low in the pit of despair I no longer thought escape was possible. I couldn't go back— not that I would want to relive any second from the past, but I loathed the future. I just wanted to be in heaven. Job was right—maybe it would be better if I'd never been born.

I heard them first—the snarls and gnashing of teeth. The creatures circled me, inching closer and closer. They were like wolves, vipers, snakes, vultures—I didn't know what they were. As each one neared, I thrust the laser sword toward them. Each time they backed away. "I'll shoot you with the laser," I mumbled. I rose to my feet which were numb from sitting for so long.

I cried to God, "Please, save me." The horror of my future was too much. I wanted to die, but not because my throat was slit by demonic animals.

The chimera edged closer. I tried to shoot the laser, but nothing happened. Maybe it was ruined when I took it on the dive. I tried once more to no avail.

I thought about throwing the injured bat at them, but that would be cruel. Then I remembered the pistachio nuts I'd stuffed in my pocket. I yanked them out and threw them as far as I could. The hybrids scurried off, giving me precious seconds to get away. I climbed up the side of the pit with a strength that wasn't mine.

As I struggled up the incline, the lava flow receded. I reached the top and sensed someone walking alongside me. I heard a tap-tap-tap of a walking stick and saw sandals matching my stride. I looked into the man's face, but I didn't recognize him.

"Do you remember the Twenty-Third Psalm?" he asked.

I began to recite it. "The Lord is my shepherd I shall not want…he makes me like down in green pastures…he restores my soul…" I knew I was forgetting parts of it. I just couldn't remember the whole Psalm right now, but I recognized the voice as the one I heard earlier reciting it.

"Though I walk through the valley of the shadow of death…" he said.

I finished the line. "I will fear no evil, for thou art with me; thy rod and thy staff, they comfort me…" and my eyes were opened. "It is you."

"Things aren't as they appear," he said. "Do not let the evil one deceive you," and then he was gone.

Encouraged, I looked through the torn veil at the lingering vision. My nemesis was hiding in a foxhole. A guard walked up to the ledge, stared down at me, and laughed. "Great job."

Another soldier joined him, and they kicked a handful of dirt into my face. "Let's dispose of him."

One of them fired gunshots, and I became a burning heap of melted wires. Awareness of my surroundings increased as my despair lifted. I saw others escaping out of the same pit and remembered the famous words of Corrie ten Boom. Gratitude filled my heart, but what if God wasn't done? What if there was more? I was learning absolute surrender without counting the cost.

CHAPTER 49

The spiritual dimension opened up to me once again, and this time I was a part of the drama and not just a spectator. The flapping of wings startled me until I realized the bat flew away. This whole time he had been clinging to my shirt. I lost sight of the creature as he ventured off to wherever it is bats go.

I don't know how I got there, but I was walking along the Outer Court of the Temple Mount. Overhead gray clouds stretched out like an accordion, and the air was cold and clammy.

For the first time I noticed the cameras that hung from light posts and street signs—and then realized they weren't cameras. They were 5G antennas. Big Brother had invaded Jerusalem.

Gangs lollygagged on the streets outside the Temple area. Discarded cigarette butts, used syringes, and beer cans littered the streets. This wasn't the Jerusalem I remembered. The perversions of Tel Aviv had found a home here.

The Third Temple, newly built, stood at the far end of the Court of the Gentiles. I remembered hiding in Herod's Temple during Passover Week when I witnessed the trial and execution of Yeshua. The porches, outer courts, colonnades, chambers, gates, and gold-filled walls were extravagant artifacts from that time and didn't exist in this Temple.

What mattered most were the religious rites and sacrificial offerings of animals as required by the Torah. Prince Adonikam met the Jews' preconceived Messianic expectations. As Jesus prophesied, they received an impostor who came in his own name.

A short distance from the holy site animal rights activists held up signs protesting the killing of animals. The Dome of the Rock and Al-Aqsa Mosque took up a portion of the Temple Mount. There was no illusion the Outer Court belonged to the Gentiles.

Oohs and aahs erupted followed by cheers and applause as Prince Adonikam, surrounded by a plethora of dignitaries and bodyguards, was seated.

Someone wearing a white cassock, whom I didn't know, stood at the podium. On his head was a jeweled three-tiered crown. The crowd applauded for a full minute before he could speak.

An on-site reporter described the scene. "What can I say? Prince Adonikam is alive and well after being assassinated by a troubled Israeli with a long history of mental illness. The search for him continues."

A photo of me flashed up on a giant outdoor screen with a number to call or text if I was sighted. And here I was among the gathering in total anonymity. I wasn't concerned. I no longer counted the costs.

The announcer spoke again. "Let's listen to the Minister of Truth, Father and Prophet Haman Urhammu."

When I tried to read the holy man's mind, I couldn't. His DNA was probably corrupted, and I surmised he was the false prophet. I sensed an important moment in the making. The audience cheered and applauded with rapt attention. When the assemblage quieted down, he spoke into the mic.

"We have witnessed the greatest miracle in the history of humankind. Our esteemed leader, Prince Adonikam, is here—in spirit, in person, and in power. We all witnessed his coronation three days ago when he was attacked by a man wielding a sword. You saw with your own eyes that he lay dead on the palace floor in Samaria."

Father Haman Urhammu focused his eyes on the prince in reverent awe. "We're blessed to have him with us today. He's alive and well—as he's risen from the dead."

Fear hushed the listeners.

Waving his hand blissfully, Urhammu said, "I present to you Prince Adonikam."

Mesmerized by his presence, more cheers and applause erupted. Some prayed, some bowed, and some, overcome with emotion, collapsed on the stone pavement. Many weren't sure what to do. The prince stood, soaking in the praise from adoring fans and followers before approaching the podium.

Prophet Urhammu and Prince Adonikam stood side by side at the rostrum. Cameras clicked amid a flurry of nonstop flashes to capture the historic moment. After the crowd settled in, Father Haman pointed to a structure that until now was hidden by a covering. Several guards stood by the colossal mystery.

"At this time, we will unveil the statue for everyone to see," Prophet Urhammu said.

The guards removed the cover from the nine-foot-high artwork. More oohs and ahhs filled the air followed by a holy silence.

The Minister of Truth smiled. "Thank you, thank you." Adonikam edged over to get a better view of the hewn creation. Soldiers held the people back as the newly-crowned prince admired the graven image.

Prophet Urhammu addressed the onlookers. "For the last three days, the statue has been under construction. I consulted several dozen artists. We came to a consensus on what the final rendition should look like. I hired scores of stonemasons to carve the image into blocks of stone. Then we called in the gold artisans and those skilled in working with brass. We brought in ironworkers and those gifted in working with clay. Day and night the artists worked. The statue was erected in three days.

"Chrislam leaders joined me for the dedication this morning and prayed for the grand ceremony we're holding now. Today is the third day since Adonikam's death. This morning, we placed his lifeless body in front of the statue. As I prayed for the miracle of resurrection, as prophesized by the prophets, the statue spoke life into him. The prince opened his eyes.

"We will share the full story in an upcoming special about his global rise to power and unparalleled genius in a documentary entitled, 'The Messiah Has Come.'"

Most of the people cheered at this proclamation, but I noticed a few didn't.

The camera focused on the lifeless carving. I saw nothing resembling what Father Haman was describing. I expected some kind of artificial intelligence to bring the statue to life. After all, I'd seen such A.I. with Tariq and my nemesis. A mocked-up Chimera would be more compelling.

Besides its allure and beauty, the statue was nothing to brag about. The head was carved in fine gold. The arms and chest were silver, and his belly and thighs were brass. His legs were iron, and his feet were partly iron and partly clay. This statue looked like a replica of the image in Nebuchadnezzar's dream found in the book of Daniel. It was just a lifeless piece of carved stone. I was unimpressed. However, I was impressed that the prince was alive.

As I lamented the crime my nemesis committed, God spoke to me. "Daniel, your nemesis did not kill the prince. Remember, I told you things were not as they appear."

Stunned by the unexpected word of knowledge, I replayed in my mind what I saw. Had it been an illusion? Satan made it appear as if I had done it? Even my nemesis was deceived.

The crowd was growing impatient.

"Now, for the big moment," Father Haman said. "You see, this isn't an ordinary statue. Prince Adonikam's essence—his body, mind, and soul—is encapsulated inside this statue."

Murmurings stirred as Prophet Urhammu spoke. "Our esteemed has become what we knew him to be all along. The statue is a representation of his likeness. Now, let's welcome Prince Adonikam."

The throng roared as he returned to the podium and took the mic from Father Haman.

As the prince spoke, his voice came from everywhere. "Friends, family, and all who are with us on the World Wide Web, you should be able to hear me."

I wasn't sure what he meant, but then I understood. The statue was speaking as well as the prince. From his head to his ten toes, the icon that was made in his image took on a life of its own. The figure and the prince were one, a fake omniscience, no more than a cheap imitation of two parts of the Trinity—Yeshua and the Holy Spirit. I stared at the 5G antennas. They were projecting his voice. He and the World Wide Web —666 in Hebrew numerology—were one entity. I couldn't imagine what could be more powerful or more persuasive for anyone who had eyes to see and ears to hear.

A hushed reverence filled the Temple Mount. Many fell to their knees and bowed at the king and statue. Then he did something no one expected. He opened the chest of the statue, and inside the statue was a Black Stone.

"The Kaaba Black Stone will be the cornerstone of the Third Temple," Prince Adonikam said. Immediately, an Imam—I presumed since he wore the identifying rounded skullcap—lifted the Black Stone and placed it on the wing of the Third Temple. A special place had been carved out of the side so that it could be inserted. A dozen guards with high-powered machine guns stood all around to make sure every-thing went according to plan.

I stared at the Black Stone along with those around me and imag-ined what people were thinking. How did they remove the Black Stone from the Kaaba without anyone knowing it?

CHAPTER 50

The musicians played in a minor key on kitharas and harps, mesmerizing the listeners. As the music dipped to a soothing whisper, Prince Adonikam hypnotically took control with his enchanting voice. Touching the soul of the people, the mystery surrounding his resurrection elevated his status to god.

"Come to me," he shouted, "all of you who are weary, and I will give you rest. Take my mark upon you and learn from me because I am gentle and humble in heart, and you will find rest for your souls. My mark is easy, and my burden is light."

The charm with which he spoke was spellbinding. The worship went on for several minutes, and I sensed far more happening in the spiritual realm than was evident in the physical.

After a short while, the music ended. The courtyard and Temple Mount were filled with V.I.P.s, military attachés, dignitaries, U.N. peacekeepers, Jews, Muslims, Christians, tourists, and curious onlookers.

The militia pushed the increasing crowd farther back, and a brief moment of concern swept through the gathering. Prince Adonikam allayed growing fears. "We have a special package that has been delivered from CERN, and we need to make room."

He pointed to a loading and unloading area on a side street next to the Temple. A drone-like plane with extra-long wings occupied a landing strip.

Nobody knew what he was talking about, and the television cameraman for a brief moment didn't know whether to focus on the prince or on the oversized drone. The stork-like plane had thin legs with wings tipped in black with reddish paint on its bill and lower legs. The wings were feminine, long, and graceful. The rest of the drone was white. A platoon of soldiers surrounded the aircraft waiting to unload its cargo.

When the doors protracted, two cylindrical objects became visible. Lead handles secured the tops of the rolls so they wouldn't open unexpectedly. The outside of the cylinders was covered in ancient writing, but I wasn't close enough to read the words. The objects were about nine meters long. The handlers carefully escorted the two packages down a plank similar to what passengers use when entering and exiting a plane.

Prince Adonikam resumed his narration. "These magnificent pieces of art will be placed on either side of the Third Temple after a special ceremony."

The television reporter added, "I've been told these packages from CERN are a special gift. What's inside the cylinders has remained a secret, but I sense an upcoming demonstration will answer our questions."

Once the packages were moved to the proper location, the guards pushed the crowd back farther. "We don't want anyone to get hurt," they kept repeating.

After several minutes, Haman Urhammu and Prince Adonikam stood beside each other before the captive audience. The cameras were rolling, and curious eyes darted back and forth between the cylinders and world leaders.

"We need your attention," Prince Adonikam said. "You may not know that Prophet Urhammu isn't only a brilliant religious leader, but he performs miracles."

Those watching became quiet, and the cameraman split the screen between Prophet Urhammu and the mysterious objects. As everyone waited for something to happen, a zephyr blew through the gathering. As the wind swirled in and out of the stunned onlookers, it descended on each of the two cylinders, and fire materialized underneath them.

In an instant, the objects took on the appearance of rockets. The crowd, astonished, stampeded en masse to safety.

"Who can call down fire from heaven?" Prince Adonikam asked.

Everywhere I looked I saw stunned faces. I heard the rabble of noisy oglers asking questions. "Who can make war with Prince Adonikam and Prophet Urhammu? Who can come back from the dead unless he was divine?"

After a minute, Haman Urhammu ordered the fire to cease. Once everyone was assured the apparent missiles wouldn't explode, subdued cheers filled the Temple Mount. I noticed a few people quietly slipping away

Prince Adonikam stood with his hands raised, and Father Haman bowed. The assemblage took their cue from the prophet.

"Thank you for your devotion and worship," Prince Adonikam said. "Much is happening as we speak, and to facilitate the transfer of power, Father Haman has another important announcement.

Haman Urhammu faced everyone. "The worship of the prince is now mandatory. Because food shortages are severe and will get worse due to climate change, it's imperative that everyone receive the Kaaba Black Stone tattoo, known simply as the mark." He pointed to the Kaaba Black Stone that was now the cornerstone of the Temple. "Those who don't receive the mark won't be able to buy or sell.

"Receiving the mark will add your name to the World Wide Web database that will allow the New World Order to ensure you receive your fair allotment of food. Receiving the mark also demonstrates your worship of our divine leader. It's an outward manifestation of who is lord of your life.

"While some misguided people have called it the mark of the beast," Father Haman said, "that negative connotation is a ruse from the devil. He doesn't want you to accept it. He's made it sound like a bad thing so you will die instead. A loving God would never want you to die, would he? And unless you receive the mark, you will die. Prince Adonikam wants you to live, and the mark on your hand or forehead will ensure in the fairest way possible you receive what's rightfully yours—and live.

"We belong to each other, right? We want everyone to enjoy the same benefits, and once you receive it, your name will be entered into our 666 database. You must wear the symbol on your skin because it's linked to your DNA. You don't want your food allotment stolen, do you?"

No one responded.

Father Haman repeated his question, "You don't want your food allotment stolen, do you?"

This time the crowd responded in unison, "No."

"The mark will ensure no one can steal your food."

The crowd nodded its approval, and any negative murmurings appeared to have been appeased.

"In addition to the elimination of all other religions, animal sacrifices will be stopped. They're no longer necessary. Why should innocent animals die?"

I noticed a slight delay in response to this announcement. Claps could be heard here and there, but not the overwhelming support exhibited earlier. Some wanted to leave, but the militia now squelched any attempt.

Any Jew would know something was amiss with the cessation of animal sacrifices. The Jews waited two thousand years to rebuild the Temple so they could carry out the ritual as commanded in the Torah. Then I noticed a few Muslims seemed unhappy—I presumed they were Muslims because the women wore a hijab. And some who wore crosses around their necks appeared concerned.

However, Prince Adonikam didn't notice and continued. "I have another demonstration." He nodded toward Father Haman.

The prophet handed him a crystal orb and took the mic as Prince Adonikam walked over to the cylinders. "Worship of the prince will be a blessing," Father Haman said. "As earth-dwellers, we hold the future in our hands, and Prince Adonikam promises us peace and safety. Blessed be our leader, Prince Adonikam."

Many rose to their feet, clapping.

Prince Adonikam stood behind one of the cylinders, turned the handle, and lifted off the lid. A small amount of black vapor escaped as he slipped the crystal orb inside the container for a few seconds. Then he quickly pulled it out and resealed the top.

He raised the crystal ball into the air. "What do you see?"

"A black substance," someone shouted.

Inside the crystal orb was a black formless vapor. Watching the substance mesmerized me. I peeled away my eyes to break the hypnotic effect.

"Watch," Prince Adonikam said. "Don't take your eyes off the crystal orb."

Prince Adonikam pointed to the cameraman. "Please follow me and focus on the image in the crystal ball."

While that was happening, some men picked up the statue and moved it inside the Third Temple.

CHAPTER 51

The crystal sphere containing the black concoction filled up the flat screen around the Court of the Gentiles. Murmurings swept through the crowd. Even if something seemed wrong, who would dare oppose the prince or his right-hand man? Father Haman nodded his approval, but apprehension shadowed the face of the cameraman. Reluctantly, he followed Prince Adonikam inside the Temple.

"Is your camera running?" the prince asked.

"Yes," the cameraman replied.

"We're standing inside the Holy Place," the onsite reporter said, "next to the Holy of Holies where only the High Priest can enter." I heard gasps. "What is happening?" someone ask.

"This is a stupendous event," an excited voice proclaimed.

Prince Adonikam raised the crystal sphere and drank the formless substance. The television screen on the Temple Mount showed everything. As he drank, a dark spirit lingered over him.

The substance reminded me of what I'd seen on the dive with Maurice. I thought back to what he told me. CERN had captured something in the particle accelerator from the other side. The new leader's joy eclipsed the horror etched on the faces of many. Stirrings and faint cries from onlookers filled the Temple Court as the strange events became even stranger.

The prophet, Father Haman, standing next to the prince in the Holy Place with the cameraman and a couple of others called down fire, and the newly crowned prince laughed in a high-pitched voice. A swirling, flaming tongue leaped through the Holy Place and wrapped itself around the statue.

Seconds later, the tongue released its grip, swept through the room, and entered the body of the prince. It was eerily similar to what I had witnessed when Judas was possessed by Satan. Iciness swept over me as I waited for the fiery tongue to exit his body. It didn't.

Prince Adonikam shouted in an unknown language, and Prophet Urhammu, who had exited the Third Temple, interpreted. "I speak for the prince," he said. It wasn't Father's Haman's natural voice. It was the projection of the prince's voice. "I am God, and my new name is Prince Banu Hashim. Everyone must worship me and receive the mark or be imprisoned, beheaded, or burned."

The prophet's natural voice returned. "Prince Banu Hashim will be moving his headquarters to Jerusalem. When he comes out of the Holy Place, you'll be expected to bow."

We were surrounded by armed militia. Would we be shot if we refused? In an attempt to dispel the tension, light applause rippled through those remaining. Many had left despite the military's attempt to stop them. My spirit was heavy. Since I could read the minds of those nearby, I knew I wasn't the only one horrified by what we'd seen. While great fear overshadowed many, others were cheering, applauding, kneeling, and worshipping.

Prince Banu Hashim exited the Holy Place with a different aura about him. He and Prophet Urhammu shook hands. That handshake cemented their absolute power. Between the two, almost everybody on the planet would die, and billions of earth-dwellers would go to hell. I couldn't read the prince's mind anymore—not that I even wanted to.

The signal was given for the musicians to play, and music befitting the new ruler filled the Temple Mount.

"We're blessed to have such a strong leader," Prophet Urhammu said. "The New World Order has now vested all military power in Prince Adonikam, and as our divine leader, the Mahdi shall be worshipped as Prince Banu Hashim."

The Minister of Truth continued. "Please show your respect and bow." Most were already kneeling. I was not going to kneel and wondered if the military would shoot anyone who didn't.

Suddenly, we lost our audio and video feed at the Temple Mount. A moment of confusion followed, and I saw the camera ditched on the ground. The cameraman was speeding through the crowd with security chasing after him.

After several seconds of empty airwaves, the broadcast on the overhead screens returned to the studio. The television anchorman displayed an annoying smile, and his eyes flashed that familiar reptilian gaze. He pulled back his hair from his forehead and showed a prominent tattoo.

"I received my mark this morning," he said proudly. "We'll be back right after this message."

As I sat in the Court of the Gentiles, I knew I needed to leave while I still could, but immediately God gave me another vision. In this one, the scene was familiar. I was looking at the room that housed the stargate that Shale and I used when we traveled to the first century. Hidden underneath the Old City, it was also the command center for believers until the rapture.

I didn't see anyone, and the only sound I could hear was the humming of abandoned computers. Clothes were strewn about, some lying in heaps on the floor, and others were draped on chairs. Eyeglasses and watches lay on desks. A thief could have made a fortune on the black market. However, the people left behind didn't know the room existed.

I heard a noise, and the camera panned to a woman sweeping the floor. I was wrong. Someone did know about the room—my sister, Martha. Tears were rolling down her cheeks. She prayed, "Lord, I know now Prince Adonikam isn't the Messiah. If Yeshua is the Messiah, make that clear to me. I want to believe he is, but how can I know?"

I noticed something caught her attention, and she stopped sweeping. She walked over to one of the computers, and next to it was a Bible. She picked it up and opened it. Light entered her eyes, and I knew in my heart the Holy Spirit was speaking to her. I choked up—I wished I could be with her.

Martha pulled the chair out from the desk and sat with the Bible in her lap.

I prayed, "Dear Lord, help her to make it to Petra before it's too late."

CHAPTER 52

I'd seen enough. I wanted to go to my sister, and this might be my only chance. I wouldn't count the cost of capture. The Old City was nearby. If I could make it to the underground, the stargate might be operational. My thoughts jumped ahead to possibilities. I could arrange for Martha to get to Petra. I could find out if my mother was still alive.

As I quickly left the Temple Mount, I heard the familiar sounds of horses and chariot wheels. When I looked up, a fiery chariot pulled by white horses was coming out of the seventh dimension. Did God have other plans? No one else seemed to see the visitor. When he landed on the ground, I recognized Clarence as the driver, and he motioned for me get in.

"So you're also a charioteer," I quipped.

He flipped the reins. "Yes, indeed. Your desire here, Daniel, is too treacherous. Why should you die before your time? I must take you myself. The enemy knows his days are numbered."

"Where?"

"I'm taking you to Ma'loula. You will find followers hidden in the cleft of the rock. They need your leadership."

Ma'loula—one of the places my father did business, and his family lived there in the recent past. I was afraid to ask if my dad was there.

However, the angel could read my mind. "You will not be disappointed."

As we soared into the heavens, I saw two holy men dressed in sackcloth preaching on the city streets. "The disasters coming upon the world are the end time judgments of God. Flee from the wrath to come. Go to Petra. Come down from the rooftops without delay. The false Messiah has desecrated the Third Temple. Believe in Yeshua Hamashiach and repent…"

As we left Jerusalem and approached interdimensional travel, I noticed in the distance around Israel's borders thousands of troops and tanks gathering. The abomination having been committed, desolations were about to follow.

I prayed, "My people, through whom salvation came, open your eyes. See the glory of the risen Lord. Yeshua Hamashiach, lives. He lives in me and he can live in you."

As I'd come to know all too well, time is an illusion, and often God's appointed times had shortcuts. I didn't know how I arrived in Syria. My first awareness was when I heard a voice behind me.

"Hold up your hands," the man demanded.

I did as instructed.

I thought he was holding a gun, but when I looked closer, I saw a flashlight.

"What do you want?" the man asked.

I wasn't sure where I was. "I'm looking for my father in Ma'loula."

The man lowered the flashlight. "A Jew speaking Hebrew? I haven't seen a Jew in these parts since ISIS. You are either very brave or very stupid."

"My father came here from Nepal several years ago. That was the last time we heard from him."

"Much of Syria has been destroyed. I can assure you he either died or left. The only ones here are the insane, the nuked, and the missionaries."

What category did that put this guy in? Was he speaking Hebrew or Arabic? How could I even know?

The man said, "No one would believe me if I told them I found a Jew outside my shop, or what used to be my shop."

"Sorry for trespassing."

The man mumbled something under his breath that I couldn't hear, adding, "You need to stay off the streets. There is no food, and those savages out there will eat you."

The guy didn't make any threatening move toward me. I wasn't sure if he was a friend or an enemy.

"Stay here," the man said. "You can sleep in my shop, but you should leave first thing in the morning. There's an abandoned Russian tank a short distance up the road from here that has fuel in it. It might be enough to get you to Ma'loula."

All things considered, that was very gracious. "Thank you."

The man started toward a stone building, dragging his left foot. I followed. He unlocked the door and pushed it open with a great effort. "I don't have any food I can share, but God's food is more nourishing in these last days anyway."

"God bless you," I said as he left.

The man paused, as if he was going to say something. Then thinking better of it, he left without uttering another word.

I watched him through the window as he disappeared.

CHAPTER 53

The next morning, I left the abandoned building and started looking for a Russian tank. Anything with wheels would get me to Ma'loula quicker than walking—and would be safer. I wanted to thank the man for letting me stay, but I didn't see him.

The day was neither light nor dark, but once again, something in between. Even that didn't affect my mood. When was the last time I had seen my father? The only thing that could make today better would be to have Shale and Shira with me.

The area was deserted. The few buildings that remained were empty shells. I reached the paved road and would keep walking until I came to a Russian tank. I saw nothing living, not even birds.

After I'd walked about half a mile, two men on the other side of the road approached. They held out their hands, but I didn't have any food. The road took a sharp turn, and when I came out of the fishbowl, I saw the abandoned tank. Skepticism plagued me. Could I even drive the thing? I climbed inside, and to my delight, the engine fired up immediately.

Soon I was creeping down the road in a Russian T-90 toward Ma'loula. After the initial excitement, several uneventful moments followed. Then I saw two men. As I passed them, they didn't give the tank a second thought. Years of fighting robbed them of normalcy. They didn't care.

The paved road was full of potholes. I passed more bombed-out buildings wasted by war until I came to the top of a hill and saw several men running—unusual for these parts. I slowed down to see why. About a half dozen Chimera were chasing them.

I maneuvered my way in front of the Frankensteins and prayed, "Yeshua, help the men to get away." My interference would give the fleeing humans a chance to escape. The hybrids scurried in the other direction, and after a few moments of constructive chaos, the humans were out of sight. I was exhausted. My emotional and physical energy spent, hunger intruded.

It took me about an hour to reach the outskirts of Ma'loula. The small town was built into the side of the mountain. I left the tank a little ways down the mountain. I'd walk the rest of the way. Many of the buildings were still standing, but I saw no one. I hiked up the steep road that hugged the mountainside. Clothes, dangling off porch railings, flapped in the wind. As I walked, I peered into windows and through doorways. A surprising number were open, but I didn't see anyone.

I was about to give up when I saw two women sitting on a doorstep. They wore scarves over their heads and looked to be in their thirties. I asked them in Hebrew if they knew my father, Aviv Sperling. Blank eyes stared back at me. They didn't understand.

As I walked away, I lamented how pathetic my Arabic was. How could I talk to the people here? Then God reminded me Ma'loula is one of the few places where people still speak Aramaic. I knew Aramaic. Excitement filled my heart. Should I go back and speak to the two women again? I decided not to. I'd look for someone else.

As I walked, my hunger increased. I trekked for over an hour up and down the mountain searching for people. The village was quiet. The gentle breeze would occasionally kick up a gust of wind. Without flowers, insects had no food. Without pollination, the trees were bare. Of course, the fact that Ma'loula had any trees at all was a miracle.

When I was about ready to give up, I saw two men walking along the street. I ran up to them and asked in Aramaic if they knew my father.

"Sorry, I don't recognize that name," one of them said. The other man shook his head.

Malaise filled their persona. Discouraged at my lack of success, I walked away. My father's family had lived in this village for several generations. I needed to keep looking.

I prayed. "Yeshua, please give me a word of knowledge."

CHAPTER 54

I heard a high-pitched shrill behind me and felt wings fluttering near my head. "My God, am I being attacked by one of those supernatural locusts?"

I soon realized it was a bird as I felt pecking on the back of my head. I covered myself and ran, shouting a few choice words. The bird followed me as I tripped on the uneven walkways. There wasn't a soul anywhere. The Russian tank was too far away—I'd never make it there. I could pull out the laser sword, but that seemed overkill, plus the last time I tried to use it, it didn't work. No wonder no one was on the streets with these creatures flying around.

I was afraid to look to the left or right. It might poke out my eyes. Could no one else hear the high-pitched shrills? The incessant pecking continued. I brushed my fingers through my hair, and blood tinged my fingertips.

The creature whispered. "Your blood is sweet."

This wasn't an ordinary bird—he was demonic. I ran through the abandoned town going toward the Russian tank when I stumbled upon an ancient monastery. If the door was unlocked, I could hide in there. No demon would want to enter a place of worship.

Much of the monastery property was defaced as a result of ISIS, and saintly statues, icons, and crosses lay scattered on the ground. Climbing up three flights to the entrance would exhaust me. Between hunger pangs and blood loss, I felt woozy. Every step up felt like a step into eternity.

Why is it we forget to pray until we're at the end of ourselves? I threw up a prayer, and I felt God's strength energizing me. When I reached the top, I squeezed through the door and slammed it shut. The noise was loud enough to wake the dead.

When my eyes adjusted to the darkness, I found myself in a small vestibule that opened into a foyer. I went into the foyer that was the doorway to a larger area. I peeked around the door and noticed a few people in a huddle. I pulled back. What should I do? I was surprised they didn't hear the door slam.

Then I heard singing—the sweet sound of voices. I peeked into the room again, and hanging on the walls were religious symbols and Christian paintings. In the nave was a center aisle, and on each side were wooden benches. Behind the pulpit, a crucifix and artwork decorated the front of the chapel.

The people were dressed like Westerners. A priest stood in front of them on an ambo. Suddenly the priest saw me in the doorway. He stopped the service and walked up to me. I tried to regain my composure, but blood was dripping from my head, and I was exhausted and hungry.

When he drew closer, I saw a cross draped around his neck. He extended his hand, and I reached out to shake his.

I introduced myself. "I'm Daniel Sperling."

The man smiled. "The Lord told me someone was coming today from far away. Just now, we have been praying for you."

I glanced at the worshippers and then noticed my blood on the parishioner's hand. "I'm sorry about the blood. Something attacked me."

He smiled. "No need to apologize."

"I'm from Jerusalem," I said, "and I'm looking for my father, Aviv Sperling. Do you know him?"

"Aviv is your father?" the priest asked.

"Yes." I started to explain more, but he interrupted me.

The man smiled. "My name is Yarpov, and I know your father. In fact, you and he speak with the same Aramaic accent."

I felt goosebumps come up on my skin. Overcome with emotion and exhaustion, I didn't have the strength to reply.

"Sit here," the man said, "before you faint."

Yarpov spoke to one of the women in the congregation. "Sue, can you come take a look at Daniel's head? I think one of the birds got to him."

Yarpov focused his eyes on me reassuringly. "Just relax for a minute, Son, and I'll share the wonderful story of your father."

Sue quickly cleaned me up and provided a washcloth for me to wipe off my hands. "Your blood pressure is low," she said. "When is the last time you ate something or drank water?"

I bit my lip. Too much had happened and my ability to focus was poor. "I don't remember."

She finished up and said, "I'll need to change the dressing once the bleeding stops. It's superficial. You were lucky. I've seen some a lot nastier than yours."

"Why are they attacking?"

Yarpov produced a Bible from the deep pocket of his cassock.

"You've a Bible?"

He spoke gently. "Because of radiation, no one comes up here to confiscate the Bibles. We have extras for anyone who asks."

"I'd love one."

Yarpov spoke to another parishioner. "Can you give Daniel one of those Bibles we have in the pews?"

I examined the front and back and ran my finger along its spine. Then I opened it to a random page and kissed it. "Thank you."

"So you haven't owned a Bible in quite a while, it seems."

"You can't appreciate the Scriptures until you no longer have them."

"I understand," Yarpov said. "That's why it's good to memorize verses, so they're written on your heart. No one can take away what's inside your soul."

As I reflected on his words, he continued. "To answer your first question about the animal attacks, and then I'll tell you all about your father, let me read to you Ezekiel 5:17: 'I will send upon you famine and evil beasts, and they shall bereave thee, and pestilence and blood shall pass through thee, and I will bring the sword upon thee. I, the Lord, have spoken it.'"

I nodded. "Even the Old Testament spoke of the end times."

Another young woman arrived with bread and water and placed them in front of me.

"Thank you. You don't know how much I appreciate it."

She smiled and left Yarpov and me alone to talk. Soft instrumental worship music played from the chapel. For the first time in a while, I felt peace and strength returning as I ate, but I was still at a loss for words. After years of searching for my father, to believe I was nearing the end of my quest seemed too good to be true. My biggest fear was disappointment. Yarpov didn't say if he was alive."

"What do you know about my father?"

CHAPTER 55

The priest reminded me of what anyone would want in a grandfather—someone willing to listen to a story with great patience. He leaned into me. "Your father was a great man, so great that when the rapture happened, he was taken."

"So—my father is in heaven?" I asked.

Yarpov laughed. "Don't look so disappointed. He waved his hand toward the parlor. "Many of those people you see are believers because of your father."

He made it sound like many people. "I've seen about six."

Yarpov's smile froze. "Six people, that's all you see?"

"Are there more?"

He chuckled. "Are they more? I'll show you."

The priest motioned for me to follow him into the adjoining room. God opened my eyes, and I saw three or four dozen people.

We walked down the nave past the wooden benches toward the front.

"Look up," Yarpov said.

I did as Yarpov said, and I saw an open window to heaven. The worshippers in the chapel were worshipping with the redeemed in heaven. God's kingdom was already here.

"So God used my father for his glory," I said, quite proud to be called his son.

"Yes, indeed," said Yarpov.

"I want to hear everything you know. Anything you can remember, please tell me."

"Come this way," Yarpov said.

I followed him to a small room off the side where congregants could pray with the priest in private.

Once we were seated, Yarpov began. "First, let me tell you about Ma'loula. You have a rich ancestral heritage. The whole world does—they just don't know about Ma'loula.

"When ISIS overran Ma'loula, they damaged this monastery as well as Mar Taqla, the Greek Orthodox Monastery. ISIS controlled this area and retained control until 2014 when the Syrian army was able to win it back.

"Thousands fled. Many were killed, but ISIS still held a large swath of territory. The United States sent more troops and obliterated the caliphate ISIS built. The U.S. took control of the lands ISIS mowed down, and they returned control to the local people. As you know, being a Jew, without land, you have no caliphate. When the Ezekiel War broke out, Ma'loula escaped the worst of it."

Sadness covered the priest's face. "After the Syrian army won Ma'loula back, your father arrived. A few people knew him from business dealings. That's when I met him for the first time.

"Since Mar Sarkis is one of the two monasteries still standing, and St. Sergius is the oldest chapel, dating back to before the Council of Nicea, your father came here and shared his testimony. Not many Jews, at least back then, believed Yeshua was the Messiah."

"What did he tell you when he first came?"

"He told me he was a Jew. He said his family lived in Ma'loula until the 1970s when almost all of them moved to Jordan. He said he went to Jerusalem, but he kept close ties to the area because of his business dealings—in textiles, I believe."

I nodded.

Yarpov rubbed his neck. "Yes, I remember now. Your father was returning from Nepal, where he was imprisoned for a couple of years by terrorists who worked for a secret elite organization—I don't think he knew who they were—but he came into possession of some scrolls. These men kidnapped him for the manuscripts.

"When your father refused to turn them over, they left him to die in a castle. One day a white dog visited him. The dog brought him food, and each day he came, he gnawed on the rope and eventually set him free."

Yarpov paused for a second.

"A white dog?" I repeated. Could it be Much-Afraid? If so, God rescued my father with Shale's dog. Our lives were so intertwined, as if God planned it that way from the beginning. There were no coincidences in heaven.

"Yes, and this is where it gets interesting. God told me in a dream to expect a visitor. I believe God was referring to you. To find out you are Aviv's son is most amazing."

I nodded. "However, I'm surprised my dad would come inside a church."

Yarpov jumped on my words. "Yes, I'm getting to the best part. He told me these scrolls were older than any other scrolls, except the Dead Sea Scrolls where they were found, and they're the oldest scrolls that speak about Jesus. That's what made them so valuable, and they were written in English. No one could explain that.

"He told me he didn't appreciate their real significance in the beginning. To him, they were just another antiquity, although he did question how they could be written in English. He believed they were a forgery, but why would scientists or anybody want them if they were a forgery?

"When the dog rescued your father, he thought God was speaking to him. The scrolls were addressed 'Dear Dog,' and then a dog saved him. That was a sign to Aviv that Yeshua must be the promised Messiah, as written in the scrolls, and God sent the dog the scrolls were written to—to rescue him."

Yarpov's words brought tears to my eyes.

"You don't know this?" Yarpov asked.

"No. We thought my dad had died. That's what the Israeli authorities told us."

Yarpov assured me. "No, your father is very much alive"—he pointed his finger toward heaven—"up there. When he saw all the suffering here, he stayed. He told outsiders he was a Christian to hide his Jewishness. By that time, there was little contact with the outside world, no cellphone service because of the war, but he stayed to witness to the Muslims and anyone else that would listen."

Yarpov smiled as he remembered my father. "People didn't know what to make of Aviv, especially those who knew he was Jewish. A few people became believers while he was here, but when the rapture happened, and he was taken, many who heard his testimony and had not believed accepted Jesus."

I pointed at Yarpov. "Why weren't you taken in the rapture?"

The priest bowed his head. "I was a good Catholic priest, but I didn't believe Jesus was the only way to heaven. I thought I could get there by my good works. I was mistaken, as are many Catholics. The only way to heaven is to confess our sin, repent, and believe in Jesus.

"I thought too highly of myself. When the rapture came, I was left behind. I wasn't ready. Because of my errant teaching about good works, many in my congregation were left behind also. When your father was taken, and we were left, our error was made clear. Your father's testimony that Yeshua was the only way to heaven helped all of us to see the truth."

CHAPTER 56

Yarpov shared his favorite memories about my father as well as the painful ones—the shelling and bombing, and the heartbreaking accounts of children who were injured or killed. The blessing in all that horror was the children were now with Yeshua.

"Most of the world isn't aware of the real story of Syria," Yarpov said. "Once there were thirty-two churches here. Now there're two, this one and Mar Takla."

"Do you still get visitors?"

Yarpov nodded. "In fact, we do, because we provide a meal once a day to the people in Ma'loula and those in the surrounding area who come. You can't reach a person's heart with spiritual food if he's physically hungry."

I glanced around the chapel. Scrawled across one of the walls were the words, "Martyrs of Syria." Dozens of names were listed. Paintings hung on the rest of the walls. "How old are the paintings?"

"Some of them are a thousand years old. It's surprising any survived."

I didn't see any stoves, ovens, refrigerators, or food except for the loaves of bread. The priest must have noticed my puzzled look. "Do you have a question?

"How do you cook? I don't see a stove or fridge."

Yarpov smiled. "That's a secret, but I'll tell you. Yeshua provides it, once a day in the early evening."

"What do you mean?"

Yarpov crossed his arms. "The food appears, and there is always bread left for the next morning. We've never run out."

"Like the Israelites in the wilderness."

"Yes," Yarpov replied. "We're exiles relying on God, except for one difference."

"What's that?"

"We're too thankful to complain. We're eating the food of heaven, knowing our deliverance from exile will be soon, and we won't have to wait forty years."

Yarpov stood. "Let's go outside. I want to take you to the other monastery where a late convert has led many to Christ."

I followed Yarpov through the chapel, shaking hands with several congregants. To know that my father played a significant role in the conversion of many here filled me with joy.

We walked outside, and although the demonic bird was gone, the gloominess never left. With the days shortened and so much cloud cover, it was always chilly.

"Do you have cannibalism?" I asked.

Yarpov seemed surprised by my question. "Cannibalism?"

We were sitting at one of the stone tables by the monastery as I admired the Qalamun Mountain Range that ran along Syria's border with Lebanon. Nearby, the Safir Hotel lay in ruins. "Yes. I saw it in Israel."

Yarpov appeared choked up by my question. "I didn't realize it was that bad in other places. After the Ezekiel War, Damascus was unlivable. Syria suffered so much nuclear fallout, no one wanted to come here, so we've been isolated. I didn't realize God protected us from such wickedness."

We sat for a few minutes so Yarpov could catch his breath. When he was ready, he stood. "I hope you will come with me to Mar Takla."

I followed Yarpov along the meandering rocky streets, passing stunning rock walls along the way. "Do you know the story of St. Thecia?"

I shook my head.

"Mar Takla is a Greek Orthodox monastery built in honor of St. Thecia. She was the daughter of a Seleucid prince and became a believer when she heard Paul the Apostle's teachings.

"There are several levels. We'll need to climb to the top, but it's worth the climb. It's a modern church that feels ancient with a domed ceiling that covers the cave. Many miracles have been received here because of its healing waters."

Yarpov opened the door, and the monastery's immense size and beauty took my breath away. Even though the temple was damaged from extensive bombing, its sereneness remained. Someone had hand-painted the dome ceiling in colorful images. As was typical of Catholic worship, iconic drawings covered the walls around the pews. A dozen or more believers greeted us.

"Daniel, there is someone I want you to meet," Yarpov said.

I followed him to another area where a priest was praying with someone. When the cleric raised his head following the prayer, his face turned ashen when he saw me.

The surprise was mutual. "Nidal?"

Nidal embraced me. "Daniel."

CHAPTER 57

My world became surreal. As if awakening from a forgotten past, memories returned in blinding clarity—the races, the stolen money, the return trip from Eilat—how I wanted my nemesis charioteer to die near Jericho, how much I hated him in the seventh dimension, oh, how I struggled to forgive him.

I remembered how difficult it was to get him to the inn so Dr. Luke could bandage his wounds from when he was robbed—and save his life a second time. Suppose I'd let him die in the wadi? Suppose Shale and I didn't share Yeshua with him at Pentecost? All the people of Ma'loula whose lives he touched might never have heard about the Kingdom of God.

When Nidal ran away at Pentecost, I never imagined I would see him again. I never gave it a second thought he would heed my words. All these years later, a former Hindu turned Muslim turned Christian was now a priest.

Yarpov broke the stunned silence. "So you know each other?"

I nodded.

"What a surprise."

Nidal spoke first. "Can Daniel and I have a moment alone?"

"Of course, by all means," the priest said.

We walked outside the monastery and sat on a stone bench. I stared at Nidal. My father almost died at his hands. Maybe God saved his life because I forgave Nidal.

As if reading my thoughts, Nidal interrupted my musings. "You see, Daniel, your life touched mine. My life touched the lives of the people of Ma'loula. If you hadn't saved me in that wadi, I wouldn't have been here to share Jesus with the people of Ma'loula.

I shook my head in disbelief.

Nidal continued. "Shale's words in her infamous scrolls touched your father, and your father's testimony touched the lives of those he met, and those he touched then touched the lives of others."

I smiled. "Even Shale's father saved my life."

Nidal finished his thoughts with a profound statement. "God redeems. Isn't that the way it is? Despite all the heartbreak and mistakes we make, either willful or through ignorance, God reaches down and redeems what seems unredeemable."

"I can't add any wisdom to that, Nidal. You said it better than I could. But, tell me, how did you end up here?"

Nidal smiled. "When I heard the truth from the Apostle Peter, I wanted to return to the twenty-first century. Remember, I told you in the beginning I didn't want to come back. I wanted to keep racing chariots. Unlike you, I was foolish. When I was robbed, I wanted to race again for the money, but after God saved me at Pentecost, I didn't care about the money anymore.

"When Dr. Luke removed the tracker, I didn't know how to get back. However, it was a blessing. My handlers could no longer follow my movements, but I wanted to rescue your father, so I prayed.

"God answered my prayer. He told me to return to the inn, and he would send someone to help me. Jacob, the inn's owner, was God's answer. I learned he was from the future, and he helped me to return to my own time".

"However, when I went back to Perlsea Castle, your father was no longer there. The good part was the rope was in two pieces, so somehow he escaped.

"I tried to think where he would go. Since he was in Syria when we kidnapped him, I thought he might have returned, and he even mentioned Ma'loula a couple of times as a place where he did business. Meanwhile, something pretty significant happened while I was in the first century."

"What's that?"

"The rapture took place. When I arrived in the outskirts of Syria in the twenty-first century, few people remained. Some died in the Ezekiel War; others were ill with radiation sickness and disease.

"However, I asked everyone I met if they knew Aviv Sperling. Many did. His fame had spread among the churches. I heard story after story how he befriended the Syrian people and brought Jesus to those who lived in darkness. Many believed because of his testimony and were taken in the rapture. Many became believers after he was gone.

"Those left behind were searching. The Syrian people wanted to know where all those people went. I heard some crazy stories—like aliens came and took the wackos and left the good people on earth. People wanted the truth. Most rejected those ridiculous stories.

"You have to remember, in Islam, there is no forgiveness, so people were trying even harder to earn their way to heaven. But it's impossible —it's a self-fulfilling prophecy. No one can be that good. Only Jesus is good, and I saw with my own eyes what happened at Pentecost."

"So you stayed here?"

Nidal smiled. "Yes. As a former Hindu turned Muslim turned Christian, my testimony was powerful. If God could reach me, God could reach anybody. Over the last two years, hundreds from surrounding towns have come to Ma'loula. This place has always attracted those who were spiritually searching. People come for food. We give them that and spiritual manna."

"Did you know Tariq isn't human? He's a humanoid. Did you know that?"

Nidal shook his head. "No, but he was heartless. No conscience."

We sat for a few minutes in silence. Then I recalled something Nidal said. "Jacob, the man who brought you back to the twenty-first century, is my brother."

"Jacob from the inn, he's your brother?"

I nodded.

Nidal chuckled. "I didn't know."

I stood. "Let's we go inside. I'm sure Yarpov would love to hear our story."

"God's story," Nidal corrected me.

I couldn't wait to share it with Shale.

CHAPTER 58

"Nidal, come here," a man shouted through the open door. He took off toward Mar Takla. As he ran, my eyes were drawn to his feet. They were moving in slow motion, leaving behind pebbles that floated in the air. I stepped forward, and an angel appeared in a chariot with his sword drawn.

"Never forget God has given you his weapon," the angel shouted. "The powers of darkness are rising, but we're advancing God's kingdom blow by blow. Come with me."

I touched my light saber and I climbed in. "The last time I tried to use it, it didn't work. Will it work now?"

"Rest assured, it will work now," the angel replied.

Once again, the horses took us beyond the boundaries of earth, and I saw the bejeweled decks of light and heard the heartbeats of millions of angels. The glory of the King filled the second heaven. Even the horses anticipated victory as their ears strained forward. Snakes lunged out at us, and their forked tongues swayed clumsily back and forth.

"No fear," the angel shouted. "No fear."

I pulled out my laser sword and thrust it toward the enemy. Green blood spewed forth, and one of them fell into the abyss. Out of the darkness came more demons. Laser weapons lighted up the heavens as the light and dark angels clashed. God's angelic warriors, the defenders of God's throne, fought hard against Satan's minions.

New arrivals strengthened God's kingdom. Lightsabers lit up the celestial city as God's army advanced. Outnumbered three to one, one by one, the dark angels fell. The trumpet sounded. The serpents, snakes, and demonic creatures, subdued, met their fate in Shambhala.

The thunders of heaven spoke. "Prepare the way of the Lord."

The angel shouted, "Remember who made you and for whom you were made."

The drumbeats became more distinct as we drew nearer the lights of heaven. The stringed instruments called my name. I remembered the beautiful garden, the magnificent fountains of living water, the sweet songs of the birds of heaven, and the colorful flowers in their radiant glory. I wanted to be in the midst of trees of divine gifts. I wanted to be reunited with Shale and Shira in the garden of my King. I longed to take my bride by the hand, hold her in my arms, and kiss her lips.

A voice interrupted my thoughts. "We're nearing the Kingdom of God. The demons will try to stop you."

"Gird your loins to fight for the King," another angel shouted.

The powerful hindquarters of the horses exploded as God called them onward. Yeshua's glory could not be stopped or contained. The winds of heaven breathed on me and gave me strength.

"Hurry," I shouted. "Come, Lord Jesus."

"Remember, the battle belongs to the Lord," a voice declared.

I saw another vision of a shattered world consumed with wickedness. Clouds cleared and a window opened to my soul. I needed God's love to cover my scars. Everything needed healing, including me. I wasn't drawing near to heaven—it was drawing near to me.

The white steeds drew closer to heaven's gates. I saw Shale in the garden. Then the angel pulled back the horses.

"I don't want to return," I said. "Can we not go to the garden?"

"You must go to Yarpov," the angel said. "Tell him everyone must leave Ma'loula and travel to Petra. God wants to save all who believe and extend his mercy to those who have not made a decision, but time is running out. The judgments are coming. Don't waste a moment. Everyone must leave as soon as possible to escape the wrath of God."

And just like that, I was back— standing in front of the door to Mar Takla. I took in a deep breath. I wanted to be in the presence of the Lord. I wanted to be in Shale's arms and take her hand in marriage.

I bowed my head in submission—I still needed to learn how to love my Lord better. I needed to occupy until that day. I asked my Lord, "Will the people of Ma'loula listen to me?"

CHAPTER 59

I went inside and sat on one of the pews. Yarpov, all smiles, walked over to me. "You must share this amazing reunion of you and Nidal with the others. Everyone would be encouraged, even those who doubt God's goodness. Longsuffering is hard for those new in the faith."

His unabashed warmth was reassuring, putting into perspective God's plan even when we didn't understand. I motioned for him to join me. "Can I talk to you?"

"Sure." He sat beside me.

"Yarpov, God has provided for all your needs in Ma'loula. God has protected the believers here, but that's about to change."

Yarpov frowned. "What do you mean?"

"You're no longer safe. We must get everyone to Petra as soon as possible."

The Catholic priest stood and shook his head. "Unless I hear God speak such things to me, I would not put my flock's life in danger to make such a dangerous trek—right through the heart of nuclear fallout —to Damascus, Mount Hermon, the Golan Heights. I've heard too many stories of strange creatures wandering in the desert. The lost come here looking for refuge because Petra is a lot farther to travel.

They arrive exhausted. God has provided for us here. Why would that change now?"

I placed my hand on Yarpov's shoulder. "I understand your hesitancy, but I'm telling you what God told me. Soon nowhere will be safe except Petra. The Scriptures tell us that."

A few members from the congregation edged over. I could feel tensions rising.

"Go get Nidal," one of the listeners said.

Urgency was paramount, but to press too hard too soon would not be wise. "Could you pray about it?" I asked. "Ask God to give you a sign?"

"A sign for what?" someone asked.

Yarpov turned his focus to the questioner. "Daniel says all of us should leave Ma'loula and go to Petra."

"Petra? That's for the Jews, not Christians," another person commented.

I shook my head. "Not just the Jews. God has provided Petra as a fortress for everyone."

Another of the congregants spoke up. "Daniel, you come here and tell us things as if God speaks to you and doesn't speak to us. He has protected us here for three years. You're young—well-meaning but perhaps misguided."

Another person added, "We have a direct doorway to heaven. God is here. He will not abandon us. I'm staying."

The discussion became heated as more people weighed in. Nidal entered the sanctuary and pulled me away from the others. "Daniel, is this something God told you?"

I nodded. "Yes. God impressed on me time is short. The people of Ma'loua must leave as soon as possible."

The discussion ended with Yarpov telling everyone to pray. "We'll resume discussion in a few days," he said.

A week passed with no decision being made. I noticed the shortened days were now even shorter. That meant safe passage would be more difficult with less daylight for traveling. I needed to convince Yarpov because the people of Ma'loula would listen to him and not to me. I had also noticed Yarpov's worship was still wrapped up in Catholic rituals, dogma, and tradition. I didn't doubt he was a believer, I knew that he was, but he carried much baggage from the past that could be redeemed if he prayed about it.

Nevertheless, God continued to provide each day. I began to doubt if I heard from God or if I misunderstood what the angel told me. Was Petra a hiding place only for the Jews? I didn't think so. I saw Christians in Petra. I talked to Nidal, but I couldn't convince him. Each day that passed without us leaving was one day less we would have to make it to Petra.

Ten Days Later

I heard shouts from a woman in the kitchen. "No, God, no." Within seconds, she ran into the sanctuary. "The water has turned to blood!"

The windows of the monastery rattled. I ran to the door and opened it. Frogs were falling from the sky. Others joined me at the doorway, and horrified screams filled the foyer.

One of the men flashed his eyes at me. "This is your fault. You brought this on us with your words of satanic prophecy."

Horrified by his accusation, I let go of the door and stepped back. The door flew open, and frogs poured into the foyer.

"Shut the door," someone shouted.

After slamming the door, the frogs that jumped inside hopped onto the man who verbally assaulted me. Sweet revenge was my first inclination until God's love prompted me to repent.

"Get them off before they kill him," I ordered.

Everyone was afraid, so I pulled them off the man and threw them into a discarded bucket. After several minutes, once we knew we found them all, Nidal took them away.

The man who accused me, humbled and scared, apologized. "I'm sorry. I didn't mean what I said."

"This must be the work of the two witnesses," Nidal said.

"How do we know if they're here?" Yarpov asked. "Without any outside contact, we don't know what's happening."

"I saw them," I said. "The two witnesses are in Jerusalem."

One of the women ran up to Yarpov trying to get his attention. "You must come into the sanctuary," she urged.

We ran into the room, and she pointed at the ceiling. "Look."

CHAPTER 60

Yarpov girded his loins and fell to his knees. "The Day of the Lord is here."

I offered words of comfort. "Even though God has closed the storehouse of his provision, his offerings won't cease. However, we must leave as soon as possible."

As I was speaking, the door flew open and howling wind gushed inside. An old painting fell off the wall, and broken glass clinked as it hit the floor. The cold wind pierced my skin—it wasn't just cold. It was supernaturally cold.

"Yarpov," a man shouted as he rushed inside, "fires have sprung up all over Ma'loula."

Others from Ma'loula arrived weeping and crying.

"Fire is razing our land," a woman said.

"What do you mean?" someone asked.

"Fires are burning around Ma'loula destroying our little harvest. It's all perishing."

"A plague has hit Ma'loula," Nidal said. "The land is becoming desolate, and our provisions are cut off. The plagues have reached us. We'll not be spared as I'd hoped."

I stood and addressed everyone. "All of you listen to me, please.

God isolated you here as a witness. You know what's happening. People from the surrounding area have told you. The two witnesses are sending the plagues to encourage the Jews to flee to Petra while they still have time. Once Prince Adonikam realizes he can't get to the Jews at Petra, he'll turn on the Christians and martyr them. Christians are fleeing to Petra as well. I saw the supplies provided by God. There is plenty of food for everyone.

"I was in Jerusalem when Prince Adonikam defiled the Temple. The Bible tells us when the desecration takes place, the Jews and believers must flee to Petra."

Yarpov spoke to the gathering group. "We must sanctify ourselves and call a solemn assembly. We'll gather for prayer and pack and meet here as soon as everyone is able."

Yarpov focused his eyes on me. "Daniel, God sent you here to warn us, and we didn't listen. Now we'll go to Petra. We'll trust God to bring us there."

I clasped Yarpov's shoulder. "Remember what Yeshua said when the people saw the abomination?"

His eyes lit up. "He told those in Judea to flee into the mountains."

"Not to waste time packing," I added.

"No more delay," Yarpov said. He clapped his hands to get everyone's attention. "We're going to leave immediately. We'll pray as we flee."

A woman ran up to Yarpov. "Nooda just delivered her baby a few days ago. How will she make it? It's a long journey, two weeks or more. Can't we wait a few days? The baby is well, but Nooda is weak. She's not well enough to travel such a long ways."

I interrupted. "Every hour we delay puts everyone at risk. Yarpov is right."

Panic filled her eyes.

I glanced at Yarpov.

"It's okay, Uri," Yarpov comforted her. "We'll all help with the baby and Nooda."

Uri backed away from Yarpov grumbling under her breath as she walked toward the door.

Yarpov moved closer to me and whispered, "Daniel, I need your help—"

Someone caught Yarpov's attention, and he disengaged from me.

"Zain?" He rushed toward the front. "Zain, you and Daniel search the buildings. You know where our people live. Take Daniel with you. We'll meet back here within the hour. Make sure no one packs."

Nightfall arrived. This couldn't have been a more dangerous time to travel. I looked up at the darkened sky. Only two-thirds of the stars were shining, and all the constellations were out of proper alignment. The desert looked the same in all directions. Compasses no longer worked because of the polar shift. How would Yarpov know which way to go?

Women outnumbered men three to one. Yarprov divided everyone into groups of ten and paired each person up with someone they knew. Altogether, there were seven groups. Yarprov, Nidal, Zain, and I led four of them.

I couldn't remember a time when I felt more vulnerable. As we left Ma'loula, it looked like a ghost town wrapped in smoke. The icy air dissipated as we traveled giving me a tiny shred of hope we could make it and not freeze to death.

We walked for seven hours straight without a single complaint when we came to an abandoned well. Yarpov drew water, and one of the men found extra rations hidden in a cave. Soldiers had used the area as a staging ground during the war.

We rested for a few hours. I noted nights were lasting about sixteen hours as the days were getting shorter. I remembered something Yeshua said to his disciples shortly before his crucifixion. If the days were not cut short before his return, no flesh would survive, but for the elect's sake, they would be shortened.

We saw no one over the next two weeks. Not even a car passed us. The war caused many to move away, and of those who stayed, most probably died from radiation exposure. Many hastily dug graves haunted our trip. Since Muslims treated dead bodies with respect, at least the bodies were buried—I could only hope their departed souls were in heaven.

Once we crossed the border into Jordan, we wouldn't have that much farther to travel. However, to think testing wouldn't come was farfetched, and when it did, I couldn't have imagined the consequences.

CHAPTER 61

An explosion awakened me, and frantic cries came from all directions. I tore open my eyes and scrambled to my feet. Were we being attacked? It sounded like a bomb. No one seemed to know. I ran around checking on my small group, but I could only find a handful of them. I noticed fire, and thick, black smoke covered a sizable area nearby. Several brave men were running toward it as women were scrambling away. I saw others hiding under whatever they could find.

As I darted after the men, I checked the sky for drones or aircraft, but I saw nothing. I caught up with them looking for answers. They slowed down as they eased their way into the saltbushes.

One of them, Eli, a group leader, spoke. "Yarpov, you're a man of the cloth. Wait here, as well as the rest of you. Let me check it out. I think I know what it is."

We all agreed to stay back and let Eli go by himself. A few minutes passed. I read his mind and hoped it wasn't what he thought.

He returned a few minutes later with his head bowed. "One of the men went off to relieve himself and stepped on a landmine. There is nothing we can do for him."

"Who was it?" Yarpov asked.

"Who are we missing?" someone else asked.

"Zain," Eli replied. "It was Zain."

We all lowered our heads. Zain was one of our leaders.

"We should bury him," Yarprov said.

Eli shook his head. "There is nothing to bury."

Yarprov's eyes watered. "We'll meet with the others and pray, thanking God for his life."

"Yarprov," Eli said, "we need to leave this area as soon as we've prayed. If there're any enemies around, even wild animals, the smoke and sound have alerted them to our presence. We aren't safe."

Yarprov nodded. "Eli and Daniel, take six of the ten that were in his group and add three each to your group. The remaining four can be added to mine."

We returned and shared the news. With heavy hearts, we took off, but we hadn't gone much farther when I heard the sound of chariots. It seemed as if everyone heard it, not just me, but no one else raced chariots besides me. It wasn't chariots.

They came upon us like bullets out of nowhere. The demonic creatures flew on the wings of supernatural locusts, appearing and disappearing in and out of the first and second heaven.

The attack was immediate and unanticipated as they whizzed by us. I couldn't believe how much bigger the locusts were than when I had first seen them pouring out of the hole in the Red Sea. Their wingspan was about a meter now, maybe more, and their bodies looked like miniature horses.

I remembered the crowns, the hideous golden crowns that glowed in the water. Their contorted, smooth faces under water were even more grotesque on land. They were Frankensteins— evil, nightmarish creatures from hell.

The wings fluttered like the din of racing chariots and horses plunging into battle. I saw them underwater the first time, but here, as they flew in and out of our ragtag group, they were hunting. One buzzed right in my face, a feminine face staring straight into my eyes, with hair as long as icicles, snorting at me before she peeled away.

The creature was so close to me, I could smell sulfur on her breath.

I saw the stinger on the back of the tail and slashed it with my sword. "It is by grace we're saved through faith. Blessed is the name of the Lord, Jesus Christ."

The creature howled and took off without a tail. I knew I couldn't kill her, but I could make her miserable and force her to flee.

I was sick at heart. When the locust stung a person, the demon slipped inside the victim's body. To my dismay, several in our group were hurt. They howled in unbearable pain, and demon possession followed.

Within minutes, the locusts were gone, similar to when I saw them disappear over the Red Sea sky. Silence followed except for the heart-wrenching wails.

Even now, however, I knew the unbelievers could be saved. If they called on the name of Yeshua, the demons would be forced to flee and their pain would end.

Great confusion filled the people. No one understood what happened or why certain ones were stung and not others. Yarpov was up front. I was in the back, and I rushed up to him.

He sat on the ground, so stunned he seemed inconsolable.

I squatted beside him. "It appears as if one or two in each group was stung." I placed my hand on his shoulder. "Do you know why?"

He nodded. "One of the trumpet judgments. I thought all who came with us were saved."

"If they confess Jesus as Lord, they'll be healed."

"They're already possessed."

"As one of the one hundred forty-four thousand Jews, I can cast out evil spirits, but the person must turn to Jesus and become a new creation in Christ."

Yarpov lifted his eyes. "Do it now."

I nodded. I explained to Nidal and Eli what happened and asked them to bring forward those stung. The victims were in such pain, they weren't hard to identify. We made a large circle and put ten people in the middle. We took turns praying over them.

One brave woman spoke. "You who were stung were masquerading as believers, eating with us, breaking bread with us. You tasted God's goodness but did not make him Lord of your life. Accept Jesus into your heart, acknowledge your sin, repent, and join us. Time is short. The judgments are coming. Don't harden your hearts. Don't delay."

I noticed the faces of those stung were turning gray. Their immense pain was to draw them to Jesus. One by one, as I prayed with them, they called upon the name of Jesus. I asked each one as I stood in front of them, "Do you accept Jesus into your heart?" All said yes until I got to the last person—a young woman.

The woman, having witnessed the other nine be healed, hardened her own heart. I looked into her eyes and saw the demon's eyes. I placed my hands on her and asked God to heal her, to have mercy on her, to call the beast out of her, but to no avail. She had been stung on her back and was bent over from pain.

A horde of flies flew into the midst of us. They swarmed around our gathering, and the circle broke up as people drew away to protect themselves. I flailed my hands to keep them off me until I realized they weren't coming after me. They were swarming around the woman.

She hollered, cussing under her breath to be left alone, but the flies were relentless. Soon they covered her entire body. They flew into her mouth and sneaked inside her clothes. She writhed on the ground as they bore into her nose and eyes. Her wails continued for a few more minutes, and then they ceased. She was dead.

No one said a word as everyone stared at the woman covered in flies. At last, someone spoke. "We should bury her."

Yarpov bowed his head as tears fell down his face. "She was my daughter."

CHAPTER 62

There were secrets no one knew, or if people did know, no one dared to talk about. Yarpov's confession drove home the sinfulness of all of us, a reminder that God's grace was sufficient, but pain would be part of our existence until Jesus returned. No one was immune. So now Yarpov grieved—he grieved for the daughter conceived in sin who chose to die in sin. Sadness overwhelmed me as she was about my age. It took me a while to get my focus back.

Two more days passed.

"Do you know how much farther it is to Petra?" I asked Yarpov.

"Two hundred twenty-five kilometers."

I calculated. "Nine more days?"

Yarpov nodded. "About."

We walked three more days, making good time, without any more incidents. We might get there in five if we hurried. We would walk until we came to a watering hole and stop to rest. God provided sustenance—fish, fruit, nuts, edible roots. One day we found an abandoned storehouse. The food we took lasted three days.

Day five a visitor came. No one doubted he was a supernatural being. He was too tall to be human, and far too muscular, and powerful. I was the first one to see him since I was with the last group to ensure no stragglers got left behind.

I saw him when he was still a ways off coming in from the northwest. At first, I saw a white dot streaking across the horizon. He covered a great deal of distance in a short amount of time.

I pulled out my sword given to me by the angels. The blade glistened even without natural sunlight. As he neared, the air became electrically charged. His power was disturbing. The wind kicked up energy particles that set off small fires.

Gasps arose, and our forward progression halted. No one moved. I couldn't swallow. The visitor's eyes focused on the sword, something he could not have anticipated hiding among God's people. The sword stood in the way of his mission. I thought I'd seen the worst of the fallen in Shambhala, but he appeared even more terrifying—and handsomely illusionary. Why did he seek us out now?

"My dear, beloved children," he said with beguiling affection, "did you not know you're headed in the wrong direction?"

"How do you know where we're going?" Yarpov asked, skepticism in his voice.

He replied reassuringly. "Why, my Lord, King Yeshua, sent me here. He was very concerned because you've veered off course. He wants you to get to Petra before it's too late. More judgments are coming, and if you don't change course, you won't make it."

Yarpov's eyes showed doubt.

I wasn't sure if he doubted himself or the demonic creature who was trying to correct him. From the beginning, I had wondered how Yarpov knew which way to go. Maybe he didn't. Perhaps we'd just been wandering in circles.

"Which way should we be going?" I asked.

"You're too far southeast. You need to go northwest." He pointed. "That way."

I edged over to Yarpov and whispered in his ear. "Are you sure we're going the right way?"

He shook his head. "I thought we were, but the terrain has changed a lot with the war, the earthquakes, and plagues. I'm not sure why we haven't seen the barrier. I wanted to go east of the Naseeb border and avoid the checkpoint. I'm…now I'm not sure."

Since the revelation of Yarpov's unconfessed sin, his devout followers seemed to hedge on trusting him. I found myself wondering since Yarpov was second-guessing himself. However, I wasn't willing to trust this supernatural being that did not look like an angel befitting the King of kings.

Murmurings picked up in the crowd. Doubt crept into everyone's thinking. Exhausted after walking for many days, no one wanted to walk a mile in the wrong direction—let alone many miles. The thought they might have done so was disheartening.

Nidal came up to me, keeping his eyes on the self-proclaimed benefactor. "What do you think, Daniel? Do you think he's right?"

"I think he's a demon."

"Why would he waste his time messing with us if he's a demon?"

At that point, the baby began to cry. The mother edged off to the side, away from the main grouping to calm down her little boy. Everyone was tired and didn't want to listen to him crying. I caught a glimpse of the messenger's lusty eyes latching onto the child. I knew that demons fed on blood, and innocent baby blood amped up their power.

Sharp, tired voices murmured. Yarpov appeared to be having a meltdown, and our apparent deliverer in a short amount of time had caused a great deal of division.

The towering creature raised his hands to get everyone's attention. "Don't you want to see King Yeshua? Why waste time. Yarpov is lost. Can you really trust him? After all, if he was a true follower of Yeshua, don't you think he would have told you about his daughter?"

Doubting eyes focused on Yarpov. I saw a great leader become smaller in one fell swoop. Whether it was an illusion cast on him by what I perceived to be a demon of immense size or our opinion of him diminished because we were surprised by his lack of confession as a Catholic priest, the end result was the same. Doubt filled everyone's hearts.

The self-proclaimed new leader turned to face me. "And here is

Daniel Sperling, a young, energetic man of God, but he isn't as perfect as he'd like you to believe."

He waved his hand, and in front of the weary travelers, a form of virtual reality lit up the desert. The scene played out for all to see—my slaying of Prince Adonikam with the very sword it appeared that I now held in my hand.

A shocked silence filled the air. The crowd backed away from me with eyes focused on my weapon.

"This man is a murderer—a murderer. Did you hear me? He slew the one God sent to redeem mankind."

Confusion filled the faces of those listening. "What do you mean?" someone asked.

The demon laughed. "Yeshua has proclaimed Prince Adonikam as the Mahdi after the prince received the cup of wrath. The prince's new name is Banu Hashim. He is the dragon, and Yeshua is his right-hand man. In fact, Yeshua is with Prince Hashim right now." The accuser pointed at me. "This young man murdered Prince Adonikam. Yeshua, the prophet, raised him from the dead."

Now I was confused. Was Yeshua another name for the Minister of Truth, Prophet Haman Urhammu?

As the beautiful creature talked, his appearance became more enchanting. He spoke in hypnotic eloquence. I wanted to believe him as I heard the voice wooing me in a direction I knew was wrong.

"You see," the tall, handsome angel said, "you haven't been in touch with the outside world in quite some time. This man has come to lead you astray. He's a murderer. Of course, he's not going to tell you the truth. He's a liar. There is no truth in him at all."

Eyes stared at me. This enchanter was winning over the hearts of the weak ones.

"Trust me," the angel of light said. He transformed himself from dark into light while we gazed. "If you continue to follow these two men, you'll never make it to Petra."

Seventy sets of bewildered, tired eyes focused on me. Did I need to defend myself? Yeshua remained silent like a lamb before slaughter. What should I do?

CHAPTER 63

I raised my hand to get Yarpov's attention. "The Word of God says we should test the spirits to see if they're from God."

Yarpov nodded. Murmurings from listeners showed agreement, although what the test should be set off another round of discussion. I already knew, however, what I would ask.

"May I proceed?"

The priest, overcome with guilt and uncertainty, waved his hand toward me in egregious surrender.

I edged closer to the dubious messenger, unabashed by his condescending smirk. "Do you confess that Yeshua Hamashiach, who came in the flesh two thousand years ago, was from God?"

The overconfident creature crooned. "Why talk about two thousand years ago? He's here now in Jerusalem. Come with me. Don't the Scriptures say, 'Come to me all you that labor and are heavy laden, and I will give your rest?'"

A young man whom I did not know strutted up to me. He held up his hand and pointed at the supernatural messenger. "I think we should go with him. He knows the Word of God."

Doubtful eyes questioned the young man's wisdom.

However, he was undeterred. "All of you listen. This messenger has shown us who Daniel is. He showed us that he killed the prince, and the prophet resurrected him. How can we believe anything Daniel says?"

Whispers ran amok. I wanted to defend myself, but what the people saw was damning. How could I refute it?

I tried. "Things aren't as they appear on that…recording. They used A.I. and trickery of the camera to record a trans-human committing a fake murder."

Everyone stared at me. These people did not know how far artificial intelligence had progressed while God protected them in Ma'loula.

After seeing he'd gained some traction, the worldly-wise man stepped up his arguments. "Maybe this leader in Jerusalem is the Antichrist. Maybe he isn't, but we know this man, Daniel, is a murderer. We saw what he did." He glanced at Yarpov. "And now we know about the failures of our leader."

I interrupted. "What you saw is a lie. That wasn't me, and it didn't happen that way."

The misguided man was undeterred. "We know this visitor is supernatural. He speaks with authority. Yes, the Bible says Jesus is coming back. He's coming back for us. We've been hidden away. Could Jesus not send an angel to rescue us from our wanderings?"

I interrupted again. "What's your name?"

His eyes narrowed. "You don't need to know my name."

Division escalated as the quarreling continued.

Was it possible for the elect to be deceived? I knew false Christs and false prophets would be rampant in the last days, showing great signs and wonders, but could the elect actually be deceived?

The creature's stature seemed to grow as the people's trust in him grew. More words spewed out of his foul mouth. "I'll take you to the Christ. He's in Jerusalem waiting to receive you. Why wait another minute? See him for yourself."

The deceiver skirted my question, but I perceived the longer I allowed this dark angel or demon to speak, the worse things would become. People would start to believe him. I held up my hand again. "Just a minute."

The murmurings stopped.

"I'll go with this supernatural creature, and if what he says is true, I'll come to Petra and bring you to Jerusalem. If I don't return, be glad you didn't come. Continue to Petra. You'll be safe. God promised he'd protect his people in the fortress."

A woman spoke up. "But he says we're going the wrong way. I'm tired, my legs ache. We've made it this far…"

I finished her sentence. "Yes, you've made it this far by the grace of God. He's protected you, right?"

"Why would you go with him if you think he's evil?" another asked.

I held up my sword. "Because I have this. God's sword of the spirit is with me."

"And God wouldn't be with us if we came also?"

Nidal raised his hand, and the people became quiet when he began to speak. "Listen to Daniel. He's one of the one hundred forty-four thousand Jewish evangelists. See his forehead? That's God's mark.

"I know this man, and he belongs to God. If it weren't for him, I'd be in hell. We're headed to Petra. I came this way when God sent me to Ma'loula. We must keep going."

Nidal pointed. "There're thousands of these jinns in Islam—at least that's what I believe he is. In Muslim theology, a false prophet comes claiming to be Jesus. He comes before Yeshua Hamashiach returns. The false prophet will tell everyone that he's Jesus, but not the Christ, and he has come to proclaim who the real Christ is.

"Ladies and Gentlemen, rest assured, Yeshua hasn't returned. When he does, everyone will see him."

Several minutes of debate ensued. Nidal, Yarpov and I exchanged glances. How long should we let the controversy continue?

Nidal walked over and put his hand on my shoulder. "God will protect Daniel. He has given Daniel the sword of the spirit. We saw how expertly he wielded it on the locusts. God's Word is with him. Let's do as he advised. Yarpov is our leader. None of us is perfect. Only Yeshua should occupy that pedestal in our hearts."

The messenger of darkness scorned Nidal's words, but I knew it was me he wanted. He was using everyone else as a pawn to manipulate the situation to his advantage. Now that I was willing to come with him, I perceived he didn't want the others, except to kill them. I couldn't let that happen.

I stepped up to the unholy messenger. "Will you let the others go if I come with you?"

Yarpov walked over and shook his head. "No, you're young. I'm old. Let me go."

"No, Yarpov. These people need you. God sent me for this purpose —to help you get to Petra. I'm ready to go home if my service to God is finished, but I know it's not. I also know this is God's calling on me as one of the one hundred forty-four thousand Jewish evangelists. Your calling is for the people of Ma'loula. Go with your people and serve them well. Finish well."

After a few more minutes of discussion, the issue was settled. The people would continue, based on Nidal's assurance they were headed to Petra, and I would go with the dark one. I waited and watched as the group of seventy continued on their way.

"God be with you," I prayed. Once they were off to a good start, I turned toward the evil one. "So, are you one of the four demons that was bound for a thousand years and released from the Euphrates River?"

CHAPTER 64

As the travelers from Ma'loula disappeared in the distance, the ground began to tremble. A vast dust bowl blew in from the north. Surprised by the suddenness, I gazed at the spectacular whirlwind and was dismayed to see strange apparitions appearing in the wind. The supernatural horsemen sped across the plains on the wings of the wind, and a trumpet sounded from heaven.

I'd seen the vile creatures in Shambhala. They wore breastplates of fire, jacinth, and brimstone as they rode on horses with heads like lions. Out of their mouths spewed fire, smoke, and brimstone. Their tails were those of a serpent. Nothing would get in their way except those sealed by God. The killers would murder one-third of the earth-dwellers, the worst of the worst, those who refused to turn from worshipping idols and demons.

My knees buckled in horror. I could see the faint shadow of believers moseying along, unaware of the demonic horde behind them.

I cried out to God, "Yeshua, protect them." Within seconds the demonic horsemen were so close I could smell sulfur on their breaths. In a matter of hours, they would cover the planet—all two hundred million of them.

I glared at the army leader. "You darkened one from the Euphrates River, sent for this hour, day, month, and year, your time is short."

As we spoke, the demonic horsemen turned on each another, and a spectacular fight broke out. Explosions rocked the desert, and the suffocating hot wind blistered the desert sands.

I shouted, "Those demons can't reach the believers. My presence here is by God's divine intervention."

The enraged creature drew his sword. "Says who?"

I drew mine. "I do."

The darkened one thrust his sword toward me, but I blocked the blow. "The Word of God is quick, powerful, and sharper than any two-edged sword."

Anger flashed across his face as he touched the tip of the blade. "No more delay. I shall take you to the forbidden place. My army will have to wait until I dispose of you."

The delay would give the seventy exiles time to get to Petra. The demonic horsemen couldn't kill them, but spiritual warfare might wear them down before they made it.

We were transported by interdimensional travel. I could tell time was of utmost import to the wicked angel as Satan's rule on earth was brief. I'd do whatever I could to delay his mission.

We arrived at Mount Hermon, to a land that was desolate, scorched, and contaminated with radiation. The stench of death filled my nostrils as the hot wind howled from the nearby gates of hell. I heard the weeping of lost souls and the gnashing of teeth.

The dark angel pointed. "Go that way to Nimrod's Castle—now. Don't waste a second."

Black snowflakes began to fall, and the supernatural snow burned my skin. I ran to warm myself, and when I glanced behind me, the angel from the Euphrates River had turned into an abominable black snowman.

When I could no longer feel my extremities, the castle came into view, and I saw a beautiful young woman standing in front of the fortress—my betrothed, Shale Snyder. Or was it really her?

The swirling drifts of black snow made plowing through it difficult, but in between the snowflakes, she waited, dream-like, holding some-thing in her hand. I didn't know how it could be her, but what if it was? As I approached, I could see there wasn't a single snowflake on her innocent face or body. She was dressed in the same clothes I saw her in before the race.

"Shale?" I shouted over the wind.

A smile touched her lips—that familiar, beautiful smile. My fears melted. I longed to kiss her and embrace her. Despite my exuberance, I needed to read her mind. How else could I be sure it was her?

But I didn't want to. Ignorance was bliss. I could pretend it was her, even if it wasn't. For a fleeting moment, I could live out my dream of marrying her. I could deny reality and make it what I wanted, no matter how brief.

The snow stopped. Black flakes covered everything—except Shale.

I edged closer. "Is it you?"

"Of course it's me, Daniel. Who did you expect it to be?"

"What are you holding?"

She smiled, extending her hands. "You are soaking wet. Here is a suit for the special occasion that awaits you. You must look your best. Inside the castle on the left is a bathroom where you can change." She handed me the clothes. "Remember?"

I nodded. "Yes, I remember, when we were in the garden, and you met me at the castle. I was wet that time, too. And just as before, you've given me a towel with which to dry off."

When I tried to get close enough to embrace her, she stepped away. Again, as before—she was different.

I obliged. "Thank you for the clothes."

She smiled brightly but didn't say anything else. I glanced down as I took the clothing from her and noticed the mark of the beast on her right hand. My heart stopped. "Shale, what have you done?"

Before she could answer, she faded away. I stared, hoping she might reappear. Tears welled up. Why didn't I try to read her mind? I was weary, tired, and spent. I didn't feel like fighting anymore. I wanted to give up.

The demon stood blocking me so I couldn't go back even if I

wanted. Hatred toward him filled my heart. That wasn't Shale—it was an apparition sent to torment me. Or was it?

CHAPTER 65

"You're wasting time," the vile creature said. "You have an appointment with death. Dress appropriately."

I imagined throwing daggers at him—or slashing him with my sword, but God claimed vengeance for himself. I couldn't do that. I grudgingly turned toward the castle.

As I approached the entrance, two half-goat, half-human statues greeted me. Gray smoke billowed from their gargoyle eyes. I turned the door handle, but the door didn't budge. I pushed harder, and this time it opened. The bottom of the door scraped against the stone slab. Once I was inside, the door slammed shut and locked.

To the left, as Shale said, there was a door—along with three others that lined the foyer. Stairs to the second floor ascended, and at the top of the stairs was a portal. It was as if someone had read my mind and tapped into my memories. How could this castle be a replica of the one I'd visited in the garden?

Candles burned in sconces outside each door. The air was musty, and I wiped my nose to keep from sneezing. I turned the handle of the first door and entered a spacious bathroom. Water dripped in the sink, and graffiti covered the walls. A small window let in a sliver of light so

I could see what I was doing. I ripped off the wet clothes, dried with the towel, and put on the suit.

After securing the sword in my pocket, I stopped to pray. When I exited the bathroom, I started to go up the stairs, but a creature reminiscent of a monkey blocked my way and pointed with a bony finger toward the foyer. "You must first enter the other three doors." His disturbing gibberish lingered in my ears, and then he disappeared.

"Good riddance," I whispered. I never cared for monkeys.

I edged down the hallway. The first door I came to displayed Door Number 2. Did it matter if I entered Door 2 before Door 1?

I turned the handle. Voices filled my ears as a street filled with people came into focus. I recognized the cracked face of the Big Ben Clock Tower at Westminster Palace. I couldn't understand what the people were chanting. The clock read 6:66. How could it read that?

A woman ran up to me, and she held her tattooed hand in front of my face. "I'm now part of the New World Order."

I backed away—I wanted no part of that and ran from her. Everywhere I turned, people were holding up their hands. Others had the mark across their forehead. Then I understood the words of the protesters in Parliament Square. "Don't take the mark of the beast, Rev 13:16." Soldiers were stalking the streets and arresting the marchers.

I weaved in and out of the crowd until I came to a line of people waiting outside a government office. A strange coldness came over me. I did not belong here. Where was I going? I turned and headed back, trying to retrace my steps, but I panicked. What if I couldn't get back? Then a portal appeared as sunlight refracted through the interface. I hurried to the opening before it closed, and the suction pulled me back inside the castle.

I took a moment to catch my breath as I stood in the hallway. The quicker I entered all three, the quicker I could get out—and meet my date with death, as the demonic messenger intimated. I could see no purpose in entering these doors, and it angered me that I must.

"You're being shown the future, so you can warn others," a voiced admonished me. I looked up and down the foyer, but I didn't see anyone. I clasped the sword of the spirit and walked to the next door.

CHAPTER 66

I entered Door Number 3. When the smoke cleared, I was in a desert. Silence reflected the black and white world around me. Railroad tracks crossed the terrain that went forever in both directions. I began to walk along the rails.

I heard a horn before I saw the train. I stepped off the tracks to wait for it to pass. A long snake of cattle cars roared past me. Small eyes peered out of the cracks in the boards. Fear spoke to me—I could read the minds of the innocent—precious cargo on the way to Auschwitz. I watched as the train became a speck in the distance. Was my great-grandmother on that train?

I forced myself to think about the inner chamber where the Holy Spirit dwelt. The wickedness of man would destroy me if I didn't keep my focus on God. My eyes went from the distant horizon to the cloudy sky. An eye stared down at me from the clouds. I must have been hallucinating.

I turned my eyes to the train tracks and continued walking. In the sweetness of my worship, I saw Yeshua on his throne, and as I prayed, color returned. I arrived at the Temple courtyard filled with people. Nighttime was approaching as I strolled along the streets, and the city lights revealed hidden cameras, listening devices, and 5-G antennas.

On the Temple Mount were abandoned babies. They cried nonstop, but nobody picked them up. A man ran past me carrying an infant. A woman trailed him through the courtyard until she tripped and fell. Screams erupted as she thrashed on the stone pavement.

The man handed the child to the rabbi. The rabbi disappeared with the baby inside the Third Temple.

As I watched, the same man went around and scooped up all the other abandoned ones—apparently left as child sacrifices. Society went from acceptance of abortion to infanticide—to the pitching of aborted babies and newborns into the fires of Molech.

I remembered Yeshua's words. "Woe to them that are with child and to them that give suck in those days."

I edged my way over to the woman who lay prostrate on the ground.

I tried to comfort her. "I'm sorry."

She wept.

"Where is your husband?"

The woman replied between sobs. "I don't have one. He was martyred."

A crazy man ran up to us and ripped off her scarf. The woman was bald. The crackpot took off, and I went after him. When he fell into a pile of trash, I stood above his body. His glazed-over eyes betrayed he was high on something.

"Why did you humiliate the woman?"

He didn't respond, and I saw the mark on his hand. I pulled out my sword, but before I could carry out my misdeed, he got up and ran off. I stared at my laser sword. I shouldn't have threatened to use it. The angel told me never to use it on a human. My heart pounded as I put it back in my pocket.

Several people saw me. I wanted to hide, but where could I go? As I left the immediate area, monitors flashed the words, "Important Announcement, Daniel Sperling, the Israeli who assassinated Prince Adonikam, has been located."

I heard footsteps approaching. Where could I hide? I threw up a prayer, and a door became visible in a strange place—the Western Wall. I ran over and disappeared inside, landing on the floor in the castle foyer. Exhausted and distraught, I consoled myself—only one door remained unopened

CHAPTER 67

I stood in the foyer and stared at Door Number 1. The only choice I was given was the order of the doors. So I could know the future to warn others—wasn't that what the voice said?

I turned the handle. The door opened to a room of mirrors. However, these weren't regular mirrors; they were mirrored doorways. "Which one should I enter, Lord?"

I heard nothing. I waited a little longer, but God's voice was silent. He left the choice to me. I wanted to choose wisely. I stepped around several and came to a tall mirror. I stuck my hand in and pulled it out. I passed up that one and several others until I came to a mirror with moving images. I entered that one.

I was in a world of moving sidewalks. They went to the north, south, east, and west, crisscrossing each other, intersecting, and moving at very high speeds.

I looked down at my feet, and I was standing on the word "Go" in a multi-dimensional space. As I studied the moving tele-transports, I noticed travelers. Some of the people were anxious. Others seemed to enjoy the journey. Some disappeared and reappeared farther down the road. Others popped up and stayed.

I watched, mesmerized. I tried to see people's faces. Who was happy and who was sad? That wasn't made clear to me.

There were more than a dozen sidewalks. The longer I mulled over which one to choose, the more uncertain I became. After a while, I grew weary. I threw up my hands. Choices carry eternal consequences, and I wanted to make the right one.

"You choose," I heard a voice say. "Free will is a wonderful thing in the hands of an awesome God."

The sidewalk whisked me alongside dozens of other travelers. As the moving sidewalk carried me, I saw foods that whet my appetite. Cinnamon rolls, chocolate croissants, and other pastries called my name. I passed a brewery with a sign advertising free samples of beer. Farther along I caught a whiff of delightful scents—perfumes, essential oils, and soaps—so many choices, so much opportunity.

The exchange of money increased. Soon I saw people buying things they couldn't afford. They pulled out credits cards, signed bank loans, borrowed from friends, and more.

"I've maxed out my credit cards," someone said.

"No problem," a merchant replied. "Just sign here."

I left that conversation, and I continued along the widening sidewalk of debt.

"This car will be the best car you've ever owned," a car salesman exhorted. "It's the number one rated sports car in the world."

I looked at the price tag—a hundred thousand dollars.

Soon I came to a crosswalk. Until now, I didn't know the sidewalks were named. To my surprise, I was traveling on the Sidewalk of Necessities. I came to a store where a merchant was selling animals. The buyer offered the seller money, which was no small amount.

The merchant shook his head. "That's not enough. These animals are extinct. You can breed them and create a new Garden of Eden. Imagine the people who will flock to your attraction—people who love Mother Earth, conservationists, animal lovers, and bird enthusiasts. You'll be the richest man in the world. Who wouldn't want to visit the rebirth of the Garden of Eden?"

The bartering continued. What would be a fair price to buy extinct animals and create another Garden of Eden?

As I walked, I came to a merchant who was selling futures. "Hear ye," he shouted as he waved his hand. "Step right up. We'll release your heart-felt dream. It's reasonably priced, and you deserve it. Come and see a demonstration of the only dream reaper in the world."

A woman walked up. "What's the price?"

The wiry man whipped out his hand and pointed with a dramatic flair. "Have a seat. If you qualify after this demonstration, you'll be given a special seat in the real dream reaper." I looked behind the salesman at a most unusual contraption.

The woman was in her late twenties or early thirties and appeared to be in good health. Youth was leaving her, as it does for all of us, but she was too immature to have attained wisdom.

The woman poured out her heart to the stranger in extraordinary detail, expounding on all the unfair and unjust things that had happened to her, leading to a life in the gutter of despair. Always the victim, she wallowed in self-pity and rejection.

The merchant smiled. "You're just the right person for the dream reaper. You deserve better. Don't worry about the cost. You can pay it off in the next thirty years before your date with death."

"What do you mean, my date with death?"

The merchant replied, "Well, I can't tell you any more than that. You'll need to talk to the dream reaper. He can answer that question."

She looked around. "Where is he?"

The merchant pointed. "Step right up to the dream reaper building."

The woman hesitated.

"You want to release your dream, right?"

The woman nodded, but her enthusiasm dissipated when she realized she couldn't have it—another unjust and unfair thing to add to her trophy list of unhappiness.

I continued walking. A merchant stood out front waving a strange-looking banner—Soul Extractor. No one was at his stand, so I left the Sidewalk of Necessities and strolled up to the merchant.

"Tell me about your soul extractor business."

His eyes lit up, and he greeted me with such exuberance I felt indebted to make a purchase.

"Would you like your soul extracted?" the man asked me.

"What do you do with the soul once you extract it?"

"Oh," the merchant said, "I give it to the devil."

"What do you mean?"

"Have you ever met a person without a soul?"

"Wait a minute," I interrupted. "If I sell my soul to you, then I no longer have a soul."

"That's right," the merchant said. "But for some people other things are more important than their soul."

I stared at the merchant.

The man leaned over and looked into my eyes. "Think about it," he whispered.

"You mean people would sell their soul?"

He laughed. "Absolutely."

"What do you give them for their soul?"

The man cocked his head as if surprised by my question. "The devil sets the price."

So what do you do with the soul you extract?"

The man laughed. "As I said, I give it to the devil."

"You can't do that," I protested.

The smile left his face. "Look, I'm not discussing the moral issue of it. All I care about is selling the soul, and all the devil cares about is receiving the soul. So we have the soul extractor. Everyone is happy. The person has what he wanted, I've made the transaction, and the devil has the soul."

I shook my head. "How can you do that?"

He leaned over and whispered, "Because I sold my soul to the devil and now I do his bidding. I have no choice. He owns me."

CHAPTER 68

I woke up face down on the stone floor of the foyer. The only sound was the flickering candles in the sconces. I stood and walked to the entrance, but it was locked. I didn't expect it to be unlocked. I stepped on the forbidden staircase as deja vu pressed in on me.

I clutched the sword. "I shall not fear, for Thou art with me." The evil tormenting me left. I was relieved when I reached the top. Nothing stopped me this time. I knocked, but no one opened the door. I turned the handle.

As I opened it, I saw Prophet Haman Urhammu sitting on a golden throne wearing white vestments. Two living gargoyles were crouched on each side of him. When my eyes met theirs, they snarled and leaped toward me. I peeled behind the door and shut it, but the false prophet called them back.

"Come in," Prophet Urhammu said.

I entered and closed the door behind me. I noticed the animals had returned to their original positions. I kept one eye on the wild beasts as I looked around the room. I expected to see a library, but the room appeared to be some kind of spiritual enclave.

"Do you know who I am?" he asked.

I couldn't read his mind. "I know who you aren't. You aren't Yeshua Hamashiach, also known as Jesus of Nazareth, the King of kings, the Lord of lords, the Son of God, the Prince of Peace, the Everlasting Father. Shall I continue?"

He stood and walked over to the luminescent wall. He brushed his fingers along the bluish tile, and fire shot forth from his fingers. Tongues of fire snaked through the crystals.

"Magic," I said.

He waved his hand, and the flames disappeared. "Prophets are never accepted in their own country."

"Why have you brought me here?"

The Minister of Untruth returned to his throne. "I have called an important meeting of the ten kings of the New World Order to announce Banu Hashim, formerly known as Prince Adonikam, as the Guided One, the long-awaited Mahdi."

I started to protest.

"Resisting is bad for your health," he said.

I reached down and touched the laser sword hidden in my pocket.

He laughed. "That sword isn't going to protect you."

"You are the false prophet and the second beast in the book of Revelation. You speak like a dragon."

He twirled his fingers. "You must come to the meeting."

"Suppose I don't want to go?"

He pressed his fingers in a steeple. "You must receive the mark of the beast or be martyred.

"I prefer martyrdom."

"You murdered Prince Adonikam."

I shook my head. "You know it was contrived. Prince Adonikam was not resurrected. He faked his own death."

The false prophet rolled his eyes. "The greater illusion is when Satan made it appear as if Yeshua died on the cross two thousand years ago so Christians would believe the lie and go to hell. I never died."

"You never died? You're a blasphemer."

He stood. "I had full confidence God would open your eyes. The

Bibles were mistranslated, so we burned them. Even books have been banned to save the planet."

I interrupted. "The word of the Lord remains forever. You can burn all the books, kill all the true prophets of God, and deceive all the earth-dwellers, but your day of reckoning is coming when King Yeshua will throw you into the lake of fire. Yes, you and Prince Adonikam will burn in the lake of fire. The prince is known by many names—Lucifer, Satan, the devil, the Antichrist…"

The false prophet waved his hand. "With 666, there is no need for books. With the mark, you can tap into the mind of our world leader."

He hadn't heard a word I said.

Urhammu, ranted on. "History needs to be kept current. We can't allow the masses to be deceived by the evil one. With the mark, Banu Hashim has outsmarted him. Take the mark, you live. Without the mark, you die."

"I will never take the mark of the beast."

He ignored me. "Remember the question Pontius Pilate asked?"

"What is truth?"

He nodded. "It's essential that Banu Hashim preserve all truth. I'm sure you would embrace that. He must protect the world from the coming invasion. If people have the truth, they can overcome darkness. That's why I'm called the Minister of Truth. The Enki already took many. Of course, the ones taken were the troublemakers anyway, and we needed to reduce the population, but other Enki are coming. The Antichrist is coming, and we must prepare for the Battle of Armageddon."

"You know, Mr. Haman, Yeshua Hamashiach once said to the Jewish people, 'I came in my Father's name, and you received me not. If another shall come in his own name, him you will receive.' You are that other one, coming in your own name. You are the false prophet."

Father Haman stood. "I hoped you would not disappoint me. Your time is up."

We left the spiritual room, leaving the gargoyles behind, and I followed the false prophet down the stairs and out the door. Lightning crisscrossed the sky in spectacular fireworks, and black-winged creatures flew in circles over the mountain. The air was charged with electricity.

We walked to the base of Mount Hermon and began to climb to the top. The only two structures on the summit were an old abandoned motel and a U.N. radar station. Why were we going there? When we reached the citadel, the false prophet took me to an upside-down door. "You enter first, Mr. Sperling."

CHAPTER 69

I climbed a spiral set of stairs, and the upside-down door became a gateway, similar to the black cube. The door closed and the female voice announced, "Welcome to Bavil, Gateway of the New World Order. Today's quota met. Population in habitable territories—two billion. Good Work by the New World Order."

After descending into the mountain, the door opened to a room full of dignitaries. Seated at a large table were nine VIPs. A man stood at a podium projecting an overhead screen. It read, "Bavil, Meeting of the New World Order." Prince Adonikam, now known as Banu Hashim, sat at the head of the table. I recognized him immediately. As foretold in the Scriptures, he rose to become the beast. I could no longer read his mind. The devil owned his soul. In fact, all those present had lost their soul to the soul extractor.

All eyes focused on the Minister of Untruth and me, including the eyes of Prince Hashim. A guard came over to take my laser sword. When he reached into my pocket, he writhed in pain, holding up his fingers that were on fire. The false prophet uttered an incantation, and the fire disappeared. He ran out of the room as televisions cameras whirled.

Banu Hashim spoke to a guard. "We need more security."

A dozen well-equipped soldiers entered the room and surrounded me. They bound my hands, being careful not to touch my pocket. I noticed on the television screens scattered around the room the headline: "Breaking News, Daniel Sperling has been captured."

The reporters began describing events that were nothing like what had happened. If I hadn't been captured, my nemesis would have been here. I'm sure there were many replacements of me. But regardless, there was no doubt in my mind the media was the voice of the Antichrist. They gave him his platform.

"Your timing is perfect," Prince Hashim said. "We have one more order of business before we go live. Mr. Hussein, can you give us an update on Israel?"

The Muslim approached the podium and raised the mic to his mouth. "The most alarming development is the number of Jews reaching Petra. We have discovered an underground network of countries providing transportation."

His eyes glared. "Who is heading it up?"

"The United States of America."

The prince slammed his fist on the table. "I knew it. We must subdue them. Their recovery from the EMP attack has gone quicker than we thought."

The Minister of Defense continued. "They're using American planes to bring people to Israel by flying into Jordan. Jews take them from there to Petra. There have been scores of flights with Jewish manifests originating in the United States. Prince Hashim, this is something we can't ignore. The Jews are returning."

Banu Hashim seethed. "I must kill those two prophets. I want to see their dead bodies lying on the streets of Jerusalem. We can celebrate their deaths with a new holiday—the first one I've initiated as head of the New World Order."

The prince smiled as he contemplated their demise. "Thank you for the update. You may be seated." He shot another glance at me and then addressed Prophet Urhammu. "Are we ready for the big announcement?"

Prophet Urhammu stepped forward. "Yes. I have a couple of announcements, and then we'll introduce our guest."

Banu Hashim pressed a button on the table. "Please bring in our executioner and alert the news stations we're ready to go live."

The door opened, and a man walked in holding a scimitar. Once he made eye contact, he sauntered over and stood behind me.

"Get down on your knees," the man ordered.

I glanced up at the multiple monitors preparing to broadcast my execution. I did as instructed and lowered my head.

Prophet Urhammu, stood at the podium as the cameras zoomed in. "Good afternoon. We're coming to you live from Bavil. You can see we have assembled here the leaders of the New World States. Our Prince of the Air, Prince Adonikam, now known as Banu Hashim, is also here. Let's give our esteemed leader a warm greeting."

A round of applause erupted from the ten leaders seated at the table.

Prophet Urhammu continued his introduction. "Banu Hashim has brought peace to the world. He has united us into a one-world living, breathing, global organism through the mark of the beast, codenamed 666.

"As many of you know, the mark is mandatory now to ensure that necessary economic reforms are implemented throughout the New World States.

"As the Minister of Truth, more widely known in some circles as Yeshua, a public confession is in order. Much misinformation about my mission and purpose has been disseminated. I'm working hard to update 666 by removing all references to me at my first appearance.

"The Jews were right in 30 A.D. I'm not the Messiah. All the Bibles, books, and reference works have been corrupted by the devil and evil men. Banu Hashim is the Messiah, the Mahdi," the false prophet emphasized. "He has brought peace, and he's committed to continuing that process.

"However, we need everyone's cooperation. By receiving the mark, you'll be able to buy, sell, trade, carry on business, and lead your lives as respectable citizens of the New World Order. You'll be protected by 666. Prince Hashim will make that his utmost priority.

"After all the famines, plagues and diseases we've faced and overcome through his leadership, we can show our appreciation by wearing the microchip like jewelry. It is no bigger than a seed of rice and is easily implanted underneath the skin.

"Let's give another warm round of applause to Banu Hashim for his hard work and dedication to preserving our planet and its global citizens."

Applause came from those seated at the table and others watching via 666 around the world. The television stations showed quick snapshots of people going about their daily lives, sitting in living rooms, restaurants, fitness centers, and business establishments.

Prophet Urhammu continued. "Now, we have one more piece of business. As was announced earlier, the young man who murdered Prince Adonikiam, surrendered himself to authorities. Daniel Sperling has come here to express his deep-felt remorse, and he has agreed to demonstrate how easy it is to receive the mark underneath the skin. The young man has been re-educated so he can become a respectable citizen of the New World States.

"Without more ado, we'll allow Mr. Sperling to speak, if he so chooses. All that's required is he must acknowledge Banu Hashim, who is the prince of the air, as the Mahdi redeemer, known by Jews as the Messiah and Christians as the Christ. Then Mr. Sperling will be able to receive the mark. Mr. Sperling claims to have renounced all prior religious beliefs, and he's here to demonstrate how painless the process is."

There was a slight delay as the cameras focused on me, and I noticed at just the right level and angle, there was a mic for me to speak into. I closed my eyes and said nothing.

Prophet Urhammu prompted me. "Mr. Sperling, are you ready to worship Prince Banu Hashim and receive the mark?"

I looked up into the camera and spoke into the mic. "Yeshua Hamashiach is my Lord and Savior. Never will I renounce my faith in him or worship anyone else."

CHAPTER 70

The lights flickered, and the room went dark. A brief moment of silence ensued, followed by several loud booms. Somebody yelled, "Earthquake!"

Multiple alarms went off as the floor buckled. I lost my balance and fell. I felt the movement of air against my skin as my executioner slammed the sword within inches of my neck. The darkness saved me, but with my hands bound, I struggled to stand.

Chaos ensued, and above the frantic screams, someone shouted my name, "Daniel."

Anyone looking for me would kill me, and I wasn't going to help him by answering.

Someone tripped over me, and I got an earful of foul language. I needed to get up, but with my hands bound and the unstable floor, I couldn't.

"Daniel, are you in here?" someone shouted with more urgency. The voice sounded like Maurice. A demonic creature or chimera was imitating him to locate me in the dark.

Or could it be Maurice? God gave me the gift to read minds, but even that didn't persuade me. I could be deceived. I tried harder to get my hands unbound, but all my attempts were futile.

The voice called my name a third time. Security barged into the room shining flashlights. They were going to find me, especially if they brought in dogs. I felt myself sliding on the floor that now tilted at an angle. The building was being swallowed. "Over here," I called out.

Within seconds the person was behind me and began to remove the bindings. Once they were off, I turned to see who it was.

"Hurry," Maurice said. "Let's get out of here."

Loud booms split the air as the building broke apart. He handed me a light, and we wobbled around the widening crevasses trying to keep our balance and avoid debris.

"Follow me," Maurice shouted.

We made it to the hallway, but we couldn't go farther. Possible escape routes were blocked by fallen walls and bodies. Maurice pointed. "We'll have to take the stairs. There're a bunch of them."

I followed him to the stairway lit by emergency lighting, and we climbed at least a hundred steps to reach the surface. The door was blocked at the top, and after several anxious seconds, we managed to open it.

The gray sky welcomed us—that supernatural grayness that I hated. For once, however, I was thankful to see it. We took off running, and when I looked back at Mount Hermon, the top of the mountain was a ruinous heap. A few people were coming out, but many were still trapped.

I checked Maurice's face in the natural light to make sure it was him. Every minute was too precious to waste asking questions. "Let's get out of here."

As we ran down the trail to the base of Mount Hermon, we dodged falling rocks from continuing aftershocks. I shouted, "I thought you were dead."

"An angel saved me," he hollered.

When we reached the bottom, mounds of boulders were in our way. It was quicker to climb over the debris than to go around it. We picked our way through it and returned to the trail until we came to a historic location. "Do you know where we are, my friend?" Maurice asked.

"Caesarea Philippe." I noted the earthquake had caused fallen rock to block the cave entrance.

Maurice pointed to the entombed entrance. "King Yeshua told his disciples, 'On this rock, I will build my church, and the gates of hell will not prevail.' Looks like the portal has been sealed."

As we stood in awe at the devastation, radiant light poured down from the heavens. A mighty angel stood clothed in spectacular white clouds with a brilliant rainbow over his head. His face glowed like the sun, and his feet were as pillars of fire. He held in his hand an open book. Another angel appeared beside him, and he began to blow the trumpet.

Maurice shouted, "The mystery of God is almost finished. The kingdom of heaven is near."

I raised my hands triumphantly. "God's kingdom is expanding. The gates of hell will not prevail."

Aftershocks rumbled.

"What happened?" I asked my friend. "When I saw Pierre walking on fire, I assumed you must have died."

In between shallow breaths, Maurice answered. "When Pierre ran off, I went after him, and I fell into a pit. An angel rescued me."

"I looked for you."

"Oh, you wouldn't have found me, Daniel. That underwater explosion we experienced was set off by CERN. Portals opened and antimatter entered our world. That's what caused that chasm. You wouldn't believe the explosions happening in the unseen realm. The angel saved me so I could rescue you."

"You were sent here?"

Maurice didn't hear my question. "Look."

A doorway was straight ahead. A carpet of grass quickly grew up between us and the door, and a trellis of bright red roses sprouted blossoms as we watched.

"Maurice, do you know what's on the other side of that door?"

He stared. "The angel said a door would appear where Yeshua promised he'd build his church." He looked at me. "Why are you so dressed up?"

I wasn't listening—I was running. I opened the door, and on the other side, I couldn't believe what I saw.

CHAPTER 71

My betrothed, Shale Snyder, stood in a magnificent white wedding gown in the garden of the King. Thousands of flowers covered the hills and valleys, and the trees were in full bloom with the fruits of the spirit. Wedding guests were still gathering in the center of the garden, and many already sat in pews facing the Chuppah.

"We're getting married right now?"

Shale's eyes glistened in the sunlight, and her face glowed in the dreamy, golden hues of the sun. "You must cover me with the veil first."

I smiled. "With great honor." I lowered the veil, but not before lingering on her radiant features. Her thoughts swept me off my feet. I did not deserve her. The scent of Opobalsamum perfume filled my nostrils. I clenched my eyes. How could I be sure I wasn't dreaming?

After covering her face, Shale stepped to the side. I wanted to admire my beautiful bride and hold her, but I forced myself to look ahead. When I did, my father stood in front of me. His face beamed as one of the redeemed. I glanced at Shale. How had she pulled this off?

I rushed to my dad and threw my arms around his neck. He embraced me with that familiar hug from long ago, with his strong arms that held me as a child. His grip was the grip of security and love. My search was over.

"Are you ready?" he asked.

I adjusted my suit as I admired my father dressed in the robe of the redeemed. I wouldn't wear that robe for a thousand years, but I hadn't arrived without being appropriately attired. I noticed Maurice was also now wearing a suit—and grinning from ear to ear.

I nodded. "I'm ready."

We stood tall and began the ritual walk on the flower-covered path to the Chuppah. The free-standing structure was decorated with the flowers of heaven—love, joy, peace, patience, kindness, goodness, gentleness, and self-control—flowers I'd never seen on earth, but that are found in the garden of heaven.

I looked around. Who helped Shale to make this possible? Besides her, who knew all the people that were closest to me? Much-Afraid barked. My father and I stopped walking, and she rushed up to greet me. I wrapped my arms around her, and she kissed me with her wet nose.

Nothing felt sweeter to me at this moment. I took a moment to reflect on how it all began. Much-Afraid brought Shale through the door to the King's garden. Shale's dog met me at the door to our apartment before I went to the seventh dimension. She was waiting outside the door of the synagogue when Shale and I returned. She'd taken food to my father while he was chained in the Perlsea Castle, and she helped him to escape. Much-Afraid inspired Shale to write her diary, and it was through Shale's scrolls my dad met Yeshua Hamashiach.

Glorious music filled the garden. The flowers, the birds, the trees, even the angels sang. I saw Shira, our newly adopted daughter, happily dropping seeds for the birds as Cherios, Shale's favorite bunny, hopped alongside her.

The donkey and the pig, Baruch and Lowly, were following around in their best wedding attire. Lowly, the pig, wore a blue ribbon attached to his curlicue tail, and Cherios wore multi-colored flowers on her head. Baruch didn't need anything to be a distinguished donkey. That's just how he was.

I longed to hold Shira in my arms. She turned her gaze to me, and her eyes latched onto mine. Without hesitating, she dropped her basket. Seconds later, I wrapped my arms around her.

Home in the King's garden, I prayed, "Come, Lord Jesus."

Shira pointed. "Look."

Everyone turned. King Yeshua was riding on a magnificent white steed. He gazed out over the wedding celebration. I remembered his words, "Marry quickly."

"It's time," the rabbi said to me.

I set Shira down, and an angel took her by the hand and led her over to Mari. My sister was sitting in the front wearing a robe of the redeemed. Brutus and Jonathan sat together—wearing white robes of martyrdom. Next to them was Nathan, the boy I mentored and Shale's half-brother, wearing a robe of the redeemed. Lilly sat beside Nathan. Dr. Luke was here—what a nice surprise he came to my wedding. Sitting beside Dr. Luke was Theophilus, Mari's adoptive father. And beside Theophilus was Martha, Mary. Simon, and Mark, and others I knew from my journey to the seventh dimension.

I saw Amir and Omi. They must have become Followers of the Way. Alongside them was Cynisca, the woman who trained me to race chariots; and Dominus, who took a chance on me and allowed me to race for his team. My cousin, Rachel, Shale's closest friend, was sitting next to someone I didn't know, wearing a robe of the redeemed. Judd was next to her. General Goren was seated in the pew—wearing a robe of the redeemed. Lying on his lap was the cat from the nursing home—the blind cat. If I were a betting man, I'd say he was no longer blind. What an awesome surprise to see General Goren here.

Then I noticed a very special woman. I knew it was her because God gave me a word of knowledge. I couldn't wait to embrace my great grandmother. Around her neck was the green Star of David. She wore the robe of the redeemed.

I looked around for my brother Jacob—he should be here some-where. Then God opened my eyes—my brother Jacob was the rabbi. How had I not recognized him?

Shale began her walk with the King of kings at her side. Everyone rose. The angels sang. The birds and animals stopped what they were doing to watch. I gazed at my beautiful betrothed beside our heavenly Father, our Lord and Savior, and our King.

"Are you ready?" my brother asked.

I nodded.

The ceremony was short—we'd waited a very long time—and Rabbi Jacob Sperling put the glass, wrapped in cloth, on the ground. With great exuberance, I smashed it. Singing and celebration spread through the garden, and I lifted the veil to kiss my bride.

CHAPTER 72

Only the Lord's return could top this day.

Shale whispered in my ear, "It's time for the Yichud."

Shale knew Jewish tradition? I accompanied her to Baruch as he stood waiting for us a short distance away.

"I promised I would let him walk me," Shale said.

"Where are we going?"

Shale smiled. "You'll see."

Everyone stood and watched with great interest as Shale sat sideways on Baruch's back. Memories of when I met Shale the first time warmed my heart. Once situated, Shale captured me with her stunning eyes. "Can you place Cherios in my lap?"

I smiled. "Like before." I picked up the rabbit, that was spotlessly clean, and placed her next to Shale.

Everyone knew where we were going but me. "It's a surprise," Shira said. I couldn't wait to find out. Much-Afraid and Lowly went ahead of us.

A few minutes later we arrived. The mansion was lavishly decorated. Much-Afraid greeted us with a happy yelp at the open door. I placed Cherios on the ground, and she disappeared inside. I helped Shale off the donkey and kissed her once again.

"Let's give Cherios and Shira a minute so they can have everything ready," Shale said.

I was quite content to give them a minute. I embraced Shale with another extended kiss.

Much-Afraid barked, and Shale translated. "They're ready for us."

When we walked inside, I was impressed and took a moment to admire the loveliness. "Did you do all of this?"

Shale smiled. "No, others helped." She glanced at Shira, Much-Afraid, Lowly, Baruch, and Cherios. Then her eyes met mine. "This is our home, Daniel, in the garden, until King Yeshua takes his rightful place in Jerusalem as the King. Then we might move our house to Galilee. Or not. Yeshua wants us to take care of his garden while he wages war against his enemies on earth."

I swallowed hard.

Shale clasped my hand. "Come, let's have a snack before we return to our guests."

We walked into the dining room, and on the table were shortbread cookies and tea. Cherios and Shira were our servers.

I embraced Shale once more. "Would you like to have tea with me?"

She smiled. "I would love to."

We sat at the table and prayed. Shira poured tea into our small teacups and gave one shortbread cookie to each of us. "I'll give you more if you eat that one," she said.

"You are a very good cook, Shira," I complimented her.

"Thank you," she said. "My mommy taught me."

Shale smiled. "Shortbread cookies are Shira's favorite."

Cherios handed me a flower from her hat, and I gave it to my beloved bride. She tucked it behind her ear.

Baruch watched through the dining room window, and Much-Afraid guarded the door so no one could disturbed us. Lowly stayed with Much-Afraid to keep her company.

I looked into Shale's eyes. I wondered, what happened after I left? I didn't need to read her mind to know it was all good because God is good. We had a thousand years of marriage ahead of us, to share our journeys, to grow as husband and wife, and to remember. After that, eternity would follow when we would be able to worship our beloved King forever. That was hard to fathom.

For now, this sweet moment with my new wife and family was all that mattered. The King had built us a mansion and made us the keeper of His garden—it just didn't get any better than that.

COMPLETE BOXED SET

ALSO BY LORILYN ROBERTS

Children of Dreams

Children of Dreams as an Audiobook

The Donkey and the King

Food for Thought Cookbook

Am I Okay,God?

Am I Okay, God? as an Audiobook

The Door

The Door as an Audiobook

The King

The King as an Audiobook

The City

The City as an Audiobook

The Prescience

The Howling

The Castle

Tails and Purrs for the Heart and Soul

ABOUT THE AUTHOR

When not writing books, Lorilyn provides closed captioning for television. She adopted her two daughters from Nepal and Vietnam as a single mother and lives in Gainesville, Florida, with many rescued cats.

Lorilyn has won over thirty awards for the *Seventh Dimension Series*. She graduated Magna Cum Laude from the University of Alabama with a bachelor's degree in social sciences/humanities that included an emphasis in Biblical history with on-site study in Israel. She received her Masters in Creative Writing from Perelandra College.

Visit Lorilyn Roberts' website to learn more at LorilynRoberts.com.

The devotions *Am I Okay, God?* in the *Seventh Dimension Series* are also available from Lorilyn's website.

EPILOGUE

If you have not accepted Yeshua Hamashiach as your Lord and Savior, today is the day.

There won't be a better time than right now. As has oft been repeated in the *Seventh Dimension Series*, time is an illusion until God's appointed time. You may not have tomorrow. Today is God's appointed time. If you have not done so, ask Jesus into your heart and repent of your sins.

I am a fellow traveler, like you, on the way to the Celestial City.